INTO
THE
FIRE

ANNE STUART

INTO THE FIRE

MIRA®

MIRA®

ISBN 0-7394-3644-9

INTO THE FIRE

Printed in U.S.A.

This one's for Spike and Yoshiki.

1

It was a cold night in November, and the heater in her old Volvo had died forty miles back. Jamie stared straight ahead into the darkness, ignoring the warning lights on her dashboard, ignoring everything but her final destination. She'd put soothing New Age music on the CD player, but it hadn't managed to calm her. She'd grown even more tense, trying to fight the soporific effects of the soft music, until her hands were numb from gripping the steering wheel.

What the hell was she doing here? Nate was dead, murdered three months ago—coming here wouldn't change anything. It wouldn't stop the pain.

She focused on the road, trying to stay alert after seventeen hours of driving. Nate was dead and no one could tell her what happened. He'd been found bludgeoned to death in an old garage in Cooperstown, Wisconsin, and no one seemed to give a damn. The police had given up after what had been only a cursory investigation. It was a drug deal gone wrong, they said. They had more important things to spend their time on. Three months had passed and everyone had forgotten.

Everyone but Jamie Kincaid and her mother. Nate had come into their family when he was ten years old, his own parents dead in a tragic fire, and he'd always been more of a brother than a cousin. More of a son to Isobel and Victor Kincaid than a nephew. Maybe even more of their own child than Jamie, it had seemed at times, but she always quashed that paranoid, disloyal thought. Her parents loved her, just as they loved Nate. Everyone loved charming, feckless Nate, with his glorious smile and easy charm. And he even looked like her parents, with his dark Kincaid good looks and brown eyes. A resemblance the paler, adopted Jamie had always lacked.

It didn't matter, never had mattered to her. There was enough love in their small family to go around, no matter what disasters befell them. And disasters had followed Nate like a vengeful guardian angel. Ending in his own murder, a thousand miles from home, a thousand years away.

The police didn't care. Isobel did. After she'd learned of his death, she'd sunk into a deep, angry depression, not eating, not leaving the house, mourning her lost nephew with a fierce, almost biblical passion. But both Isobel and Jamie needed answers before they could let him rest in peace. And after a bleak, broken Thanksgiving, Jamie had gotten in her old car and driven a thousand miles to get those answers.

If she'd thought twice about it she never would have left Marshfield, Rhode Island. The roads had been crowded with holiday travelers, rushing to and from warm family gatherings. Her car was on its last legs, barely reliable enough to get her to and from work at the small private school where she taught. It wasn't up to heroic efforts, and it was telling her so.

The windshield wipers had stopped working hours before. Fortunately the rain had stopped, as well. She'd passed the Wisconsin state line hours ago, left the interstate to wander on the dark, wet roads outside the city. It seemed like the final indignity, to die in Wisconsin, Jamie thought. Nate was such a flamboyant, larger-than-life character—he should have died spectacularly. Not in some squalid room over top of a garage.

But Dillon Gaynor had seen to it that he had. Nate's lifelong best friend, his nemesis, the person who'd dragged him into the gutter and held him down there. The man Nate had called Killer. Who might have lived up to his name three months ago. The police had even taken him in for questioning. But they'd let him go. Never filed charges and simply closed the case when other, more important issues took their attention. And the question that haunted Jamie was simple. Had Dillon Gaynor gotten away with murder?

Sometime in western Pennsylvania she'd wondered what the hell she was doing, going after a man she knew was capable of killing. A man who'd scared the shit out of her when he'd been a teenage delinquent. She hadn't seen him in twelve years— he hadn't even bothered to come east for the memorial service for his oldest friend. Even if he hadn't beat her cousin to death, he was still guilty. He'd kept Nate supplied with drugs, he'd taken him down the dark path that had ended in a sordid death. He was to blame, even if he hadn't actually killed him. And she would have been happy never to see him again.

But by Ohio she'd stopped thinking about it. She needed answers, her desperately grieving mother needed them. And Dillon wouldn't dare hurt her. He might be little better than pond scum, a high-school dropout with a record and an ongoing history of trouble with the law, but he was very, very smart.

Almost frighteningly so. He'd be too smart to com-
mit another murder and think he could get away
with it.

She even had a plausible excuse for coming. Dillon was holding on to a box of Nate's possessions,
and despite Isobel's increasingly virulent requests,
he hadn't bothered to send it back to them. God
only knows what was inside—maybe the Patek Phi-
lippe watch that had been handed down through
generations, maybe some clue to what happened. Or
maybe dirty laundry and unpaid bills. It didn't matter. Isobel was fixated on having anything that had
ever belonged to Nate, and after that bleak Thanksgiving meal Jamie had agreed to go and get it.

Exhaustion set in by Indiana. She'd been surviving on black coffee and Ritz crackers, and the blind-
ing headache was such a familiar companion that it
almost felt like a friend. She tried turning off the
New Age tape to listen to the radio, but all she
could get was angry hip-hop or mournful country
music. The classical music station put her to sleep,
so she cracked the window and turned the New Age
music back on. She gripped the steering wheel
tightly.

Illinois had passed in a blur. She didn't even
mind Chicago driving, when she usually panicked
over city traffic. It was late by then, the commuters

were home in bed, and she sped through, half daring the police to stop her.

No one did. She was close now, within just a few miles of her destination. She had an address, she had a map, she had determination.

She also had a car on the verge of dying and a light snow that had begun to fall. She turned on the windshield wipers, forgetting that they were broken. The night seemed darker still on this narrow back road, the lights barely cutting through the darkness.

And then she realized it wasn't her imagination, it wasn't exhaustion. The lights were getting dimmer, the car was slowing, cruising to a sudden, coughing halt in the middle of the road. The New Age piano was still going, but it sounded like a warped record. And then even that stopped, and the last of the light gave up the ghost, and she was left sitting in the darkness.

Crying was an option, an appealing one, but she resisted. She hadn't really cried since she'd heard that Nate had died. She was afraid that once she started she'd never stop.

She certainly wasn't going to start crying right before she came face-to-face with Dillon Gaynor. She wouldn't give him that pleasure.

She rolled down the window, put the car in Neutral and stepped onto the wet pavement. The car was on a slight rise, and she couldn't leave it sitting in the middle of a road, even one as deserted as this.

Pushing a car onto the shoulder was a lot harder than it looked, even with the aid of a slope. And it was just about impossible to steer through the open window. God knows there was no stopping it when it began to roll, picked up speed and knocked her onto her knees on the pavement. She watched it slide off the road, ending up on its side against a copse of trees.

She flinched at the crunching sound. Volvos were strong—they could take a lot of punishment. Even a twelve-year-old one was tougher than a lot of new American cars. She'd get someone to tow it out tomorrow, fix it.

Hell, Dillon lived in an old garage. Maybe someone still worked there, and she'd kill two birds with one stone.

Her watch was an elegant antique, a family heirloom. It needed to be wound every day, having been made long before aquaglow was invented, and it had stopped hours ago. There was no way she could tell what time it was. It had to be after midnight, but that was as close as she could come. She hadn't seen another car since she'd gotten off on this secondary road that led into the small mill city of Cooperstown. She had a choice—climb down the embankment, crawl into the back seat of her car and wait for morning. The snow had picked up a bit, but one night in below-freezing temperatures wouldn't kill her.

And maybe she'd wake up in the morning stiff and sore, and think better of her impulsive trip. Maybe she'd rent a safer car, abandon the Volvo and drive straight back home. What did she think she could learn from a man like Dillon Gaynor? A man who always kept his secrets?

That wasn't going to happen. She'd come too far, worked herself up to face him. She left her second thoughts back in Rhode Island. She wasn't turning back now.

She'd been heading in the right direction—she was certain of that. Her only choice was to follow the empty road and hope that eventually she'd find what she was looking for. All she had to do was manage the snowy bank and grab her purse from the car without falling again.

In the end it was almost too easy. Her feet were numb, from the cold, from walking. She'd scraped her knee when she'd landed on the hard pavement, and her winter coat was back in Rhode Island, where the weather had been unseasonably balmy. She kept walking, huddled in a thick sweater that had seen better days, plowing forward through the slowly drifting snowflakes.

The building where Nate died sat alone on the edge of the run-down little town. She hadn't even been able to find Cooperstown, Wisconsin, in the road atlas—it had taken the Internet to find a route. The place was little more than a ghost of an old industrial town, and the building itself looked as if it had once been some kind of factory back when this had been a viable community. Now it simply looked abandoned, and she would have walked on if she hadn't seen the glimmer of light behind one of the filthy windows. And the sign by the door— Gaynor's Auto Restoration.

After so many miles, so many hours, she simply stood outside the closed door, afraid to take the last step. She could hear voices, and a moment later the door opened, light and noise spilling out into the night as two men flew forward, locked in an embrace of fury.

She stumbled back, just in time, and the two ended up in the thin layer of snow, one on top as he methodically pounded his fist into the other man's face with a casual violence that would have horrified Jamie at any other time. She hadn't seen anyone hit someone in twelve years. And it had been the same man administering the beating. She knew it with a kind of sick fear.

He dropped the man back on the ground and rose. She could see blood on his fists, and he wiped them casually against his jeans. "Don't come back," he said.

It was the same voice. Huskier, but the same. Nate had been beaten to death, beyond recognition, in this very building. Maybe by those very hands.

She stayed in the shadows, silent, motionless, horrified. He saw her, anyway, his head jerking up as he peered into the darkness.

"Who's there?"

He wasn't alone. The small figure of a man stood in the doorway, blocking the light from spreading out onto the little tableau. The man on the ground was groaning, cursing, but smart enough not to move. And Jamie wondered if she had time to run.

She wasn't going to, she reminded herself. She had a bad habit of running from trouble, and this was what she'd been determined to face.

She stepped out of the shadows, moving up to him. He wouldn't know who she was, of course. He'd barely been aware of her back then, and he hadn't seen her since that night so long ago, when both their lives had changed. She'd be the last person he expected to show up on his doorstep.

She was right about one thing. "What the fuck are you doing here?"

He knew exactly who she was. It was one shock on top of another, and she came out with the only answer she could muster. "I'm looking for answers."

"Nate's dead," Dillon said, his voice as flat and expressionless as his eyes.

"I know that. I want to know why."

He said nothing. He looked just as she remembered, and yet nothing like it at all. He stood with the light behind him, and she couldn't see his face. She could only see the blood on his hands.

"Go home, Jamie," he said after a long moment. "Go back to your safe little boarding-school world. There's nothing for you here."

She didn't even stop to wonder how he knew that she taught in a boarding school. "I can't. I promised my mother. We need answers."

"Your mother," Dillon said with a throaty laugh. "I should have known the Duchess would have something to do with this. I don't give a shit what you and your goddamned mother want, I only care what I want. And that is for you to get in your car and get your scrawny little ass out of here before I lose my temper. I'm already in a bad mood, and you should remember that I'm not very nice when I'm in a bad mood.''

The notion was so absurd she found she could laugh. ''You're never very nice,'' she said.

''True enough.'' He glanced past her. ''Where's your car?''

''Broken down somewhere.''

''And I'm supposed to rescue you?''

''Aw, Dillon!'' The man behind him spoke. ''Let the poor girl in out of the cold. You're scaring her.''

''Easy enough to do,'' he said carelessly.

''C'mon, man. We're finished our game, anyway. We can't play two-handed, and I don't think Tomas is going to be in any shape to play cards for a while.'' He stepped out into the alleyway, a short, skinny little man, smaller than her own average height. He probably wouldn't weigh more than one hundred and twenty pounds soaking wet. Less than she did. If there was one thing she didn't possess, it was a scrawny ass.

''I'm Mouser,'' he said. ''And your name's Janie?''

''Jamie,'' Dillon corrected. ''Jamie Kincaid. Nate's sister.''

Mouser took an instinctive step back from her, looking rattled. ''I didn't know he had any sisters. I thought he hatched from a snake's egg.''

"Cousin," she said, startled. "We were brought up together."

"Then you knew what he was like," Mouser said, nodding. "Just ignore Dillon. He gets like this when someone cheats at cards, especially when they do it badly. It insults his intelligence. That's why we've got Tomas over there in the mud. He's not going to make you stand out here in the alleyway and freeze to death."

"Who says?" But with that caustic remark Dillon moved back inside. Leaving the door open behind him.

"That's as close to an invitation as you're gonna get," Mouser said. "Better get moving before he changes his mind and locks us both out in the snow."

The room beyond the door was hot and smoky, and Mouser closed the door behind her, shutting out the cold. Shutting off escape.

The place was a mess. They'd been playing poker around an old table, and chips and cards lay scattered on the floor. Two chairs were overturned, bottles of beer lay spilled on the floor, and Dillon stood in the corner, smoking a cigarette and looking at her out of hooded eyes.

She stifled a cough. The room was a sty, but what else would she expect of someone like him?

"So you're Nate's sister," Mouser said, getting a better look at her in the smoky light. "Not much of a resemblance, is there?"

"Cousin," she corrected him again. "We were just brought up together. And I'm adopted."

"Lucky you," Mouser said obscurely. He glanced up at Dillon. "Maybe I'll just leave you two together to relive old times."

"Not likely," Dillon said.

"Well, then, to work out your differences. Be nice to her, Killer. It's not every day you have a pretty waif show up on your doorstep. Be a hero for a change," Mouser said, his voice stern.

"Jamie'll tell you that's not in my nature. Scrape Tomas off the sidewalk on your way, will you? I don't want any more complications tonight. She's enough."

"Will do. But I'm warning you, I expect to find her safe and happy next time I see her," Mouser said.

"She'll be safe enough," he said. "I can't be responsible for 'happy.'"

"Funny, that's not what your women say," Mouser murmured.

"In case you hadn't noticed, she's not one of my women," Dillon snapped.

"Oh, I noticed," Mouser said in a cheerful voice.

"I notice everything. Don't let him browbeat you, Jamie. He's mostly bark and very little bite."

That wasn't what she remembered. But the door closed behind them, leaving the two of them alone in the smoky, trashed room.

He moved then, picking up the overturned chairs on his way to the sink. They were in a kitchen of sorts, with a microwave, a hot plate, a tin sink and an old refrigerator. Which would undoubtedly be filled with beer. The old oak table in the center of the room took up most of the space, and he had to come way too close to her to reach the sink. He made no effort to avoid her, and she had to stumble back, out of his way.

He was washing the blood off his knuckles, and she stared at his hands. They were big hands, strong, with a webbing of little nicks and scars. His knuckles were skinned—it hadn't just been his victim's blood. He didn't seem to react to any pain—he just rinsed the blood off and dried the raw knuckles with a paper towel. He tossed it in the overflowing trash can by the sink, but it missed and floated down to the floor in a lazy, graceful swirl.

He turned then, leaning against the sink to look at her, letting his eyes run from the top of her head to her wet, aching feet.

It was very nice of Mouser to call her a pretty

waif. She couldn't disagree with the waif part, but "pretty" was pushing it. Particularly right now, when she hadn't slept for two days, wore no makeup, and her pale brown hair straggled around her face. She'd never been Dillon's type, thank God, even at her best, and at her worst she was definitely safe. If anyone could be safe around Dillon.

"You can spend the night," he said abruptly. "It's after three, and I'm not in the mood to haul your car out of a ditch. Tomorrow I'll get someone to tow it here, I'll fix it, and you can get the hell out of here."

"You'll fix it?" she repeated.

"I'm a grease monkey, remember? I can fix any car. I just don't happen to have a tow truck. I count on other people to drag them to me." He opened the fridge, but to her surprise she couldn't see any beer. They must have drunk it all. "I suppose you came to collect Nate's stuff. Fine with me—it's been just taking up room."

"Then why wouldn't you send it?"

"Couldn't be bothered." He took a carton of milk, opened it and drank.

She wondered what he'd do if she fainted. She was tempted—she couldn't remember the last time she ate, and after her long, cold walk she was too hot, dizzy, ready to collapse, and he hadn't even offered her a chair. She should walk to the nearest one and sit, but for some reason she couldn't move.

She realized he was looking at her again. His eyes were just as cold, just as blue as she remembered. "You look like shit," he said.

"Thank you."

He pushed away from the sink. "Come on. I don't feel like carrying you upstairs if you pass out."

He was more observant than she realized. There were at least three closed doors leading off the small kitchen. He opened one to reveal a dark, narrow flight of stairs.

He took them two at a time. She hauled herself up with the handrail, slowly, knowing he was waiting for her at the top of the stairs.

He didn't move out of her way when she reached the second floor. He moved to take her arm, and she jerked away from him in sudden panic.

She could feel nothing beneath her—she was falling, and she was going to break her neck on these rickety stairs, and then what would her mother do, and what the hell did she care, and...

He caught her arm and yanked her back onto solid ground. "Are you trying to kill yourself?" he snapped.

He was very strong. Stronger than she remembered. She'd have bruises on her arm.

"You can let go of me now," she said.

"And have you take a header down the stairs? I don't think so." He moved down the hallway, dragging her after him.

The bare lightbulb overhead did little to illuminate their way. The place smelled of gasoline and cooking and all sorts of other smells she didn't even want to think about. He pushed open a door and pulled the string from overhead. The light didn't come on.

"Shit," he muttered. "Stay here."

At least he let go of her. She stood in the hallway, waiting, while he disappeared behind another door. When he came back he was carrying a sleeping bag and a small lamp. He pushed past her into the room, and in a moment the light came on. He'd plugged it in and set it on the floor next to the mattress that lay there, the only thing in the small, bare, dismal room.

He tossed the sleeping bag on the mattress. "You'll have to make do with that. The bathroom's down the hall. You want something to sleep in?"

"I'll keep my clothes on."

His smile was cool and fleeting. "I'm sure you

will. Go to sleep, Jamie. Tomorrow you'll be safely on your way home.''

And before she could respond he closed the door, shutting her into the tiny, empty room.

Someone was there, in the huge old building. He knew it without seeing, without hearing. Knew that someone had finally come, to break him free from the stasis that had held him.

Was the newcomer afraid of ghosts? He didn't want to scare whoever it was. Not yet, at least. First he had to see if they were of any use.

And if they'd help him kill Dillon Gaynor. He'd been waiting too long. It was time for Dillon to pay.

2

Jamie found the bathroom, a mixed blessing given its condition. She never could figure out why men were such utter pigs—it must have something to do with that extra chromosome. The only towel in sight was a dismal shade of gray, so she simply used her hands to wash her face, then glanced up at her reflection.

Waif, was it? At twenty-eight years old Jamie Kincaid looked much as she'd always looked. Pale skin, gray eyes, hair an indiscriminate shade between brown and blond.

She pushed her hair away from her face, staring at her reflection thoughtfully. Good bones, good skin, even features. Nothing to write home about, but nothing to be ashamed of, either. She was never going to attract the kind of dangerous attention from the wrong kind of man. The only reason Dillon had known of her existence was because of her cousin. If it hadn't been for Nate he never would have noticed well-behaved Jamie. They'd hardly run in the same crowd in high school.

If you could even say he'd *been* in high school. There had never been anyone at home to make sure he attended regularly. His mother had left when he was young, and his father had died in a drunken car crash when Dillon was sixteen. He'd dropped out just before graduation, and there'd been some story that had been effectively hushed up. Maybe he'd gotten someone pregnant, though that seemed a relatively mild offense. Beaten someone, been arrested? All she knew was that the school and her family were furious with him, Nate was amused, and Dillon, when she saw him from a distance, defiant.

He was still defiant. Living in this rattrap, living his marginal existence. It was probably the best he could manage with his alcohol and drug problems. The addictions hadn't yet made their mark on his face. He still looked very much like he'd looked twelve years ago, with a few lines added for interest.

As if he needed anything to make him more interesting. Jamie shivered, turning away from the mirror. This was harder than she'd expected, and she'd expected it to be tough. Seeing him again brought all sorts of feelings back, unwelcome mem-

ories flooding through her mind, through her rebel-
lious body. He made her feel young and vulnerable
again, just by being there. She'd been a fool to
come.

She'd leave, first thing tomorrow. As soon as her
car was up and running. He wanted her out of there,
and she wanted to go. She'd grab Nate's things and
take off. Dillon wasn't going to give her the answers she needed. She should have remembered that
much about him. He never gave up anything he
didn't want to.

No lock on her bedroom door, of course. Not that
it would have made any difference—as far as she
knew she was alone in this old building with Dillon,
and he wouldn't let anything as flimsy as a lock get
in the way of what he wanted. And why in hell
would he want her?

She shut the door, anyway, then picked up the
lamp and held it over the mattress. It was thin,
stained, but there was nothing crawling on it, and
she was so bone tired she could weep. If she were
in the habit of crying. She shook out the sleeping
bag, unzipped it and crawled in.

And immediately scrambled back out in a panic,
knocking the lamp over. It was an old down sleeping bag, and it smelled like Dillon. Like his skin,
an ineffable scent that was unmistakable and dis-

turbing. Almost...erotic. She couldn't possibly sleep with that thing around her—it was like being wrapped in his embrace.

She sat on the thin mattress, shivering. There was no way she could attempt the long drive back home, no way she could escape without sleep. And no way she could sleep without some kind of cover.

She stretched back out on the mattress and pulled the sleeping bag over her. It settled against her like a silky cloud.

There was no escaping him, not that night. She'd chosen to walk straight into the lion's den—she might as well accept it.

Tomorrow she'd be gone. Come to her senses. If her mother needed more answers she'd have to hire a private detective.

Nate was dead. Nothing would bring him back, and right now answers, justice, even revenge seemed too dangerous a quest. Maybe when she'd gotten some sleep she'd see things differently, but she didn't think so. One look into Dillon Gaynor's cold blue eyes reminded her of just how dangerous he could be. And she was a woman who valued safety.

She turned off the light, and the room was plunged into a thick, inky darkness, punctuated by a blinking neon sign somewhere beyond her window. He hadn't given her a pillow, and there was no way she was going to go looking for one. She punched her sweater into a ball and put it under her head, pulling the sleeping bag up to her chin.

He was everywhere. Beneath her, above her, surrounding her. There was no fighting it, not now. She closed her eyes and remembered.

Twelve years ago

It was a beautiful late spring night in Rhode Island when Jamie Kincaid grew up. She was sixteen years old, privileged, beloved, living in a dream world with nothing more to worry about than grades and dates. Grades were no problem—as her cousin, Nate, always told her, she was too smart for her own good.

And dates weren't usually an issue, either. She'd had a pleasant, nonthreatening boyfriend who'd done no more than give her a few closedmouthed kisses, and when he dumped her on the eve of the junior prom she was more annoyed than hurt. She had the dress, she'd worked on the committee, she had every intention of going, anyway, and dragooned her cousin Nate to take her.

Nate was more a brother than a cousin. He'd lived with his aunt Isobel and uncle Victor for the last nine years, since his parents had died in a fire. Jamie was an only child, and she'd always wanted an older brother. And ten-year-old Nate was a dream come true for young Jamie.

She still adored him, though nine years together had worn off some of the novelty. But then, everybody adored Nate—he was incredibly handsome, with a dazzling smile, dark eyes, silky black hair and the kind of rugged body that made him perfect for sports and teenage fantasies. He was beloved by teachers and students alike, his surrogate parents, and most especially by his besotted cousin, Jamie.

"What's up, kitten?"

Jamie looked up from her spot on the floor. The pale pink prom dress billowed out around her, and she wondered if unshed tears made her makeup run. Being dumped wasn't worth crying for. It was just…annoying.

She managed a crooked smile. Her cousin Nate hated emotions. With his easy charm he breezed through life, and he preferred those around him to do the same, and since Jamie adored him she did her best. "I just got dumped. Zack told me he was breaking up with me and taking Sara Jackson to the prom."

Nate shook his head. "Great timing. I could have

told you Zack was a loser. Want Dillon and me to go beat him up for you?''

Jamie controlled a little shiver. Her cousin was only kidding, but when it came to someone like his friend Dillon Gaynor there was no telling what might happen. "Don't bother. I'll get revenge sooner or later.''

"I suppose you still want to go to the prom? Forget it, precious! I may love you like a brother, but I'm not going to take you to a high school junior prom. I've already suffered through one once.''

She shook her head. "I wouldn't ask you. I'm not going.''

"So what are you going to do? Aunt Isobel and uncle Victor have already gone out, and I've got plans with Killer. Wanna come along?''

Killer was Nate's affectionate name for his low-life friend Dillon. Unfortunately there were times when Jamie wondered whether or not it was a bit too appropriate. "That's all right. You don't want a sixteen-year-old tagging along after you. I'll be fine. There's a book I want to read....''

"Nope," Nate said flatly. "You aren't going to miss out on your prom to curl up with a good book. You're coming with us. Time to visit the wild side of life. See how the other half lives. Try a little danger.''

"I'm not big on danger."

"Your big cousin will be there to protect you," he said. "And Dillon will make sure nothing happens to you."

"Like I trust him?" she scoffed.

"Trust who?" Dillon said, lounging in her doorway.

That was only one of the things she didn't like about him. He always walked in, appearing out of the blue. He seemed to know when her parents were gone—Victor and Isobel Kincaid neither liked nor approved of Nate's friend, and he was wise enough to make himself scarce when they were around. But anytime they were gone he'd be lounging in front of the big-screen TV, eating their food, smoking cigarettes, watching her out of his cool, insolent blue eyes. When he bothered to pay any attention to her at all.

"My little cousin thinks you're a dangerous man," Nate said with a laugh. He was a few inches shorter than Dillon, dark hair to Dillon's bleached-blond shag, sunshine and good nature to Dillon's mocking deference that always bordered on rudeness. It was no wonder her mother disliked him.

"She's right," Dillon said, looking down at her. "So are you ready?"

"I'm trying to talk Jamie into coming with us.

She just got stood up, and I thought it was time to broaden her horizons.''

She half expected Dillon to object, but he simply looked at her and shrugged. "If you think she's up to it.''

"She's my biggest fan," Nate said. "She'd never rat us out. Besides, Jamie can be your date since you don't have one.''

"No!" Jamie said, her horror overriding her usual courtesy.

If anything, Dillon seemed more amused than offended. "I don't need a date where we're going. I think you're asking for trouble here, Nate.''

Nate's smile was wide, the kind that won over friend and foe alike, clouded men's minds and women's, too. "But you know I love trouble." He reached out a hand to Jamie and pulled her to her feet.

"She's not wearing that," Dillon said.

"Killer, you are no fun at all," Nate protested. "I think we should show up at Crazy Jack's with my cousin the prom queen.''

"I don't think this is a good idea," Jamie said nervously.

"Of course it is. Go change into something sexy. Dress like a bad girl for a change. Wouldn't you like to be a bad girl, just once?''

"Not particularly." She cast a wary glance up at Dillon. He tended to ignore her, and she'd probably exchanged maybe a dozen words with him in her entire life. "What do you think, Dillon? Should I come with you guys?"

She should have known she'd get no answer from him. "Suit yourself. Just hurry up."

She was crazy to do it. Her parents only tolerated Dillon because of Nate, but there was no way they'd approve of her going out with them. Dillon came from the wrong side of the tracks, and his behavior befitted his upbringing. He'd already spent three months in juvie for stealing cars, and no one had any illusions that he'd changed his ways. He'd just gotten more careful.

Jamie could never understand what Nate saw in him. Maybe it was his to-hell-with-you attitude. Nate charmed everyone he came in contact with, needing their approval; Dillon didn't care one way or another. He just did what he wanted and let the chips fall where they may.

And she was going out with him. Well, not with him, really. She was just tagging along with her cousin and Dillon and as soon as they got to Crazy Jack's, wherever that was, he'd find someone to keep himself busy. Nate would look after her—she trusted him with her life.

The prom dress ripped slightly when she yanked it over her head. She tossed it in the corner, found a pair of jeans and a big white shirt. She buttoned it up high, just so Dillon didn't get any ideas, and headed back out to the sound of their voices before she could change her mind.

They were in the kitchen drinking beer. Her father wouldn't like that one bit—the boys were only nineteen and one of them would be driving. Dillon was to blame, of course. Maybe after tonight Jamie would have some kind of idea of what Nate saw in him. And if she did, maybe she'd help her parents figure out how to get Nate away from such a dangerous influence.

"That's better, precious," Nate said approvingly. Dillon said nothing, draining his beer.

"We'd better get going. Rachel will be pissed."

"Who's Rachel?" Jamie asked. Maybe Dillon had a girlfriend, after all. In fact, he was very good-looking. A polar opposite to her cousin, he was tall, blue-eyed, teenage skinny with endless legs. He had the best cheekbones she'd ever seen on a man, she had to admit that much. And the kind of mouth a susceptible girl might find attractive. If she liked danger.

"Never you mind about Rachel," Nate said fondly. "She's nothing serious. Just for fun."

"Is she your date or Dillon's?" she asked.

"Carry these." Dillon shoved a six-pack of beer into her arms. "And you've forgotten. You're my date for the night."

She looked at him warily, not certain whether he was kidding or not. With Dillon you could never quite tell.

Her only choice was to ignore him. She wrapped her arms around the beer, hoping the white cotton of her shirt would disguise her bundle, and followed them out into the driveway.

It was a warm night in May. The peepers were in full voice, and there was a soft breeze ruffling through the bright green leaves overhead. The kind of night that always put an ache of longing in the pit of her stomach, though she never could quite figure out what she was longing for.

Dillon's old car was parked in the driveway. There was no mistaking it—a very old yellow Cadillac convertible that he'd fixed up himself. It was fast and big, and he could outrun the police if he really wanted to. As far as Jamie knew, he'd never wanted to.

He'd always tinkered with cars. He'd been driving since he was thirteen, and she had no idea if he had a driver's license even now. He went around to the driver's side and climbed in, not bothering to open the door. Not bothering to open hers, either, of course.

She reached for the rear door, but Nate was ahead of her. "You sit in the front, kitten. I want the back seat for me and Rachel."

He smiled at her, beguiling as always, and there was no way she could object.

"The doors don't work," Dillon said. "You'll have to climb in. Hand me the beer."

She hesitated. She could still go to the prom— there was no shame in going alone, and she had the dress. That stupid pink dress that she'd torn.

Safety or danger? Dillon was looking up at her, his cool blue eyes daring her. She climbed over the side of the car and slid down onto the worn leather seat of the Caddy, putting the beer beside her.

He took one, opened it and set it between his legs. Immediately drawing her attention to his crotch. She jerked her head away, staring straight forward. He wouldn't notice the blush of color on her face. He wasn't that interested.

He drove fast but well. He'd jury-rigged a cassette tape player into the dashboard, and he had it playing loud heavy-metal music. He finished one beer, tossed the can in the bushes and opened another, all without sparing a glance her way.

She had no idea where they were going, and the

little shiver of excitement in the pit of her stomach mixed with fear as he turned down a dirt road, barely slowing the car. It sped along the rutted surface, moving deeper into the woods, until he finally came to a stop in a clearing. A battered old pickup truck was parked there, accompanied by a couple of rusting wrecks, and a narrow path led through the woods to a tumbledown building almost out of sight.

Nate had already jumped out of the back seat. "You guys stay here. I told Rachel to meet me at the house. I'll just go get the stuff and be back in a minute."

Dillon switched off the car, stretching out in the front seat. "Take your time," he said lazily. "My date will keep me entertained."

Was that excitement or dread in her stomach? Or a heady combination of both? "Maybe I should go with him..." she said nervously.

"I don't think so. He and Rachel will want some privacy. He'll be back eventually."

"Eventually?" she echoed, and she could hear the panic in her own voice.

"Don't look so terrified, sweet cakes. I don't bite. Much."

She was already as far from him on the wide front seat of the Cadillac as she could get. He reached between them, ripped another beer from the plastic ring and then set the remainder on the floor. Leaving nothing between them. "Have a beer," he said. She wasn't sure if it was an offer or an order.

"I don't think..."

"I thought this was your big night of rebellion. Take the beer, Jamie."

She took it. It wasn't as if it was the first beer she'd ever had. She just didn't like it much. However, she was so nervous her stomach was doing flip-flops, and maybe the beer would calm her down, help her to relax. She didn't want Dillon thinking she was a total idiot. Though she didn't even want to consider why his opinion suddenly mattered.

The beer was lukewarm, yeasty, and she took a long drink. Dillon lounged against the door, making no move toward her, watching her out of hooded eyes. "Nate will be bringing some more stuff if you'd prefer grass."

"I don't!" she said quickly.

"Just say no?" he mocked. "I bet you're good at that, sweet cakes. I bet you say no all the time. Do you ever say yes?"

She didn't answer, and he didn't seem to expect her to. He leaned back against the seat, looking up into the darkening sky, totally relaxed, while Jamie sat miles away on the other side of the car, clutching her beer.

So he was every young girl's secret fantasy, she mocked herself. Latter-day James Dean, bad boy with a killer smile and a mouth that could tempt a nun. And she was no nun.

"Do you want to make out?" she asked suddenly.

He turned to look at her, slowly, lazily. "Is that an offer?"

She squirmed, uncomfortable. "Well, if I'm really your date..."

"You're not," he said. "Much as I appreciate the offer of a virgin sacrifice, I think I'll pass this time. I don't make out."

She took another swig of the beer. It was almost gone, and she wondered if he'd offer her another one. Probably not. "You don't? Don't you like girls?"

His smile was the most dangerous thing she'd ever seen in her life. "I like girls just fine. I don't make out, I don't neck, I don't kiss as a recreational activity."

"Then what do you do?"

"I fuck."

Jamie choked on the last of her beer. "I beg your pardon?"

"You heard me. I fuck. I don't kiss women un-less I want to fuck them, and I sure as hell don't kiss jailbait like you unless it's a sure thing. And I don't think you're going to be slipping out of those jeans anytime soon, are you? Not for me."

She just stared at him. Night was falling, and the breeze had picked up just slightly, running through his shaggy blond hair like a lover's caress. "No," she said in a small voice.

His smile was small and mocking. "I didn't think so. Not from the way you're hugging that side of the car. Don't worry, baby girl. I won't touch you." He turned his head, peering through the gathering darkness. "It won't be long now. Nate doesn't have much staying power."

"Staying power? What are you talking about?"

"He and Rachel are having sex. He goes for quantity rather than quality, and Rachel's a good match for him. They'll be out in a few more minutes, smelling of sex, half drunk with it. That, and the dope he went to get."

"Whose house is that?"

"Mine."

"Are they your drugs?"

"Yes."

She was silent. She'd gone through all the man-datory drug-education classes, she knew the dangers. She'd been around marijuana enough to know the smell, to see people get giggly with it, then numbed out. "Are you a dealer?"

"Why? You looking to score?"

"No. I was just curious."

"I think you ought to stifle that curiosity, sweet cakes," he said. He glanced at his watch, a cheap Timex, and swore. "Maybe Nate's being more creative than usual." He looked over at her, considering. "Maybe I've changed my mind."

"What?" It came out as a nervous little squeak.

"Come here."

3

Jamie woke up in the shadowy gloom, lost, disoriented, fighting back panic. There was a loud, roaring noise coming from somewhere, she was cold, her back hurt, and for a moment she had no idea where she was. The neon light flashed on again, illuminating the small room for a brief moment, and she remembered. And felt her panic increase.

She sat up, taking deep, calming breaths. She never liked sleeping in unfamiliar beds—one of the many reasons she'd driven straight to Wisconsin without stopping at a motel along the way. Even in the familiarity of her own bed she seldom slept well—the slightest sound would jar her awake and she would lie there, for hours on end, staring into the darkness.

At least this time she had a reason. The windowsill was eye level from her seat on the floor, and she looked out over the alleyway, into the dismal gray light of a November dawn. She had no idea how long she'd slept—it might have been hours, or minutes. The room was cold, and in the unforgiving light of day it looked like a cell. Though she could finally identify the roaring noise as heat pouring into the room from a vent near her mattress. At least this place came equipped with an extremely noisy furnace.

She lay back down again, closing her eyes. There was no use getting up—Dillon would be sleeping off the effects of whatever he'd had the night before, and he wouldn't be in any shape to help her. Not that he'd be interested in doing anything for her—they'd never gotten along. But he'd be motivated to get her out of there, if for no other reason than he'd never liked her.

She shivered. It had never really left her—that haunted night so long ago. Months, even years, went by without her thinking about it, without remembering the painful embarrassment and shame, but one look into Dillon's cold blue eyes had brought everything back, with a vengeance. The rough pleasure in his hands. The shattering misery of how it ended.

She took a slow, deep breath, willing her tense body to relax. Long ago, she reminded herself. And by the end of the night Dillon had been so wasted there was no way he could remember any details. If he even remembered that night at all.

She must have been out of her mind to think that she could come here unscathed. Though maybe that was part of the reason she'd come, jumped in her car before she thought better of it, taking off into the dark November night like an angel on a mission. She wanted answers about Nate's death. But she needed to face Dillon Gaynor and put any lingering emotions to rest. To let go of the past before she could get on with her future. And like it or not, Dillon was part of her past, inextricably entwined with Nate.

She'd been wearing the same clothes for forty-eight hours, and she was feeling beyond grungy. As soon as she got away from here she'd stop at the first motel she found, take a two-hour shower and even try for a nap. And then drive straight back to Rhode Island, with no more answers than she'd had when she started on this idiot quest.

At least the room was warming up, and she could dispense with the sleeping bag. She shoved a hand through her tangled hair, scrambling off the thin mattress. And then she saw her suitcase.

She stared at it, not making the mistake of thinking it a good sign. If Dillon had managed to fix her car, then he wouldn't have brought her suitcase up—he wouldn't do anything to prolong her stay.

She opened the door to the long, narrow hallway.

The bare lightbulb at the end illuminated the empty bathroom. All the other doors were closed, and she wondered where he slept.

Not that it mattered. At that moment the bathroom was looking pretty damned good, and a shower was becoming more and more appealing with the arrival of clean clothes. She wasn't getting out of here until Dillon woke up and she was able to get Nate's things, and there was no way she was going to sit around in these clothes for another minute.

At least there was a lock on the bathroom door. One of those old skeleton key things—if she'd had half a brain the night before she could have taken the key and locked her own door. And then Dillon couldn't have come in the darkness to dump her suitcase. Had he stood there and stared at her while she slept? Doubtful.

The bathtub was a grimy, claw-footed antique with a shower overhead, but the water was hot and the grayish towels smelled clean. She combed her wet hair with her fingers and grimaced at her reflection. She'd thrown T-shirts and jeans in her suitcase instead of her usual professional clothes. She looked like a twelve-year-old, with her scrubbed, makeup-free face, wet hair and boy's clothes. Any other twenty-eight-year-old woman would be happy to look so young. For Jamie it just reminded her of when she was sixteen and Dillon Gaynor was the terrifying center of her universe.

She'd had all sorts of fantasies about what it would be like if or when she saw him again. She'd be cool, calm, mature, with perfect hair and makeup, maybe a subdued suit and the string of pearls her parents had given her. The person she was raised to be.

Instead she'd shown up at his doorstep like a snowy waif. And he wasn't going to look at her today and see the calm, professional woman she'd become. He'd see a kid, and he'd remember.

Maybe. Or maybe that night was just a blur, along with a thousand other nights. Maybe he didn't remember.

But the problem was, she did.

The hall was still dark and silent, all the doors closed. She dumped her dirty clothes in a corner in her room, then glanced outside. It was getting lighter—maybe seven o'clock in the morning. She had two choices: wait for Dillon to get over his hangover and drag himself out of bed, or go down and start taking care of things on her own. It was a no-brainer. She needed to find out where her car was, get it towed, call Isobel, find some coffee, find something to eat....

The stairway was narrow and dark, and if there were any lights she couldn't find them. She went down carefully, holding on to the rickety railing, feeling her way in the shadows. She got to the bottom, reaching for the door into the kitchen, when she stepped on something soft and squishy. Something big.

She screamed, falling back in the shadows, and then immediately she felt stupid. It was probably nothing, just a discarded piece of clothing....

The door to the kitchen was yanked open, and Dillon stood there, filling it, radiating impatience. "What the hell are you yowling about?" he demanded. "Did you fall?"

"I—I stepped on something," she said, trying to control her stammer. "It was probably nothing...." She glanced down at the small square of floor at the bottom of the stairs. She gulped. "Or maybe not."

"It's a rat," Dillon said, his voice as flat as his expression. "We get them every now and then."

"You have rats?" she demanded in horror.

"Sorry, princess, but this ain't the Taj Mahal. It's an old warehouse, and rats come with the territory. They show up occasionally, but at least they're dead. Someone must have put some rat poison behind the walls years ago and it's still working.

Every now and then there's a nice fresh corpse, and I don't have to worry about them getting into the food.''

Food, Jamie thought. She glanced down at the dead rat, but even a corpse wasn't enough to distract her. ''I'm hungry,'' she said.

''Then go on into the kitchen and find yourself something to eat. Unless you were thinking of fried rat?''

She rose from her seat on the stairs and glared at him. Two steps up put her eye level with him, and the result was disconcerting. ''Maybe you could move the rat first? I don't want to step on it.''

Big mistake. Before she knew what he was doing he'd simply picked her up, swung her across the small square of floor and set her down in the kitchen. Letting go of her immediately, as if she weren't any more appealing than the dead rat. Maybe less. ''There you go, Your Highness. There's bread on the counter and beer in the fridge.''

''Or course there is,'' she said, hostile. ''But I'm not in the habit of drinking beer for breakfast.''

''You oughtta try it. Good for what ails you.''

''Nothing ails me.''

''Nothing but that stick up your ass,'' Dillon said

pleasantly, picking the rat up by the tail. It swung limply from his hand, and she shuddered.

"I'll save the beer for you," she said, controlling her shudder.

"Good of you." He carried the rat over to the back door, opened it and flung it out into the alleyway. "All taken care of," he said.

"You're just going to leave it out there? Spreading disease and God knows what else?"

"The bubonic plague is over. And if it comes back I'm willing to bet you'd be happy to have me get the first case."

"You got me there."

He seemed to consider the idea for a moment. "Besides, there are enough scavengers around that he won't be there for long. He'll either be eaten by his brothers or carried off by some stray dog."

"What makes you think it's a he?"

"That was for your benefit. I assumed you think all rats are male."

"Good point," she said. The kitchen didn't look much better than it had last night. The bottles had been swept off the table, but the smell of cigarettes and stale beer lingered in the air, with the faint note of exhaust beneath it.

"Bread's on the counter," he said. "I'll make coffee."

There were exactly two pieces of bread in the plastic bag, both of them heels. "Where's the toaster?"

"Broken. There's some peanut butter over the stove—make yourself a sandwich."

Isobel would have fainted with shock at the idea of peanut butter sandwiches for breakfast. Jamie was just grateful for the protein. She sat down at the scarred oak table to make her sandwich, watching as Dillon reached for the coffeepot. He poured out the dregs, filled the carafe with water and put it back in the machine.

"Aren't you going to wash it out first?"

"Why? It's going to hold coffee, and that's what it held before. What's the big deal?" He leaned against the counter, watching her lazily.

"The old coffee oils will make it bitter," she said, not even getting to the cleanliness part. From the look of Dillon's littered kitchen, cleanliness wasn't high on his list.

"Maybe I like bitter."

"I have no doubt that you do," she said. The bread was slightly stale, but it was solid, and she devoured her makeshift sandwich. "I don't suppose you have anything as mundane as a soda?"

"They call it pop out here in the hinterlands, Your Highness. Check in the fridge."

He'd been lying about the beer. They must have finished it all during their late-night poker game. The contents of the refrigerator consisted of a chunk of moldy cheese, half a quart of milk and enough cans of soda to satisfy anyone. She grabbed a Coke and shut the door, snapping the top and taking a long drink, letting the sugary caffeine bubble down her throat.

He was watching her, an unreadable expression on his face. Not that she'd ever been able to guess what he was thinking. "What?" she demanded irritably.

"You don't strike me as the type who'd drink straight from the can."

"Maybe I don't trust your idea of cleanliness."

"I'm sure it's not up to your standards."

"It's not. When did you get my suitcase? Is my car here?"

"Your car's still stuck in a ditch out on the highway. And I didn't get the suitcase. Mouser was running an errand for me and he stopped and got it. You made quite an impression on him, but then, he doesn't know you as well as I do."

"You don't know me at all. We haven't seen each other in twelve years, and back then you had nothing to do with me."

"That's not the way I remember it."

It felt as if she'd been kicked in the stomach. She didn't even blink. "And your memory is so clear after all these years?"

"Clear enough." She wondered if she was imagining the faint thread of menace beneath his smooth tone. Probably not.

"I need to call my mother."

"Why?"

"To tell her I got here safely. And to tell her I'll be leaving as soon as the car is ready. This afternoon, I hope."

"Hope away," he said. "Mouser said your car was pretty messed up."

"This is a garage, isn't it? I'll pay you to fix it."

"I work on old American cars, not imports. Different tools."

"Then I'll call Triple A. If they can find someone to fix it I'll stay in a motel until it's ready—otherwise I'll rent a car."

"Honey, this town is the armpit of despair. The only motel around rents rooms by the hour, not the night, and no one rents cars but me."

"So?"

He glanced at her. "So I don't rent cars to drive out of state. No way to get them back."

"I'd think you'd be motivated to get me out of here."

"Now, that's where you're wrong," he said lazily, reaching for the coffeepot, which was now filled with thick black sludge. "I think I'm going to enjoy reliving old times. The halcyon days of my youth and all that."

"Your youth wasn't particularly halcyon."

"Neither was yours, princess."

"That's not the way I remember it. I had two loving parents, a secure life, I had Nate as my brother and best friend. Until you got your hooks into him."

He took a chair at the table, reaching for his cigarettes. It seemed like years since she'd been around anyone who smoked, and she watched with fascination as he lit the cigarette with a flip of his silver lighter. "Memories can be faulty," he said, and blew smoke at her.

She would have liked to summon up a hacking cough, but in fact she'd never been particularly sensitive to smoke. Besides, he was clearly trying to bother her, and she wasn't going to give him that satisfaction. "Maybe yours are. I think I'm a little clearer on details than you would be."

"Suit yourself."

"Where's the telephone?"

"In the garage. It's a pay phone—be sure you have plenty of quarters."

"How do you manage to do business without a phone?"

"I don't like people intruding on my privacy."

"Then I'll be doing my best to get the hell out of here. Just find me Nate's stuff and I'll give AAA a call."

"What's the hurry, princess? Nate's been dead for three months—he's not going anywhere."

"Don't you even care?" she demanded. "He was your best friend! A brother to you, and he died when he was under your roof. Don't you feel anything? Grief, regret, responsibility?"

"I'm not responsible for Nate's death," he said in a detached voice.

"I didn't say you were. But you're the one who should have protected him. If he'd gotten in with a bad crowd you should have done something, anything, to help him...." Her voice trailed off in the face of his ironic expression.

"Maybe you better make those phone calls," he said, rising and pouring himself a mug of steaming sludge. "You want any of this?"

"I'd rather die."

"Sooner or later, angel face, you're going to have to learn to lower your patrician standards."

"You aren't going to be around to see it."

"Oh, that's where you're wrong. I'm looking forward to it."

The smell of the coffee was tantalizing. She knew it would be awful—too strong, too bitter. It would wreak havoc on her stomach and her nerves, and even milk and sugar wouldn't make it palatable. And she wanted it, anyway.

She rose, shoving a hand through her wet hair. He was watching her, and she didn't like it. The sooner she was out of there the better. "So my car's still in the ditch on...what road did you say it was?"

"Route 31."

"Fine. I'll call AAA, I'll call my mother, and I'll make arrangements to give you back your privacy as soon as possible. That's what you'd like, right? Have me get the hell out of here?"

"Do you have any doubts about that?" He stubbed out his cigarette, looking up at her above the thread of smoke.

In fact, she did. It didn't make sense, but he didn't seem in any hurry to have her leave. "I'll just go get my purse. Maybe my cell phone will work here."

"Maybe," he said, taking a sip of his coffee and not even grimacing. "But I wouldn't count on it. I wouldn't count on anything if I were you."

She didn't bother arguing with him. She didn't bother wasting another word on him—she simply headed up the dark, narrow stairs, stepping over the stained spot where the rat's corpse had rested, going straight to her room.

In the gray light of a November morning it looked even less welcoming than it had before. The room was Spartan—just the mattress on the floor, the sleeping bag and her suitcase.

And no sign of her purse anywhere.

It was cold up here. Nate never thought he would be so cold, looking down on them. It was an odd sort of feeling—floating, dreamy, and then everything coming into focus. He should have known she was coming—he just couldn't understand what had taken her so long to get here. His death would have shattered her, and there was no way she could move on with her life without getting answers. She'd come here to face his old buddy Dillon. The man who had let him die.

He wasn't sure what he was going to do about it yet, even though he'd had a long time to think about it. Time had stopped making any sense, one day blending into another. He was trapped in this old building, unable to leave, but he'd heard her moving around, and known it was her.

The dead rat had been a nice touch. He left one every few days, not on a regular schedule. He didn't want to be too predictable. He hadn't expected Jamie to be the one to find it, but he didn't mind. It meant Dillon had to come up with explanations, fast. And if he knew Dillon, he wasn't about to tell her that the old factory was haunted by the ghost of her murdered cousin.

No, infested by rats was a preferable explanation. And it was. The rat of a man who'd betrayed his best friend and sent him to his death. And the King Rat himself, Nate Kincaid.

You can't keep a good man down.

4

Jamie searched, of course. It had been there when she woke up, hadn't it? Dillon couldn't have taken it—he'd been with her the entire time. And there was no way up to the second floor except that dark, rat-infested stairway, and no one had passed them while they sat arguing at the kitchen table.

Or maybe whoever had dumped her suitcase in the room had taken the purse. She wasn't carrying a lot of cash, though her small supply of sleeping pills might appeal to some teenage druggie. And hell, what was Dillon but an overgrown teenage druggie? It had to be him.

She sat down on the mattress. She should go downstairs and confront him, demand that he return her purse. He'd deny taking it, of course. She was going to have a hell of a hard time getting out of here without her license and credit cards. No one would rent her a car, much less a room, without ID and credit. If he didn't give it back to her she was stuck.

She stretched out on the thin mattress, staring at the cracked ceiling. He didn't want her here. Why the hell would he do something that would keep her trapped here? Why, when he'd never liked her? If he even remembered that night so long ago, all he'd remember was what an idiot she'd been. What an embarrassing, pathetic idiot.

Twelve years ago

"I've changed my mind," he said, and the soft breeze of early summer riffled through his too-long hair. "Come here."

Jamie sat frozen in the front seat of the old Cadillac, practically wedged between the seat and the door. The beer bottle in her hands was empty, and in the gathering dusk Dillon Gaynor looked like every good girl's worst nightmare. And secret, shameful dream.

She'd had her share of them. They all had, all the good girls of Marshfield, Rhode Island. He was wicked, he was sexy, he was as pretty as sin. Just the sort to daydream about. Just the sort to keep away from. And she was sitting in the front seat of an old Cadillac convertible with him, alone in the woods, and she'd been fool enough to bring up the subject of kissing.

She didn't move. "I was just kidding," she said, unable to keep the thread of nerves out of her voice.

"I wasn't." He took the empty beer bottle out of her hands and threw it into the woods. And then he reached for her, pulling her across the broad front seat. The old leather was so soft and smooth she slid easily, until she was touching him, thigh to thigh, and he was looking down into her breathless face. "So where do we start?"

"You drive me home, then come back and get Nate and his girlfriend?" she suggested in a nervous voice.

"I don't think so." He picked up her hand and looked at it for a long, contemplative moment. "Baby-pink nail polish. Did that match your prom dress?"

She'd chosen the shade just for that purpose, but she wasn't about to admit it. He wasn't expecting her to. He just held her delicate hand in his large, callused one, rubbing his thumb over her palm, slowly, sinuously. "Such an innocent hand," he said. "What naughty things have you done with it?"

"Nothing."

"I can believe it," he murmured, pulling her hand to his mouth. He put his mouth against her palm, and she felt a shiver run through her body.

And then he licked it, and the feel of his tongue against her skin shocked her. ''Time you learned,'' he said. And he put her hand against his chest.

It wouldn't have been so bad if he'd been wearing the usual ratty T-shirt. But tonight he wore a faded Hawaiian-style shirt, and it was partly open, and her damp palm was pressed against his warm flesh without the safety of thin cotton between them.

He was hot. His skin burned beneath her cold hand, and she could feel the slow, steady pulse of his heart, beating against her palm, moving down her arm and into her body, so that her heart was beating with his, but faster, much faster, and she was cold where he was hot, and she stared up at him, paralyzed.

He kept her hand captured in his, pressed against his heart, as he leaned forward and flicked on the car radio. U2 was playing—Bono was singing about sex and love, just what she didn't want to hear. He leaned back in the seat again, his fingers touching hers, caressing them, one by one, as he slowly unbuttoned the rest of his shirt with his other hand.

She felt like a small white rat facing a hungry python. Mesmerized, she sat in the front seat of the old convertible and waited for him to make the next move.

This was Dillon Gaynor, the object of her teenage

fantasies since the first time he'd walked into her parents' house, whether she'd wanted to admit it or not. It was his skin beneath her hand, and he was moving his head closer, and he was going to kiss her, he actually was, and she closed her eyes, holding her breath, waiting.

He tasted like beer. And cigarettes. And sin, sweet sin. The baddest of all bad boys, and he was kissing her, his mouth moving slowly over her closed lips, his hand pressing hers against his hot skin, holding it there. She closed her eyes, telling herself this wasn't happening, and since it wasn't, she wasn't doing anything wrong or dangerous, and she could just lean back against the ratty leather seat and let him kiss her. He lifted his head.

"Is that the way you kiss your boyfriends?"

The nice dreamlike haze vanished, and she opened her eyes, trying to sit up. He held her down. "I know there've been boyfriends," he continued, and she realized he was moving her hand across his stomach, in slow, erotic circles. "Nate's told me all about them. Jimmy McCarty and Jay Thompson. You have lousy taste in boys."

"Is that why I'm here with you?" she said.

"Kitten's got claws," he murmured. "Open your mouth when I kiss you."

"I don't like that."

"Tough. You're playing with grown-ups now. This is how we do it in the big leagues." He pushed her back against the seat and forced her mouth open before she could come up with another protest. He kissed her, using his tongue, slowly, thoroughly, and she felt a heat begin to pool in her stomach, radiating outward. Dillon Gaynor definitely knew how to kiss. What had been wet and sloppy with Jimmy was slow and mesmerizing with Dillon. She hadn't even realized he'd released her hand, and she was slowly caressing the warm skin of his stomach, until she felt his hand on the waist of her jeans, heard the rasp of her zipper as his hand slipped inside.

She panicked. It didn't do her any good, he was too strong for her. His mouth silenced any protest, his body pressing against hers kept her from escaping, and his hands, his fingers, slid beneath her plain cotton panties to touch her.

She had the strength to wrench her mouth away from his. "Stop it," she whispered. "Let me go." She could have screamed, maybe. But she didn't want to.

He pushed her face against his shoulder, his mouth by her ear, and he took a small, wicked bite of her earlobe. "Just relax," he said. "Consider this a graduation present."

"But I didn't graduate," she murmured in a dazed voice.

"You're about to."

One of her hands was trapped beneath their bodies, but she wrenched the other free to grab his shoulder and try to push him away. He didn't budge.

"Close your eyes, baby girl," he whispered. "I'm about to show you a very good time."

There was nothing she could do to stop him—he was too strong, too determined, and he knew exactly what he was doing. He pushed his fingers inside her, and she wanted to die of shame. And he was rubbing her, using his thumb, and she knew what he was trying to do, but she couldn't even do it on her own, much less with a stranger touching her, inside her, rubbing her until she moaned.

"That's right, sweetheart," he whispered. "That's what I want to hear from you. Just a little bit louder."

She bit her lip to keep from making any sound, but it didn't do any good. She felt a spasm of reaction wash over her, and she shivered, her voice choked.

"Better," he murmured. "But I think I want to make you cry."

"Dillon," she said in a cracked voice. Begged, though she wasn't sure what she was begging for.

But Dillon knew. He knew exactly what he was doing to her, how to make her shiver and teeter on the very precipice, and then draw back, only to bring her forward again, stronger than ever, and she wanted to weep.

"Come on, baby girl," he whispered in her ear. "Let go. Stop fighting me, stop fighting it. Come for me."

She didn't have any choice. It washed over her like an explosive force, as her body arched, rigid, and she wanted to scream, to cry, to make it stop, to make it last forever. It was too powerful, too overwhelming, and she let out a low, keening cry that he swallowed with his mouth, keeping her silent as he prolonged her orgasm past human endurance.

And then she collapsed beneath him, in a boneless, quivering heap, lying against his strong body in the front seat of the old Caddy, shaken and tearful.

He pulled his hand free and fastened her jeans again, pulling up the zipper and snapping the snap with experienced ease. Her face was wet with tears, but at least it was too dark for him to see, until she felt his fingers wiping them away in the darkness.

"What's going on in there?" Nate's slurred voice rang out in the darkness. "Are you corrupting my little cousin, Killer?"

"Of course not," he said in a lazy voice, pushing her down on the seat, out of sight. "I tried to talk her into it but she's too prim and proper. She just got tired of waiting for you and Rachel."

"Sorry, kiddo," Nate said in a careless voice. She couldn't see anything from her vantage point on the cracked leather seat of the old Caddy, but it sounded as if it was just as well. Nate and his girl-friend climbed into the back seat, and she could smell the sickly sweet scent of marijuana permeating the air, mixing with the smell of liquor. Not the beer that Dillon had been drinking, something stronger.

"Drive on, Jeeves!" Nate ordered in a lordly manner.

Without a word Dillon started the car, the head-lights spearing the darkness. It had to be late—the sky stayed light till almost ten that time of year. Would her parents wonder where she was when they got back from their cocktail party? No, they'd assume she was at the prom, safe in the care of a good boy who'd look out for her and keep her safe.

But that good boy had dumped her. And even her beloved Nate was doing a piss-poor job of seeing

to her welfare, leaving her in the hands of a...
a...she couldn't even think of the word for Dillon.

She tried to sit up, but Dillon simply put a hand
on her shoulder and shoved her down again. "You
need your rest," he said, pushing her head down to
rest on one hard thigh. She couldn't have sat up if
she tried, but then she heard the telltale sounds from
the back seat and realized that Nate and his girlfriend were doing more than necking. And she definitely didn't want to be seeing that.

She stopped resisting, letting her head fall against
the soft denim that covered Dillon's leg. "That's
right," he murmured, so quietly that the two in the
back couldn't hear him. Not that they were paying
attention. "Just stay put and you won't see anything
you don't want to see."

Dillon had pulled out of the parking area and was
driving down the tree-shrouded back road, fast, with
one hand holding the steering wheel, the other
draped casually on her shoulder. He was stroking
her, absentmindedly, she assumed, his long fingers
brushing against her arm, trailing up the side of her
neck to brush her hair away. She had no illusions
that he'd let her sit up—every time she tried he
simply exerted enough pressure to keep her down.

She gave up fighting, letting out her breath and letting her head rest on his thigh.

"That's better," he said, softly enough that the words were torn away by the wind rushing past them. And she closed her eyes, breathing in the night air, the smell of beer and denim and spring flowers. The scent of her on his hand as he slowly stroked her neck.

She almost fell asleep. She could hear the noises from the back seat, but she didn't want to think about it. Didn't want to think about what Dillon had done to her. Didn't want think about anything but the quiet sense of calm that surrounded her as Dillon stroked her neck.

She heard the music first, echoing through the woods, loud and insistent. Dillon pulled the car to a stop, and this time when she tried to sit up he let her, let her scurry over to the far side of the car, while he showed nothing more than a faint smile.

At least Nate and his friend had resurfaced, flushed, half dressed, but finished with whatever they were doing. Nate scrambled out of the car, leaving his girlfriend to follow after him, but he paused to give Jamie a hand. A good thing, too, because her legs were still shaky. People surged around them, all of them strangers, most of them drunk or stoned, and she turned back to look for Dillon.

He already had his tongue down the throat of some girl who'd plastered herself against him. Except that he was holding on to her, holding her hips against his, and she'd already managed to unfasten the final buttons of his shirt. The shirt he'd unbuttoned for her.

She knew she hadn't made a sound, but he broke the kiss for a moment, turning back to glance at Jamie. She couldn't read his expression, and she knew she must have looked totally pathetic. "Hey, Pauly," he said to somebody standing nearby. "Nate brought his little sister along. Look after her, will you?"

She didn't even bother to correct him. Nate had already disappeared into the crowd, and Dillon had his hand on the huge breast of the girl who'd greeted him so enthusiastically. Totally forgetting about her.

"Hey, there, Jamie." And she realized with a shock who Pauly was. Paul Jameson, quarterback of the football team, president of the student council, tall, gorgeous, every girl's dream. He was slightly drunk, and his dark hair was flopped over his forehead in an endearing tangle. "Wanna drink?" He had a bottle of tequila in his hand.

She looked back toward Dillon, but he'd disappeared, without a backward glance. "Sure," she said. And he handed her the bottle.

Jamie wasn't accomplishing a goddamned thing, remembering that night. She'd put it out of her mind long ago, with a combination of determination, a good therapist and the judicious use of tranquilizers. Whenever the memories hit her she usually just popped a pill and the clawing anxiety would pass.

But the pills were in her purse, and her purse was gone. And the couldn't spend the day in her room, hiding.

She sat up, then froze in horror. The door was open, and Dillon was standing in the darkened hallway, watching her, that same unreadable expression on his face. He was so different from the boy in the Cadillac all those years ago. He was exactly the same.

"Someone took my purse," she said.

He looked neither surprised nor shocked. "Did you leave it in the car?"

"No. I brought it up here. Someone came into my room and took it." She wasn't certain of her ability to get to her feet with complete grace, so she stayed where she was, sitting on the thin mattress.

"And you think it was me? Not likely, sweetheart. I have no particular interest in keeping you around here, and the lack of your purse is going to slow your departure considerably. I know you like to blame me for everything that's ever gone wrong in your and Nate's life, but this time I'm innocent.''

''For some reason the very notion of you being innocent of anything is beyond my comprehension. And don't call me sweetheart!'' There was no question that Dillon brought out the worst in her. She'd spent her life trying to be compassionate, calm and forgiving, and Dillon made her shake with anger.

''What do you prefer I call you? Baby girl?''

It was like a punch in the stomach. He hadn't forgotten that night. She didn't even have that small comfort. At least he'd been too out of it to remember details.

She ignored it. ''So if you didn't take my purse, who did? The dead rat? Nate's ghost?''

''You never can tell.'' He made no effort to come into the room, but it was little comfort. He still loomed over her, and she decided it was better to scramble to her feet and risk looking clumsy than to keep staring up at him from such a subservient position. She knew enough about body language and politics to know this was only making her sense of powerlessness worse.

She got to her feet without stumbling, and even

took a step toward him, just to show that she wasn't afraid of him. "Where did you say the telephone was?" she said. "I need to call my mother and have her wire me some money."

"Down in the garage. But you'll have to call collect, princess."

"Don't be ridiculous. You have to have more than a pay phone here!"

He shook his head. "No need. There aren't that many people I want to talk to."

"Or who want to talk to you?"

"You got it. You shouldn't have any trouble finding it. I'm going to take a shower."

"I'd appreciate the privacy."

"Whereas I couldn't care less. If you have any interest in joining me in the shower—"

"I don't!" He was saying it just to annoy her, but it worked, to her utter shame.

"Give the Duchess my love, then," Dillon said lazily. And he closed the door behind him.

He was lying to her. Nate hovered overhead in a dreamlike state. He'd always been a good liar, and he could recognize when his old friend was lying, as well. What did Dillon want with Jamie? Maybe what he'd always wanted with Jamie and had never admitted.

It didn't mean that Nate didn't know just how fixated Dillon Gaynor had always been with little Jamie. And now she was here, stuck in the old building with no one to play chaperone but the ghost of the one person they had in common.

He was going to enjoy this.

5

At least he'd left the door open to the kitchen, so that light filtered into the bottom of the stairwell. There'd be no dead rats beneath her bare feet this time, thank God. Just the live one upstairs in the shower.

Jamie didn't want to think about that. Dillon and a shower meant Dillon naked, and that was one image she could happily do without. The only mental image she wanted of Dillon was with his head on a platter.

No, she didn't even care that much, she reminded herself as she crossed the now surprisingly neat kitchen. She just wanted to be gone. To take Nate's few possessions and get the hell out of there. Dillon unsettled her, even after all these years. Unsettled her more than the unanswered questions about Nate's death. She'd loved her cousin, deeply, but in the last few years she'd lost most of her illusions about him. Nate was a bad boy, maybe almost as bad as Dillon Gaynor. He'd done drugs, he'd broken the law, he'd broken her mother's heart. With his charm and good looks he'd managed to talk himself out of the consequences for his bad behavior. Until at the end, when someone, maybe even his childhood friend, had had enough and killed him.

Nothing was going to bring him back. Nothing would make the loss of him less painful, not the truth, not revenge. In fact, they'd lost Nate long ago. He needed to rest in peace.

But her mother wasn't about to accept that simple truth, and Jamie would have done anything Isobel asked of her. Except that this time it was too much, and she needed to get the hell out of there.

She dreaded going into the garage to use the pay phone but she had no choice. "Why in heaven's name are you calling me collect, Jamie?" she greeted her in the faint, slightly querulous tone she'd taken to using in the last few years. "You have a cell phone and a phone card."

"I've lost my purse," Jamie said flatly. And then guilt hit her. "How are you feeling, Mother?"

"The same," Isobel said with a sigh. "What can one expect? How did you happen to lose your purse? Where are you, for that matter? Have you seen that man?"

Jamie had no doubts that "that man" was Dillon.

"I'm here in Wisconsin. At his garage. My car went off the road, I lost my purse, and I need to get home."

"How unfortunate," Isobel said in her faint voice. "And a bit careless of you. How long have you been there?"

Jamie took a deep breath. "Twelve hours. Twelve hours too long. I need you to wire me some money, and any form of identification of mine you can find. Bella can look for you. She could even call the motor vehicle department to see what I need to do about my driver's license. I can't rent a car without one, even if I have a credit card."

"I try not to ask my nurse to do personal favors for me," Isobel said stiffly. "She's got enough to do, taking care of an old woman in a wheelchair."

Jamie pounded her forehead against the wall beside the pay phone, just once. Isobel never missed a chance to use her crippling arthritis as a weapon. "I don't think Bella would mind in an emergency," Jamie said.

"I don't see that it's an emergency. You're staying with Dillon, aren't you?"

"Yes, but—"

"Then that's perfect. Your cousin died there, Jamie. Our Nate was murdered there, and now you have the perfect chance to find out what happened."

"I'm not Nancy Drew, Mother."

"Don't be flippant with me," Isobel said in her faint tones. "You care just as much as I do—you can't fool me. A few days there won't do you any harm. I'll call my lawyer and have him put something in motion to get your paperwork back for you, but in the meantime you stay put and pay attention. Nothing happens without a reason. I think fate must have wanted you there."

Jamie didn't bother arguing. She loved her mother dearly, but Isobel did tend to think fate worked at Isobel Kincaid's whim. She was a Kincaid, after all, twice over. She'd even married her second cousin Victor, and Nate used to say she'd done it just to keep the name.

"I really don't want…" she tried one more time, but Isobel sailed right over her, her voice uncharacteristically strong.

"I don't think your wants should be paramount right now, Jamie. I'll call Miss Finch's—I'm sure they can make do without you for a few days. In the meantime you should concentrate on what happened to Nate. Why he was even there, what he did during his last days. Anything."

That tone of desperation had slid into Isobel's voice, the one that always destroyed Jamie's defenses. "All right, Mother," she said wearily. "I'll give it a few days."

"Thank you, Jamie. I knew I could count on you. After all, we both loved him so much."

"Yes, we did," Jamie said. "Let me give you…"

"Goodbye, darling."

"…the telephone number here." But Isobel had already hung up. Jamie stared at the phone in frustration. She could always try calling her back, but knowing Isobel's gift for getting what she wanted, she probably wouldn't answer the phone. Either that or she'd refuse to accept the collect charges.

She was trapped. She resisted temptation, putting the telephone back into its cradle very carefully. Her mother was right—a couple of days wouldn't kill her. And surely she could do something herself about getting her license and credit cards back. If only Dillon had a goddamned private telephone line.

She headed back toward the kitchen, then paused, looking at the cavernous garage.

It must have been some kind of warehouse or factory in the distant past. The place was huge, with a line of cars along both ends, half of them covered with tarps. She recognized an old Thunderbird, a Mustang Cobra and a stately '49 Oldsmobile. For some reason she had always been good at recognizing cars, and the ones she could see in Dillon's garage were beautiful and rare.

There were two more in various stages of disarray. The one missing an engine was a Ford from 1954 or 1955. The other was nothing less than a Duesenberg.

She took a step, irresistibly drawn to it. It had taken the years with surprising dignity, and even in its current state it had a certain grace and elegance that filled her with a rare covetousness. She'd never been particularly materialistic—her needs had always been more emotional and elemental. But looking at the old Duesenberg, she wanted it.

She turned her back on it, resolutely, and stalked to the kitchen. There was no sign of Dillon, thank God, and she was hungry. It was no wonder the man was still skinny—there wasn't even enough food in his cupboards to feed the dead rat. She half expected to find pellets all over the place, but whatever rodents had taken possession of the kitchen had left no sign behind.

She gave up looking, starting to eat stale Wheaties from the box, when the door opened and a very small guardian angel stepped in. Or more specifically, Mouser, with a boxful of groceries.

"Hi, there, sugar," he greeted her. "I brought

you some food. Dillon never has a damned thing in the house, and I figured you'd be starving about now. Don't eat those Wheaties—I think the guy on the box was in the 1936 Olympics.''

She set the box down hurriedly, swallowing her last dry mouthful. The little man was unpacking milk, orange juice and a bakery box that smelled like divine intervention.

"Cinnamon buns, no nuts, right?" he said.

She'd already opened the box, but she jerked her head up at his words. "How did you know that's what I like?" she demanded sharply.

Mouser shrugged. "Nate musta said something. I got a good memory for things like that."

"But Nate didn't. I don't think he had any idea whether I liked nuts or not."

"Well, hell, I musta got you mixed up with someone else. I'll get them with nuts tomorrow," he said, unabashed.

"No, this is perfect," she said hurriedly, realizing she must have sounded rude. Isobel had drummed good manners into her, good manners above all things. Besides, what did it matter if someone knew she didn't like nuts on anything?

"And some decent coffee," Mouser added, setting a tall cardboard mug in front of her. "Dillon uses the stuff he makes to strip the rust off old car parts.''

"I'd resent that if I didn't know you'd brought me some, too," Dillon said from the open doorway.

Jamie turned at the sound of his voice, and then quickly looked away. He was shirtless, his long hair wet, his feet bare. She should have known he'd look even better than he had at eighteen, the glorious golden bad boy of Marshfield, Rhode Island. She took the top off her cup of coffee, and the scent of hazelnut wafted up, as tempting as...tempting.

"Hey, I'm a sucker," Mouser said, sitting down at the table and opening the box of cinnamon buns. "Aren't you going to work today?"

"I was planning to." Before he took a chair beside her he put his shirt on, but didn't bother to button it. And his feet were still bare. "Hand over my coffee." Dillon took a big gulp from the paper cup Mouser handed him, then looked at it in horror. "What is this shit?" he demanded.

"Hazelnut coffee. I thought it was time to broaden your horizons."

"My coffee horizons are just fine as they are," Dillon said, grimacing as he took another deep drink. "Now, if you want to talk about something more interesting, like a '49 Studebaker, then—"

"I need to get out of here!" Jamie broke in.

Dillon turned to look at her, as if he'd just realized she was there. "And I'd like to get rid of you," he said affably. "The perfect partnership. What do you expect me to do?"

"My purse is gone."

"So you said. Call the Duchess and have her wire you what you need."

"I did. She says she will. Eventually. In the meantime she wants me to stay here."

She'd managed to surprise him. "The Duchess wants you in my evil clutches? Any reason why she'd choose you to be the virgin sacrifice?"

Virgin sacrifice. The phrase should have been light, comical. But it held too many loaded memories. For her, not for him. The years of alcohol and drugs had probably blotted out unpleasant memories for Dillon Gaynor. Sooner or later it would begin to show on his face. Right now he just looked older, sexier. His mouth was just as tempting as it had always been. It had tasted of cigarettes and beer, she remembered vividly. Even after all this time, no matter how much she wanted to, she couldn't forget Dillon's taste.

"What are you staring at?" he said, reaching for the pack of cigarettes on the table.

Mouser slapped his hand. "I thought you were trying to quit."

"I am. But not at this particularly stressful time in my life. I'll wait till I don't have guests," he said, lighting one. "You didn't answer my question. Why does the Duchess want you here?"

"She wants me to find out what happened to Nate."

"He died."

The knowledge still hurt, but she wasn't about to show it. "Tell me something I don't know."

He took a deep drag of the cigarette, his eyes narrowed over the exhaled smoke. "I could tell you a lot of things you don't know, child. There are none so blind as those who will not see."

"What's that supposed to mean?" she demanded.

"It means that even if I told you, showed you, you wouldn't believe it. You've set up your own belief system long ago, and nothing could ever shake it. Not that it should. You can go back to Rhode Island and live in your safe little cocoon. Didn't you ever want to leave there?" he added with a swift change of topic.

"Not particularly." It was a lie, but he wouldn't know that. She felt stifled in the small college town where she'd spent her entire life. Anything, even a run-down garage in the middle of nowhere, would have been preferable.

"So what's needed to get you the hell out of

here?'' he said, reaching for the last cinnamon bun. It wasn't until that moment that Jamie realized she'd eaten the other three, out of sheer nervousness.

"My purse with all my credit cards and identification, for one thing."

"I haven't seen it," Dillon said flatly. "What about you, Mouser? Did you run off with the lady's purse?"

"Not me, Killer," Mouser protested, absolutely innocent.

Jamie was about to finish her coffee, but she set it back down with a steady hand. "Why do they still call you that?" she asked.

He shrugged, stubbing out the half-finished cigarette. "Maybe I deserve it. Or maybe my fame follows me wherever I go. So no one knows where you left your purse. What do we do next?"

"I need to have my car working, and I need enough money to pay for gas to get me back to the East Coast."

"Little enough to ask, and I'd be more than happy to pay you off to get you out of here. But your car's been towed to a place across town, and Mick isn't sure when he can get to it. And it's against the law to drive without your license on you."

"I'll risk it," she said dryly. "Besides, when did you ever care about what's legal and what's not?"

He shrugged again. "Just thinking of your lily-white reputation, Ms. Kincaid. Accept it—the car's out of reach for the time being. You can stay until it's fixed, or you can come up with another solution."

"Like what? I need money. I need my credit cards. I need my cell phone and my driver's license. I can't rent a car or buy an airplane ticket without a credit card and proper identification."

"Then I guess you're shit out of luck," he said mildly. "And I'm doomed to have an unwanted guest for the next few days. Don't worry about it, sweetheart. Mick's an old friend, and if he knows we'll end up killing each other if you don't get out of here he'll put a rush on it. In the meantime, you're going to have to sit back and put up with me. But then, you're good at enduring, aren't you? You've had to put up with the Duchess all your life."

"Stop calling her that! I love my mother."

"Of course you do. Even though she doted on Nate and barely noticed you were alive. You're a glutton for punishment, Jamie."

"Not anymore," she snapped, pushing away

from the table. "I don't suppose you have a car I could drive?"

"None of my beauties. They're worth too much to risk in the hands of an unlicensed driver," he said in a lazy voice.

"You know I really hate you, don't you?"

"I believe you've mentioned it before. As long as your mother's whispering in your ear I wouldn't expect you to change your mind."

She was already at the door. "Would you want me to change my mind?"

She'd managed to startle him. He paused, clearly giving it some reflection. "It might prove interesting."

She slammed the door behind her.

The sound of it was satisfying. The bite of the winter air wasn't. She'd gone storming out with nothing but a sweatshirt and a pair of sneakers, and the snow was at least three inches deep on the ground.

She turned back to look at the door. There was no way she could walk back in there, not after her grand exit. She was going to have to stand out there in the cold for at least a half an hour, and in that time she'd probably develop pneumonia, which would solve everything. She'd go into the hospital, or Dillon would creep into her room at night and open the windows over her fevered, prostrate body to hurry her along. And she wasn't quite sure which of those options was preferable.

She was shivering, her body racked with cold, when the door behind her opened. She should have stomped off, but Dillon's garage was in a particularly unsavory part of an unsavory town, and even in broad daylight she didn't feel too safe exploring.

She didn't turn, keeping her back rigid, trying to control the shivers. He could apologize until he was blue in the face. Though actually she was the one who was turning blue.

"He's gone into the garage to work," Mouser said. "Come in before you freeze your...freeze to death."

She turned to look at the little man. "Dillon is an asshole," she said flatly.

Mouser's wizened face creased in a smile. "Can't argue with you on that one. He's always been a difficult son of a bitch. Doesn't mean you need to catch your death of cold. Because if you get sick while you're here I don't think he's going to be bringing you chicken soup and aspirin. He's not exactly the nurturing type, is he?"

"Not exactly," Jamie said, following him into the kitchen and closing the door behind her. It was warm, blessedly warm, and she rubbed her hands together to try to bring some life back.

"You're as stubborn as he is, aren't you?" Mouser said. "That's going to be trouble."

"No, it's not. I'm going to get out of here and never see him again. I don't know what his problem is—you can't tell me he couldn't come up with a car I could use and a hundred bucks to cover gas."

"I wouldn't tell you that Dillon couldn't do anything. He's very resourceful. Must be he doesn't want to help you."

"I can believe that. But I'd think getting rid of me would be more important than his dislike of me."

Mouser's smile exposed a set of startlingly perfect teeth. Undoubtedly dentures. "You think he dislikes you?"

"Of course. He dislikes me just as much as I dislike him," Jamie said flatly.

"Well, if you put it that way, that's a possibility," Mouser said in a dry voice. "But bottom line, Jamie, is that I've known him well for the last five years, and I know what he thinks about things. And in your case, dislike doesn't have much to do with it."

"Okay, hatred," Jamie supplied.

Mouser shook his head. "Not exactly. You'll

have a chance to figure it out in the next few days, both of you. It'll be a good thing. Too much unfinished business between the two of you.''

"What makes you think that?'' Jamie demanded. ''I can't believe he's ever even mentioned me. Even thought of me in the last five years.''

"You forget, Nate was here. You were mentioned. Why don't you ask Killer about it. He just might tell you.'' Mouser was shrugging into his heavy jacket, preparing to head out into the icy Wisconsin weather.

"You think I won't?'' Jamie said. ''I'm here for answers.''

"Good for you. And if you pay attention, maybe he'll give them to you. If you really want them.''

And he closed the door gently behind him, leaving Jamie alone in the kitchen. Wondering if she really did want all the answers, after all.

He could smell the cinnamon and hazelnut floating up toward him. Funny, he'd forgotten what it was like to eat, to feel warm, to touch, but his sense of smell was still powerful. He could recognize the smell of Killer's shampoo, he could tell when Jamie was moving far beneath him. Trapped as he was, he could feel everything, smell everything, know everything. Except how to escape.

Unfinished business, isn't that the sort of thing that kept ghosts tied to a place? Nate had unfinished business, and as soon as he figured out what it was, he'd be able to leave.

It might be as simple as killing Dillon. Or getting someone to do it. Or maybe he had to be finished with Jamie, as well. A murder-suicide pact would be perfect, but highly unlikely. Unless Jamie could be persuaded to shoot Dillon.

It wasn't outside the realm of possibility. Anything could happen, and there was a lot of history between them. They were just as haunted by the past as they were by his shadowy presence.

It still waited to be seen which of the two would prove the stronger. And the more destructive.

6

Jamie considered herself riddled with flaws, but cowardice wasn't one of them. Yes, she wanted to get the hell out of there rather than confront the past and the possibly unpalatable truth about Nate, but fate, or her mother, had decreed otherwise. She was stuck here for at least a couple of days, and she wasn't going to spend that time avoiding Dillon. Besides, the bigger a pain in the butt she was, the more motivated he'd be to help her leave.

She shoved her hair back from her face and straightened to her full height. She was too short, almost a foot shorter than Dillon, and she always thought that he would have been easier to deal with if he didn't tower over her. He thought he could bury his head inside a car engine and ignore her, but she was about to disabuse him of that notion. She was going to be a total pest until she got out of there.

She opened the door to the cavernous garage and was immediately assaulted by noise, a vast rumbling that had been almost completely muffled. She closed the door behind her and began to sort through the cacophony. The rush of white noise was actually some kind of space heater, spewing hot air into the vast expanse of the room. The music was loud, too, Nirvana, Jamie suspected, though she'd never been that fond of the group. But Dillon had always favored the raw-pain sound of Kurt Cobain.

Beneath it all was the rumble and roar of a car engine, punctuated with the steady sound of a hammer on metal. And then a stream of curses as Dillon emerged from beneath the hood of the Duesenberg.

She'd half hoped to watch him for a bit without him realizing she was there, but he honed right in on her, his eyes narrowing. It was too loud to do anything other than shout, and Dillon wasn't about to bother raising his voice. He simply disappeared back beneath the hood of the old car, leaving Jamie with two choices. She could go back into the kitchen and wait. Or she could go over there and make him talk to her.

The kitchen option sounded immensely appealing, but Jamie was made of sterner stuff than that. She wasn't about to turn off the heat—her sojourn in the alleyway still hadn't worn off completely— but she could put a stop to the cacophony blaring from the huge stereo system.

She walked over to it and punched the power button, and the noise level decreased substantially.

"What the fuck do you think you're doing?" Dillon demanded, emerging from the Duesenberg engine once more.

"Turning off the noise. I want to talk with you."

He dropped the hammer on the cement floor and headed toward the stereo. And her. "I'm working," he growled. "And when I work, I listen to music."

"If you call that music," she scoffed.

"You can't fix cars to Mozart, princess, no matter what your mother might think. Not that the Duchess would think about anything as mundane as fixing cars, but you know what I mean. I promised to get this Dusey ready sometime before Thanksgiving, and obviously I'm running behind schedule. So if you'd take your cute little butt out of here and let me listen to my music then I won't have to shoot you."

"Do you even have a gun?"

"I'm a convicted felon. Not allowed to own firearms."

"You didn't answer my question."

"And I'm not going to." He had moved up close to her, because she was fool enough to be blocking the stereo. He reached past her, pushed the power button, and suddenly the music was blaring in her ears.

She punched the power button off again, glaring at him. Until she saw the thoughtful expression on his face, and realized she might have misplayed her hand.

"Are you going to get into a wrestling match over Nirvana, Jamie?" he drawled, turning it on again. "I'm game if you are, but I can think of only one way it would end, and the floor of this garage is a rotten place to have sex."

She didn't blush, didn't flinch, though it took a great deal of effort. "In your dreams," she said.

"Yes."

The one-syllable word was even more unsettling, and she wisely decided it was time to change the subject. "Look, you've got at least half a dozen cars over there. Surely one of them is in good-enough working order that I could drive it back to Rhode Island. I'd have it shipped back to you, I promise. I just really need to get the hell out of here."

"Most of those cars belong to other people. That's what I do for a living—restore cars for rich people who don't have the soul or the knowledge to appreciate them."

"You can't convince me you haven't kept some for yourself."

He smiled then, a predatory grin that gave her pause. "As a matter of fact, three of those cars are mine, and two of them run. You want to check them out?"

She didn't trust him, didn't trust that faintly smug expression. But it didn't matter—she wanted to get out of there badly enough to risk it.

"Okay," she said. "I'm not picky."

How could a smile be infuriating, unsettling, and sexy as hell? But then, that could describe everything about Dillon Gaynor, and always had.

He strolled over to the row of cars along the far end of the garage, pulling the bright yellow tarp off the first one. At that point Jamie would have been willing to drive a stagecoach back to Rhode Island, but the sight of the old Model A Ford stopped her.

"It runs," Dillon said. "About twenty-five miles an hour, and the tires have to be replaced every hundred miles, or sooner if you have a blowout, and the hand crank is a bit tricky to start, but you're welcome to it."

"I think I'll pass. What's next? The Hindenburg?"

He yanked the tarp off the next one, and Jamie held her breath. It was gorgeous—an aqua-blue Thunderbird from the mid-fifties. "I'll take it!" she breathed.

"I didn't know cars got you that excited, kiddo," he said. "I would have tried it earlier. And no, you won't take it. The T-bird is waiting for a new engine. It's not going anywhere until then."

"You said you had two working cars. Why bother showing me ones that don't work?"

"Because you aren't the type to take my word for anything."

She didn't bother arguing. "Where's the other car?"

"Over there," he said, jerking his head in the direction of a covered vehicle in the far corner.

"Does it run?"

"Yes."

"Then what's the problem?"

He wasn't moving, he was just watching her, but she wasn't about to let him spook her. If the old junker hiding under the blue tarp was her ticket out of there, then she'd embrace it willingly. Anything to escape.

He was still halfway across the huge expanse of the garage, watching her, when she reached the car. She didn't hesitate, yanking the plastic away from the machine. The first flash of yellow and chrome should have warned her, but it was already too late.

It was the car Dillon had owned twelve years ago, the same car she'd driven to that party in, the same car, the same front seat where he'd kissed her, touched her. The same back seat where...

Her back was to him, a small blessing. She knew the color had bleached from her face, and she stood still, trying to figure out how she was going to handle this. How she was going to be able to turn around and smile calmly and tell Dillon that this car wouldn't do, either. Because nothing in the world could make her get back on the cracked leather seats of the old Cadillac.

Except the seats weren't cracked anymore. Dillon must have restored them at one point. It was a small comfort to know those weren't the actual seats where she'd been trapped...

She couldn't think about it. She took a deep breath, trying to control her reaction, so that she could calmly turn and tell him that she needed a different car. She could do this.

Nirvana was still blaring, but she knew he was watching her. Watching for a reaction. And she knew there was no way she could fool him. So she didn't even need to try.

She let the tarp drop back over the old Cadillac. And then she walked over to the door leading to the kitchen, keeping her back to him so he couldn't see her face. His imagination would fill in the gaps.

She didn't bother to slam the door—he wouldn't

hear it over the sound of Nirvana. She simply closed it behind her and burst into tears.

Dillon was half tempted to go after her. It wasn't his fault she'd gone snooping under the tarp—if she weren't so goddamned determined to escape and get back to that old bitch she wouldn't have gone poking her nose into places it didn't belong.

Of course, that was exactly what she'd do, as long as she stayed here. Maybe it was a good idea she'd found the Caddy, after all. She'd know that snooping could bring unwanted results.

The tarp was still half hanging off his old car, and he covered it carefully, so that none of the dust and paint flying through the air would harm it. It had been his first car, and he loved it like a mother. Not that his mother had been much to love. A car, even an old one prone to breakdowns, was still a hell of a lot more reliable than most people.

Jamie had dropped something on the cement floor—he could see it glistening in the dim light. He picked it up, turning it in his hand. An earring, and it could have belonged to no one else. For the simple fact that despite what he'd told her, no woman ever had the nerve to come into his garage uninvited, and he'd never invited them.

Trust Jamie to ignore the hidden warnings. She

always did have a habit of storming into a situation without thinking first. That was one of the things that got her into trouble that night twelve years ago.

He looked down at the piece of gold in his hand. Of course it was gold—only the best for the Kincaids. It was a unicorn—that was typical of Jamie, as well. She'd be the kind to have an affinity for mystical beasts who only came to virgins. But Jamie wasn't a virgin—he knew that for a fact. And while she might want to live in a fantasyland, in her safe girls' school, by coming here she'd walked into the dragon's den. Into the fire. And she was likely to get burned to a cinder.

He crossed the room to the workbench, reaching underneath and unlocking the small combination safe he kept there. He set the gold earring on top of her purse. And then locked the door again.

Jamie's hands were shaking. Why was she surprised? She'd been trapped in Dillon's garage for less than twenty-four hours and already she was re-membering, reliving things she hadn't wanted to ever think about again. There was no escaping it, and she was someone who'd take any escape she could find. If every time she turned around she was going to find herself remembering, then her only defense was to face it, squarely, instead of trying to hide from it.

Except that right now she didn't feel like facing anything. She glanced out the grimy window at the bleak street beyond. The snow should have blanketed things with a romantic shroud, but instead it only seemed to make things look more depressing. The snow was still falling lightly, but the fresh layer on the ground was already dusted with grit. She could see rusting cars parked haphazardly along the side of the building—clearly junkers unworthy of Dillon's magic touch. There were no people around. This was the back end of beyond, though how that could be the case in a city was beyond Jamie's comprehension. If she could just find decent boots and a couple of layers of sweaters she could take off and look for help. Someone around here would be of more assistance than Dillon Gaynor. Anyone would.

Mouser was her best bet. He wasn't moved by Dillon's bad temper, and he wouldn't be too intimidated to help her. At least she could ask.

The only problem was finding him. She was pretty sure he'd walked to wherever he was going—there was no sign of fresh tire tracks in the gritty snow, and he'd been dusted with snow when he'd appeared in the kitchen like an angel bearing coffee.

Or maybe he just walked from the coffee shop. It didn't matter—she couldn't just sit around in Dillon's abandoned kitchen and fight off all the memories that kept hammering at her. She needed to get home, away from Dillon and the past and old memories. Away from that damned yellow Cadillac.

If she knew where the hell her car was she could find the raincoat she had tucked in the back, but nothing on this earth could get her to go back into the warehouse to ask Dillon. She was wearing jeans and a light sweater, but she'd already discovered that was little defense against the biting Wisconsin wind. And there was nothing else in her pitiful suitcase.

There was, however, a row of hooks by the back door where Dillon had flung the dead rodent. The heavy sweater seemed the most innocuous of her choices, and she pulled it over her head. It smelled like engine grease and gasoline, and it came down to her knees, but it was warm and bulky. And better, it smelled more of old cars than of Dillon.

Except that she'd always associated the scent of engine grease and motor oil with Dillon. Mixed with the taste of cigarettes.

Hell, it was lucky he hadn't blown himself to kingdom come long ago. Or unlucky. If Nate hadn't come here he'd probably still be alive. And she wouldn't be trapped in a living nightmare, remembering things she thought she'd dealt with long ago.

The air was even colder when she stepped outside this time, and the earlier sunshine had vanished, leaving the sky gray and threatening as the snowflakes filtered down. She walked down the alleyway between Dillon's warehouse and the next, but there was no sign of life. No cars except for the abandoned ones, no voices in the muffled silence.

The main road wasn't any better. Now that she could get a good look at her surroundings she was even more depressed. Everything around Dillon's warehouse was deserted. If this had once been part of a thriving city, that city had abandoned this area, spreading out in more congenial directions. Maybe times would change and gentrification would hit Cooperstown, Wisconsin. Someone would snap up the deserted warehouses and turn them into loft apartments, someone would buy the empty storefronts and turn them into pricey boutiques.

There were footprints in the snow. Considering how abandoned that area of the city seemed to be, there were a surprising number of different tracks. The small ones were probably Mouser's. She could see the scratching marks left by the rat's brothers and sisters, and she shivered lightly. And there was another set of footprints, probably male. Narrow feet, not too big, almost graceful. The tracks couldn't belong to Dillon. He had big feet. When she'd been an impressionable teenager she'd noticed them, and she and her girlfriends had speculated about what else might be oversize about Dillon Gaynor, giggling at the salacious thought.

She wasn't giggling now, and she didn't want to think about it. Those feet were more like Nate's. Narrow, aristocratic feet, while she had always bemoaned her own wide peasant ones.

There was no traffic, no taxi she could hail, even if she had the money to pay for it. No one she could even hitch a ride with. She stood still in the deserted street and closed her eyes for a moment.

And then opened them again. Someone was watching her. She turned, slowly, but there was no one. She looked up at Dillon's ramshackle garage, up to the windows on the second and third floor, and for a moment she thought she saw movement behind the frosted glass. She blinked, but then there was no one, and she shook her head. There was no one in that garage but Dillon and her, more's the pity. Unless the rats had made their home on the third floor and had taken to spying on the human inhabitants of the place.

But she hadn't heard the scrabbling sounds of rodent feet last night. Granted, she'd been exhausted, but she'd been edgy enough to be freaked by any unlikely noise. If the building was infested with rats then they all kept regular hours.

She must have imagined the movement at the window. The narrow footprints disappeared into the scuffed snow, and she told herself she was letting her imagination run wild with her. Not enough sleep, not enough food, and the shocking effect of seeing Dillon Gaynor again had managed to make her even more neurotic than usual. She never would have thought seeing him would have such an effect on her. After all, it was ancient history, she'd moved on, and one bad night shouldn't have the ability to color her entire life. It hadn't. Until she looked up into Dillon Gaynor's cool blue eyes, and suddenly she was sixteen again.

But she wasn't. She was twenty-eight, with a master's degree, a good job, a loving mother and a sense of satisfaction in her life. While she wasn't in a relationship at the moment, that didn't mean she couldn't be if she wanted one. She'd had offers. She just wasn't ready. Besides, she was secure enough that she didn't need a man to make her feel complete.

There was no sign of Dillon when she walked back into the warm kitchen. Her borrowed sweater was covered with snow, and she shook it out all over the cracked linoleum floor before hanging it back up on the peg. It was probably the first water that floor had seen in twenty years, she thought wryly. But surprisingly enough, on a closer look, the floor didn't even need sweeping. Someone must look after Dillon.

For some reason the notion came as a complete shock. It had simply never occurred to her that there'd be a woman in Dillon's life. And how idiotic of her—there'd never *not* been a woman in Dillon's life.

The type of women Dillon had been involved with had never seemed the type to be interested in housework, but twelve years could make a lot of changes. Not that much in a unregenerate bad boy like Dillon, but maybe enough to appreciate someone who'd sleep with him and clean his house at the same time.

No, not Dillon. He'd never be that practical. He'd always chosen girls by the size of their breasts, the bigger the better. It was a good thing that Jamie was still a meager 34B. Not that Dillon was a serious threat to her.

He was trying to intimidate her with his suggestive comments. It would shock the hell out of him if she called his bluff. He had no interest in her, and never really had. That night so long ago had been a fluke. He'd been drunk, and bored, and mischievous, but the moment he could he'd handed her off to someone else.

She wasn't going to think about that. Ever again. She was going to grab that box of soggy crackers and head back upstairs. She was going to sit in her room and try to figure out what the hell she was going to do. And try not to worry about whether there were rats crawling up the curtains in the room above her. Or ghosts.

She didn't believe in ghosts. If it had been up to her she wouldn't believe in rats, either, and if she'd never had to see Dillon again she probably wouldn't have had to deal with an oversize rodent.

It wasn't fair that she was stuck here, with the last person in the world she'd ever wanted to see again. She'd done it for her mother, thinking she could dash in and out without ever having to look Dillon in the eye. She hadn't counted on her car giving out. Or her purse being stolen.

And she hadn't counted on the fact that when she looked up into Dillon Gaynor's cool blue eyes she'd feel like a vulnerable sixteen-year-old once more. Just as frightened. Just as wary.

And just as fascinated.

7

There was no sign of Jamie when Dillon finally strolled back into the kitchen. It was already dark outside, and he was starving. He opened his refrigerator and stared at it for a long moment, as if looking for the answers that had eluded him all his life. A six-pack of beer that Mouser had brought over with the donuts. Diet Coke and a soggy head of lettuce, a half dozen eggs that were probably ready to hatch, and some moldy cheese.

He shouldn't be surprised—food had never been one of his priorities. If he wanted to eat he went out and found something. Otherwise he didn't bother. Mouser was trying to reform him, but then, Mouser was trying to reform everyone. They were playing poker again tonight—he'd probably show up with another armful of groceries. Dillon could wait that long.

There was no sound from upstairs. Maybe Jamie was asleep again. He liked watching her when she was asleep—it reminded him of when she was sixteen and so innocent it made him ache with the memory of it. Her innocence was long gone, her defenses were in full flower, but when she slept he could stand there and look at her and pretend it was twelve years ago, a lifetime ago, when he still had choices.

He was turning into a sentimental asshole in his old age. Next thing he knew he'd be turning up at reunions of a high school he never bothered to graduate from. He could even drop in on the Duchess and express his sympathy for the loss of her beloved Nate. She'd always had a blind spot where her nephew had been concerned. The Duchess believed in what she wanted, and her priorities had always been clear. Her daughter had been a distant second, no matter how Jamie tried to deny it.

It was no wonder she'd come here, the last place on earth she'd want to be, to see him, the last person on earth she'd want to be with, all because of the Duchess's whim. She should have learned by now it was a waste of time trying to win the old bitch's favor. But Jamie had never been a quitter. Maybe she thought with Nate dead there'd be room for her in the old lady's flintlike heart. She was going to find out the hard way.

It was no business of his. Jamie Kincaid had come back into his life unexpectedly, and she'd be gone just as fast. As soon as he was ready to let her go, that is. In the meantime he had every intention of enjoying himself.

She'd had a crush on him when she was sixteen. She thought he didn't know, but he had. For some reason it pissed Nate off—he liked Jamie being his own personal fan club—but there was nothing he could do about it. Dillon knew because she blushed when he walked into the house, and looked anywhere but at him. He knew because she always found some reason to come into the room where he and Nate were smoking. He knew because he saw her looking at him one day, with those wide gray eyes that were an affront to his unregenerate nature.

He'd had every intention of leaving her strictly alone. For one thing, Nate was oddly protective. For another, the Duchess scared the shit out of him. And then there was the fact that he liked fast girls, bad girls, not honor students. If it had been up to him he never would have gone near Jamie Kincaid.

But it hadn't been up to him. He'd had no more than a taste, a long time ago. And a taste could build up a powerful appetite.

He sat down at the table and lit a cigarette. What would Nate think if he could see what was going on? He'd be pissed as hell—he'd never wanted Dillon anywhere near Jamie, and he'd made sure that had never happened. But Nate was dead, and there was no one to stop Dillon from doing exactly what he wanted with his unwilling houseguest. Maybe it was time to find out just how badly she wanted to go home. Nate was no longer here to stop him. No one was.

Except his own tarnished sense of honor. Or even better, maybe it was just self-preservation. For all his gut telling him he could have her, his common sense was screaming no. And maybe, for once in his life, he'd let his brain run his body, instead of his hunger.

Jamie woke up with a start, the flash of neon outside the only light in the barren little room. She'd been sleeping too much since she'd been there, which was crazy, when sleep was usually the most elusive thing in her life. Maybe the answer had always been boredom. She had nothing else to do but wait, and she wasn't even sure what she was waiting for. And so she slept.

She sat up and groped for the switch on the dim light. Her book lay discarded on the mattress—it was no wonder she'd fallen asleep. In the best of times Charles Dickens was a tedious bore. In the worst of times he was unbearable. Maybe when she got back to Rhode Island she'd forgo the yearly ordeal of teaching *David Copperfield* and switch to *A Christmas Carol* instead. For one thing, it was a hell of a lot shorter. For another, it was a better story. And not so many simpering female characters.

She shoved a hand through her hair. She was hungry, of course. She'd come upstairs planning to just sleep the rest of the day away, but luck wasn't with her this time. It was dark, she'd had nothing but three cinnamon buns earlier in the day, and it didn't look as if Dillon had any intention of feeding her. The sound of male voices drifted upward—they must be playing poker again, and if she had any sense she'd resign herself to David Copperfield and ignore them.

And then she smelled the pizza. It was like a siren call, one she didn't even try to resist. It didn't matter that it was late—the other voices assured her she wouldn't be alone with Dillon, and for the sake of food she was willing to risk a lot. She went in search of pizza.

She was right, they were playing poker. The kitchen was filled with cigarette smoke and the yeasty smell of beer, and the pizza boxes lay open on the littered kitchen counter.

"Hi, there, Jamie!" Mouser greeted her cheerfully. "I wondered when you were going to show up. Killer said you'd gone to bed for the night, but I figured with us down here making all this noise you'd be bound to emerge sooner or later.''

She smiled at him. There was another man there, as well, looking at her in shock, and behind the veil of smoke sat Dillon, a cigarette in his mouth, a glass of dark amber liquid by his side, a pile of poker chips in front of him.

''I was hungry,'' she said, drifting toward the pizza.

''Help yourself,'' said Mouser. ''The one on the left's got pepperoni and mushrooms, the one on the right's got sausage and green peppers.''

As if fate hadn't been cruel enough, she thought. ''I don't suppose you have any plain cheese?'' she asked, trying not to sound plaintive.

''Picky, aren't you?'' Dillon commented, not bothering to look at her.

''I'm a vegetarian.''

That got his full attention. He looked at her, a smile curving his mouth, and for a brief moment she remembered that mouth. ''Of course you are,'' he said. ''I bet you don't smoke or drink or gamble, either.''

''I drink. Occasionally. Responsibly. And I play poker very well,'' she said, defiant.

''Get the woman a beer, Henry. And a chair.

Looks like we don't have to make do with the three of us, after all.'' He stubbed out his cigarette and rose, moving in her direction.

She scuttled quickly out of his way. The man named Henry dragged another heavy oak kitchen chair up to the round table, opened a bottle of Corona and set it in front of her place. ''What are we playing, Killer?'' It was the first time she heard him speak, but his slow, deep voice matched his looks.

''Lady's choice,'' Dillon said. ''Sit down, Jamie.''

''I don't want—''

''Sit down.''

Jamie sat. A moment later a paper plate appeared in front of her, pizza with the sausage removed. She could have protested, but it would have been a waste of time. And, besides, she was too hungry. ''I can't gamble with you,'' she said. ''I have no money.''

''I'll stake you,'' Mouser said, shoving a pile of chips in her direction. He was drinking Diet Coke— a strange choice for a night of poker.

''Yeah, who knows, maybe you'll make enough to get your butt out of here,'' Dillon said, resuming his and taking a long pull from his tall glass. Whiskey, Jamie thought, the color dark enough to mean he hadn't diluted it. He was going to be very drunk by the time the night was over, and she would be smart to get the hell out of his way. He'd always been a nasty drunk.

"Maybe I should just take the pizza and go back to bed."

"Maybe you should shut up and deal."

"Don't be an asshole, Dillon," Mouser said. "There's no need to be rude."

"It's my nature."

"We all know that. Try to overcome it. Isn't that what we're put on earth to do?"

"Some succeed better than others," he said in a dulcet voice, looking directly at her from across the table.

"Fuck off," she said sweetly, and took a long drink of beer. Doing her best to act as if she used that particular phrase in her daily conversation, when to her knowledge she'd never said it to any-one. No matter how tempted.

"Deal," he growled.

She dealt, picking the wussiest, most complicated game of poker she could think of. It had been a favorite of her college roommates, and its rules were so complex that the game usually came to a screeching halt, but it was her best chance to beat the three card sharks looking at her, and she needed that money.

Things started well enough, after their initial grumbling, and the pile of chips in front of her began to grow. She ate the pizza, ignoring the fact that the taste of sausage still lingered *and* and tasted wonderful. She finished one beer and started on a second, all the while trying to ignore Dillon, who watched her through the haze of smoke like a python fixated on a mouse.

It put a dent in her poker abilities. You needed to be able to read the subtle body language of an opponent to tell whether they were bluffing or not, but she simply made do with focusing her attention on Mouser and Henry. Dillon was going through the tall glass at a leisurely pace, and at some point he refilled it when she wasn't looking, but he didn't seem to be showing any signs of getting drunk. If anything, he seemed sharper.

Hours passed, and the chips kept mounting up. Sometimes she'd lose a little, but mostly she'd gain, and Mouser kept up a cheerful running commentary on how she was cheating them all. If only she knew how. For once things were going her way, and if she could just manage to hold on to her lead she'd be out of there by the next morning, with enough money to get into a hotel and get her life back.

"Too rich for me," Mouser said, throwing down his cards. "I'll let you two duke it out. Come on, Henry. It's getting late, and I've got work tomorrow."

Dillon hadn't moved. "Since when do you work for a living, Mouser?" he drawled.

"Oh, I make an effort every now and then. Henry's going to help me, aren't you, Henry?"

Henry simply nodded, pushing back from the table.

"Aren't you going to cash in your chips?" Jamie asked.

"Tell you what. I wanna see Killer get his comeuppance." He leaned over and pushed his moderate pile of chips onto hers, then shoved Henry's, as well, without asking him. "Kick his butt, Jamie. I figure any time he gets a beating it's long overdue."

The door closed behind them, leaving Jamie in the kitchen with the last person she would have chosen to be alone with.

She took a deep breath and a drink of her third beer. It was more than she usually drank, but since there seemed to be no chance in hell that she'd be driving, and Dillon was drinking a hell of a lot more than she was, she figured she could risk it. After all, she was trapped here no matter what—it didn't make much difference if they were both awake and reasonably alert after midnight.

And she had nothing to worry about. She kept holding on to this absurd belief that some part of him wanted her, when common sense and experience had told her just the opposite. It didn't matter that he made suggestive comments to gauge her reaction—that was just Dillon. He liked to stir up troubled waters, and Jamie's were troubled, indeed.

She looked up at him. "I'm tired," she said. "Why don't we call it quits? Split the pot and I'll go on up to bed."

"I don't think so." He wasn't even slurring after all that whiskey.

"Look, what are we playing for? A dollar a point, right? I have enough to get out of your hair tomorrow—you should be grateful I have the chance to leave you alone."

"I never do what I should, or feel what I should. The hand is dealt—we'll play it."

She looked down at her cards. Good enough. They were back to playing five-card stud, and she had a straight, queen high. He'd have a hard time beating that, especially since both Mouser and Henry had had decent-enough cards to ante.

"All right," she said coolly. "We'll play it."

"Double or nothing?"

She took another gulp of beer. She wasn't a natural gambler—with so much riding on the outcome she should play it safe.

"Coward," he said softly. "What are you afraid of, little girl?"

It came back to her, a flood of memories, his voice in her ear, his hands on her body in the front seat of that car, and she felt hot color wash over her. She pushed her entire pile of chips into the middle of the table without a word, then looked up at him with a stony expression.

He stubbed out his cigarette, a faint smile drifting over his mouth. That mouth. It was no wonder she was feeling unsettled, crazy, wanting to hide. It was bad enough that she was trapped and helpless, a thousand miles from home.

Trapped with Dillon Gaynor was her worst nightmare. "You show me yours and I'll show you mine," he said softly.

She lay the cards out on the table, slowly, deliberately, savoring his inevitable discomfort and frustration.

He didn't look the slightest bit frustrated as he glanced down at her cards. "Very nice," he said in a lazy drawl. "But not nice enough." He spread four kings on the table.

She couldn't move, couldn't speak. There was no

way he could have all four kings—the likelihood was just too damned improbable. Not when so much was riding on it. Not the money—she'd started with nothing and she'd end with nothing. But it felt like her very life hung on the turn of a card. Or, in this case, four cards.

She pushed back from the table. She'd had just enough beer to make her foolhardy—never a good thing. She put her hands on the table and leaned across, looking into his eyes.

"Come on, Jamie," Dillon said. "Accuse me of cheating. I'm waiting for it. You probably think that's the only way I can beat you. The only way I can accomplish anything in this world. By cheating."

There was no missing the touch of acid in his voice, but she wouldn't react. "You tell me."

He simply grinned up at her. "I don't give easy answers."

"Do you give hard ones?"

An awkward, suggestive silence, but she didn't back down. "I've been known to," he said. "Why don't you try me?"

She didn't like where this was going, not at all, so she pulled back, moving away from the table, heading toward the refrigerator.

"There's not much in there," he said, rising from

his seat in front of that mountainous pile of poker chips. Coming toward her.

She held on to the refrigerator door like it was a life preserver. ''I don't need much. A glass of milk should help me sleep.''

''The beer should help you sleep,'' he said. He reached past her, into the open refrigerator, and pulled out the carton of milk. He opened it and tipped back his head to drink straight from the carton. Then he wiped his mouth and held it out to her.

Too close, but she wasn't going to run. It was a matter of pride. If she ran now she'd never be able to stand up to him. His hand was on the top of the refrigerator door, his arm effectively trapping her. ''I'd like a glass, please.''

''Of course you would. I don't have any.''

She knew that was a lie—she'd had orange juice for breakfast out of one. But he was barring her access to the sink.

''Forget it. I don't need milk.''

''Milk builds strong bones,'' he taunted her. ''What are you afraid of? Never done it before?'' He moved closer, crowding her, his hips almost brushing against her. ''Come on, you'll learn to like it, you know you will. Don't worry so much about it. You just open your mouth. Let it slide down your throat.''

"You're not talking about milk," she said in a hoarse voice.

"No, I'm not." He leaned closer, and she could smell the milk on his breath. "Be brave, Jamie. You want it. It tastes good." His mouth was almost touching hers, and she did. She wanted it. She wanted everything he was talking about, everything she'd never done, and she swayed for a moment, toward him, and it was so close, so dangerously close.

She didn't know what saved her. Maybe the ghost of Nate, watching over her. Maybe her own buried common sense. She heard a noise from outside the building and she pulled back, ducking under his arm and heading for the stairs at a run.

She expected his hand on her shoulder, spinning her around, and then he'd kiss her, and she wouldn't have any choice but to kiss him back, because she was trapped and it wasn't her fault, was it?

But he hadn't moved. She took one last furtive glance behind her as she darted up the dark, narrow staircase, and he was still standing in front of the open refrigerator, a carton of milk in one hand, watching her panicked retreat.

8

He should have let her win. He'd be a hell of a lot better off if she took Nate's box of possessions and headed back to Marshfield, Rhode Island, and the chilly bosom of the Duchess. Once she left, he'd never have to see or think about the Kincaids. That part of his life would be over, and it was long past time.

He'd been acting on impulse since he looked up from pummeling Tomas and saw her standing there like the little match girl, a waif in the snow, her eyes wide with shock. She'd probably never seen a fight in her life. Even if she'd caused at least one major one.

So he'd let her in, put her to bed and gone from there. Her Volvo was in rough shape, but it wouldn't take much to at least get it running. And he'd lied about his tools—the Duesenberg was a German car and it needed metric tools. So did any number of other ones he'd worked on. But she'd believed him, because she'd always been gullible, and clearly she still was. She'd believe just about anything he told her, a fact he found highly tempting. Then again, he found everything about her highly tempting, and always had.

Taking the purse had been an impulse. He'd liked the thought of having a Kincaid in his power, even if it was the most powerless of them. Mouser had lectured him, but it had done little good. He'd only considered letting her win at poker for a brief moment. He was a far better player than she was, and a far better cheater than the hapless Tomas. Mouser and Henry knew what he was going to do, but then, they knew him well. To Jamie Kincaid he was a total enigma.

Keeping it that way was a good idea.

It was a good thing she'd run. In another minute he would have had her ass on the kitchen counter and her thighs wrapped around her hips. And, whether she realized it or not, she would have let him.

But he'd let her run, when he'd wanted nothing more than to see how far she'd let him go. And one reason he'd wanted to touch her was for the simple reason that Nate would have hated it. For any number of complicated reasons, the thought of Dillon putting his hands on Jamie Kincaid would have driven his friend into a rage.

But Nate was dead. It was only his ghost to worry about, and Dillon didn't believe in ghosts. It had been more than twelve years since he'd kissed Jamie. Twelve years could build up a hell of a lot of hunger. Particularly when he'd spent eighteen months in jail because of her.

He should let her go. He wasn't going to. He was going to take his own sweet time, and when he finished with her she'd be ruined for any other man. And this time there'd be no Nate around to get in his way.

Because he didn't believe in ghosts.

She hadn't seen him as she she'd run into her room and slammed the door behind her. He could hear her fumbling with the lock, and he wanted to tell her the skeleton key wouldn't do any good. Even a dead bolt wouldn't stop Dillon if he wanted to get in.

But she wouldn't have heard him any more than she'd have seen him. She knew he'd died three months ago, and she wouldn't let herself see ghosts. Not when that was what she wanted to see.

She would have been the one who mourned him the most. With a clear conscience and a broken heart. Aunt Isobel would have carried on like a character in a Greek tragedy, but Jamie would have grieved quietly, deeply. The thought charmed him, almost enough to tap her on the shoulder when she least expected it.

But he wasn't about to reveal himself until he was good and ready. Until he had the most to gain from reappearing. He wasn't quite sure when that would be, but he knew that Dillon figured prominently in his timing. As long as he kept Jamie there it made matters relatively simple. And he knew Dillon well enough to know he wasn't about to let her go easily. Not this time.

Dillon would get her into bed sooner or later, he thought resignedly. He'd wanted her from the first moment he'd seen her, when she was an innocent fourteen-year-old in awe of her cousin's wicked friend. Fourteen years was a long time to fantasize about someone, and Dillon wasn't the sort to live in a fantasy world. Now that she'd delivered herself to his doorstep he was going to take her, and there was nothing Nate could do to stop him. Rattling chains, bumps in the night—nothing would slow Dillon down once he decided to go through with it.

He had no choice but to resign himself to the inevitable. At least he would have the chance to watch.

The room was dark except for the intermittent flash of neon, but Jamie was too concerned with locking the door to worry about turning on the light. She'd taken the key from the bathroom, and while it wouldn't stop a determined man, it might slow him down. Give her time to escape out the window.

Except there was nowhere out the window to go but down, into the trash-littered alley. The thin covering of snow would do nothing to break her fall, and then she'd be in even worse shape.

She pulled the key out of the lock, then shoved her suitcase against the door before throwing herself down on the thin mattress. She didn't know what she was panicking over. Dillon hadn't done anything but talk. He hadn't done more than that in years, and then it had just been out of boredom. He wasn't going to come storming up the stairs like some swashbuckling pirate and knock down her door to have his wicked way with her.

But still she clutched the key tightly in her hand, for what comfort it could give her.

He hadn't kissed her. Hadn't even touched her. And yet she felt stripped, seduced, vulnerable and shaken. He'd always been able to have that effect on her. And this time there was no Nate to interfere. Dillon would do exactly what he wanted, just as he always had. Whether she wanted him to or not.

And the wretched, miserable thing was part of

her wanted him to. To touch her. Kiss her. Even though she knew better.

She closed her eyes, but she could still see the neon flashing behind her eyelids. She had to get out of here. Maybe tomorrow she'd be able to talk him into helping her. Unless he had some other reason for keeping her there. Some reason she hadn't yet figured out.

In the long run it didn't matter. What mattered was just getting the hell away from there. She could buy a new car—she should have years ago. She could just abandon her old Volvo and buy something new. But in the meantime, if Dillon wasn't going to let her go, she'd have no choice but to take matters into her own hands.

And steal one of his cars.

She could do it. She could do anything if her motivation was strong enough. And all she had to do was think back to that terrible night so long ago and she knew what she had to do.

Twelve Years Ago

''I thought you'd be at the prom with Zack Gunther,'' Paul Jameson said. His voice was slightly slurred, just enough to put Jamie on guard. He was wearing a powder-blue tuxedo that would have made her mother faint with horror. In fact, Jamie wasn't impressed with it, either. It didn't fit him very well—it strained over his bulky shoulders and came up too high on his wrists. He was still the best-looking boy in the junior class, and Jamie told herself she should be more appreciative.

"We broke up," she said. "What about Charlene? Is she here?"

"Hell, no. She dumped me, too, on the way to the prom. Rented this fucking tuxedo for nothing. Looks like you didn't get that far."

Jamie thought of her pink confection of a dress back home on her bedroom floor. "No, I didn't get that far."

"I figure I can have a better time here, anyway. There's lots of weed, lots of beer, and I heard that someone was bringing blow. Probably that boyfriend of yours."

"Blow? Boyfriend?" she echoed, confused.

"What are you, retarded? No, I remember. You're an honors student, aren't you? Lemme explain some of the facts of life to you. Weed is marijuana. You smoke it to get high."

"I know what weed is," she said, getting irritated.

"Beer's an alcoholic malt beverage much preferred by high school students. Me, I prefer tequila, and you'll be pleased to know I brought a bottle with me. Blow is cocaine, and your boyfriend is Dillon Gaynor, who provides the marijuana and the blow around here.''

"Says who?" It was only logical, but for some reason she didn't want to believe it.

"Just ask your brother Nate."

"Cousin," she corrected absently. "And Dillon's not my boyfriend. I just got a ride out here with him."

"Yeah, you're not really Killer's type. And if you were, he wouldn't have handed you off to me." He reached out and grabbed Jamie's hand. "Let's go find us a little privacy and maybe I'll show you how to drink tequila."

"I'm sure I can manage it without any instruction." She looked around her, but the people who'd greeted them had disappeared, and they were alone by Dillon's battered yellow Cadillac. With no sign of Nate or Dillon anywhere around.

"Where'd they all go?" she asked.

Paul grinned down at her, sliding his hand up her arm. "Don't worry about it, baby. I'll keep you company."

In the end, maybe it was her fault. She'd taken one look at Paul's handsome face and known he was drunk. He didn't force her to put the bottle of tequila to her mouth and drink. And drink. He didn't force her to climb in the back of Dillon's parked car and let him put his hands all over her, kiss her with loose, rubbery lips, grinding his crotch against her as he shoved his hands under her shirt. So why should she have expected him to listen when she finally did say no?

She lay pinned beneath him, no longer fighting, as he pumped away at her, cursing and grunting, his fingers pinching her breasts, his tongue running over her teeth. She should have had more to drink, enough to knock her out, enough, maybe, to make her like what he was doing. He'd told her she'd like it. He told her she was a frigid bitch and a cock tease. And then he stopped saying anything, stopped talking, just put his hand over her mouth and unfastened his pants.

He ripped off her plain cotton underwear, and it hurt, but it was nothing compared to the pain of him pushing inside her, forcing her, and she tried to push him away. She felt like she was tearing inside, and then she was, as he ripped through her virginity without anything more than a grunt.

The longer it took the better it was, or so she'd been told by her more experienced friends. They'd lied. He went on forever, hunching, grunting, and there was nothing she could do but lie still beneath him and cry.

With a final string of obscenity he finished, collapsing on top of her for a brief moment. And then he sat back, fastening his pants again, looking at her out of hooded eyes.

"Jesus, are you crying?" he demanded. "I hate girls who cry all the time. They're just trying to get you to do what they want, but I'm not buying it. If you think just because you put out it means we're dating then you're wrong. Charlene will come back to me—she always does. And if she doesn't, no offense, but I can do better than you."

She'd found her jeans on the floor of the car and managed to pull them back on, and she scuttled into the corner of the back seat. She could see her blood on Dillon's leather seats. He wouldn't like that.

She looked at Paul, but she couldn't see him very well, probably because she couldn't stop crying. She was making embarrassing little hiccup noises, and he was looking even more disgusted.

"For fuck's sake, shut up!" he snapped. "You don't want to be making a scene, do you? Here!" He shoved the bottle of tequila at her. "Have a drink and stop crying."

The smell of the tequila made her stomach roil. She shoved at the door, blindly, but it wouldn't open beneath her desperate hands. She climbed over the side, tumbled out and made it into the woods just before she threw up.

When she finished she collapsed in the dirt, crying silently. It was too late for tears, but she couldn't stop. She just lay there, weeping, curled into a ball.

And then she heard the voices. Drunken laughter. She sat up, trying to wipe the tears from her face in case someone decided to come in search of her.

She should have known it would be her worst nightmare. Dillon and a woman had arrived back on the scene, probably to use the back seat of his car. Whether it was the same woman he'd been kissing earlier or a different one was immaterial.

"Hey," Dillon said. "We want a little privacy, man."

Paul hadn't wandered off, after all—she heard him grunt in response. "Hey, I'm outta here. Next time you ask me to take care of someone you might pick someone who knows her way around. Virgins are a pain in the butt."

"What do you mean?" Dillon's voice was casual.

"Man, all she did was cry. Do you know how hard it is to ball someone when they're crying all the time? Took me for-fucking-ever. And even then she wouldn't stop crying. We made a mess of your back seat—you should have told me she was jail-bait.''

"Killer, you're hurting me" came a plaintive female voice. "Let go."

"Hey, Dillon." Nate's voice carried into the woods.

Jamie couldn't listen anymore. She pushed herself to her feet and started running. She could only hope she was headed toward the highway. Sooner or later she'd reach the road, and someone would pick her up. She'd already had enough bad things happen to her for one night—hitchhiking no longer held the same terrors it once had.

The highway was farther than she realized, and for a few panicked moments she thought she'd been walking in circles. And then she heard the sound of a car moving fast, and she knew she was almost there.

She stumbled out onto the highway just as a pair of bright headlights speared her way. She didn't even have to put out her thumb, which was a good thing. She wasn't sure she had the energy. The car pulled up beside her, and she recognized Nate in the driver's seat.

"Get in, precious," he said, and his casual manner was oddly comforting. If he'd shown her any sympathy she would have fallen apart.

She went around the car and climbed in. She didn't recognize it, and for that matter Nate didn't have his driver's license yet, but Jamie didn't question it. She put on her seat belt and closed her eyes.

He drove very fast. She could smell the beer on his breath, and she almost wanted to vomit again. She was never going to drink anything for the rest of her life. And she was never going to make the mistake of thinking some bad boy like Dillon Gaynor was worth fantasizing about.

Except that Paul Jameson had been even worse.

Her fault, she reminded herself. She'd led him on. But she hadn't realized that Dillon had told him to. Dillon had handed her over like a ripe peach and told Paul she was his for the taking. And she'd gotten half drunk. It was no wonder she hadn't made it clear that she didn't want him to.

A little whimper escaped her, and Nate glanced over at her. One arm was draped along the back seat, the other on the steering wheel. "Cheer up, Jamie. Had to happen sooner or later, and now you've got it over with. Next time will be better."

"There won't be a next time," she said in a low, bitter voice.

"Sure there will. All Dillon has to do is crook his finger and you'll come running."

"With a gun," she said.

"Not his fault. As a matter of fact, you'd be surprised to know—" The flashing blue lights behind them shut him up midsentence. "Shit," he said.

Jamie glanced behind them. "Were you speeding?"

"I was speeding, I'm loaded, and I didn't bother to ask the owner whether I could use his car. I think we're screwed, Jamie. In more ways than one."

She just stared at him in horror.

"Come on, Jamie," he said. "You gotta have a sense of humor about these things. Aunt Isobel will bail us out, and we probably won't get anything more than a slap on the wrist. Don't worry about it. Hell, they might even let us go with a warning."

They were sitting side by side in the police station an hour later, waiting for Victor Kincaid to come pick them up, when two police came in, dragging someone in handcuffs. Someone bloody, disheveled, barely walking.

Dillon Gaynor.

He looked at the two of them out of one swollen eye, and his mouth curved in that familiar, mocking smile. And then the police dragged him away.

They shoved him up against the desk with unnecessary force, and Jamie winced, watching them. Not that she should have a moment's sympathy for him, she reminded herself. But he looked so thrashed.

"Dillon Gaynor," said the desk sergeant in a resigned voice. "I should have known you'd be back. You're going down for this one, you know. You were warned—one more fight and you'd be spending time as a guest of the state. Looks like you're about to reap the fruits of your labors."

"Worse than that," one of the cops said. "He put a kid in the hospital."

"Doesn't surprise me," the sergeant said. "What does surprise me is that the other guy managed to make such a mess of his pretty face."

"The other kid barely touched him," the cop said with a malevolent chuckle. "He...fell on the way to the patrol car."

"Nasty fall," said the sergeant casually.

"Very nasty."

"Nate! Jamie!" Isobel Kincaid appeared in the doorway of police station, in her high heels and her real pearls and her expression of horror and disdain. "Your father's waiting for you in the car. I'll take care of any papers—just leave."

"Mother..." Jamie began, but Isobel turned the full force of her disapproval on her.

"Don't start with me, Jamie. I'm extremely cross with you. With the both of you." She turned her icy glare to Nate.

"But you'll forgive me, Aunt Isobel," he said sweetly. "You always do."

Her mother gave him a rueful smile. "Out of here, the both of you. The less time you spend in the company of trash like Dillon Gaynor, the better off you are. I warned you, Nate."

"Yes'm. You did."

Nate put his arm around Jamie and led her out into the warm spring night. "You know, you gotta admire Dillon. There he is, in the midst of a drama, and he forgets all about it and gets in a fistfight with one of his buddies. The man doesn't think of anyone but himself. It must have been Jimmy Canton— they've been gunning for each other for weeks, ever since Dillon ran off with Jimmy's girl. I wonder if he killed Jimmy." He sounded no more than vaguely curious.

Jamie shivered.

"Cheer up, Jamie," Nate continued. "Don't look so stricken. When we get home you'll take a shower and forget anything ever happened."

She glanced up at him in surprise, wondering if he was serious. He was. "Don't worry about it, kiddo. The only other person who knows about this is Dillon, and he's too drunk to remember anything by tomorrow morning. Besides, he'll have more important things on his mind, like how he's going to get out of spending a couple of years in jail.''

''What about Paul?''

''Oh, he's not about to go bragging about this to anyone. Charlene would kill him. And if he does, just say he's lying. People would believe you. After all, why would a good girl like you give it up in the back of someone's convertible?''

She felt her stomach lurch at the memory. ''Good point,'' she said in a rusty voice.

''A shower and a good night's sleep will make everything better,'' Nate said cheerfully. ''Trust me.''

''I always do.''

9

It would have been nice if she'd been able to sleep. She'd spent half the day zonked out, and now, when she really needed the oblivion of a good night's sleep, it was eluding her, leaving her with nothing to do but replay that night, over and over again in her mind.

She really thought she'd put it all behind her. After all, her mother had paid handsomely for the therapy Jamie had requested without even asking why, and she'd worked hard at getting past the memory of that night.

And it wasn't that bad, really. It wasn't rape—he hadn't hit her, hadn't really hurt her. And she'd never had to see him again—when she'd surfaced from her bedroom two weeks later she heard that Paul had been in an accident and spent most of the summer in the hospital. He'd gone away to school for his senior year, and in a town the size of Marshfield, she'd never had to run into him again. She could pretend it had never happened.

If Nate hadn't kept bringing it up.

She knew why he was doing it. He must have been trying to help her face it, deal with it, get past it. He didn't understand that all she wanted to do was bury it. With Paul gone and Dillon in jail, there was nothing to remind her that that night had ever happened.

Except for Nate. And her sudden distaste for being touched by anyone. Which wasn't a problem in the Kincaid family—neither Victor nor Isobel were demonstrative parents, and if she was lucky she could go for weeks without anyone putting a hand on her.

At least the subject of Dillon Gaynor had been completely off limits. She knew only the vaguest details—that he was in jail, that he was being sent away for nearly beating someone to death in a fight, but for once Nate wasn't talking. Jamie had assumed that, for the first time, Killer had gone too far for Nate. Bad-boy misbehavior was one thing, felonious assault was a different matter.

And in the end it all could have been fine. But it wasn't. Nate was now dead, beaten to death in the home of a man who'd already been convicted of almost doing the same thing to someone else. And Jamie was still terrified to have a man touch her.

The only one who seemed to be doing all right

was Dillon. But then, he wasn't troubled by scruples or second thoughts. He just moved through life without noticing the damage that lay around him, the ruined lives. The deaths.

She sat up, leaning against the wall as the neon flashed over the thin mattress. It had to be very late. Even close to dawn, maybe, since they'd played cards well into the night. But there was no light in the sky—there was nothing but long, empty hours to remember that night over and over again.

And the damnable thing was, she could still re-member how good it felt, with Dillon's hands and mouth on her. And how bad when it had been Paul.

She pushed herself up from the mattress, unable to stand being alone with her thoughts anymore. The huge old building was silent—Dillon would have gone to bed hours ago, and even the rats were asleep. There would still be alcohol downstairs, and she intended to find it and drink enough to put her-self into a nice, lengthy stupor.

The hall light was still on. She was wearing flan-nel boxers and a T-shirt—her usual sleeping attire—and she didn't travel with a bathrobe. It didn't mat-ter—she wasn't going to run into anyone. She could sneak down there stark naked and no one would notice.

She moved carefully on the darkened staircase,

not wanting another encounter with rodent corpses, but the way was clear, and when she stepped into the shadowy kitchen she saw with mingled relief and disgust that the table was still covered with glasses, ashtrays and poker chips. No money, though, which was a blessing. She wasn't quite sure what she would have done if there'd been a nice pile of cash left there, promising her escape and freedom. She probably would have taken it, though Dillon was a dangerous man to cross.

His half-full glass of whiskey was still there, and she reached for it, intending to drain it in one gulp. She almost choked on it.

It wasn't whiskey. It was unsweetened iced tea. She set the glass back down, disgusted. No wonder he was able to beat everyone else. They were cheerfully getting drunk, thinking he was matching them drink for drink, and instead he was staying completely sober just to win. She shouldn't be surprised that he'd be that devious.

She began a slow, methodical search of the kitchen. She'd been drinking beer, and there should have been some left, but there wasn't a trace. Mouser and Henry must have taken the leftovers with them. There was no alcohol in the place at all.

''Find anything interesting?'' Dillon drawled from the open doorway.

She hadn't realized he was there, watching her, and she froze, but she had a moment to compose her expression before turning around to face him.

Lucky thing. He was leaning against the door-jamb, his jeans riding low on his hips, his flannel shirt unfastened. He still had a beautiful body—she knew for a fact that he had to be very strong, but it didn't show in his lean frame. Just the hint of muscle in his shoulders and arms. For some reason that deceptive strength was vaguely erotic.

And what the hell was she doing even *thinking* of the word *erotic?* Especially in connection with this man.

"I was looking for a drink. I couldn't sleep."

He moved into the room, closing the garage door behind him. "Now, I know it isn't a guilty conscience that's keeping you awake. You haven't lived enough to feel guilty about anything."

"But I imagine you make up for it."

"Make up for your lack of experience? Depends." He shrugged. He started moving toward her, slowly, and without thinking she began backing away.

"I mean, you more than make up for my lack of guilty conscience. You have plenty to feel guilty about."

"Yes, I do. Fortunately I think guilt's a waste of

time. What's done is done, and all the whining in the world won't change matters.''

''I don't whine.''

''I didn't say you did.'' He was circling around the table, between her and the stairs. ''What I'm saying is, sooner or later you just have to get over it.''

''Fuck you!''

''That's one way to deal with the problem.'' He'd gotten closer, with seemingly little effort, closing the distance between them.

She stopped her retreat. ''This is ridiculous. You can't chase me around a table like we're in some Road Runner cartoon.''

''Then stay put.''

She started backing away again. ''I don't think so. Just tell me where I can find something to help me sleep and I'll go back to bed.''

''Right here.'' He caught up with her, shockingly close, and backed her up against the table.

''Don't touch me.'' Her voice was very quiet, a plea and a warning. ''I don't like to be touched.''

''Get over it,'' he said again. He put his arm around her waist and lifted her, effortlessly. She heard the crash of glass and poker chips as he swept the table clean, and then she was lying in the middle of it and he was on top of her, looking down at her, pressing against her, his warm, smooth, naked chest, the unmistakable pressure of his erection against her thigh. She couldn't move.

He looked down into her face, resting on his elbows as he contemplated her obvious panic. "Nate forgot to mention this little goodie," he said, half to himself.

"What?" The sound that came from her mouth was nothing more than a terrified squeak. She was shivering, and she knew he could feel it, but he seemed totally unmoved.

"That you're afraid of men. Did Paul do this to you?"

"I did it to myself," she said. Knowing it was the truth. She could have worked through it, if she'd wanted to. But it was safer this way. Or at least, it had been.

To her horror he brushed his lips against her forehead in an almost absentminded gesture. "Good thing Paul's dead," he murmured. "I might have had to kill him."

He let his lips trail down the side of her face, whisper soft, across her cheekbone and the corner of her mouth. "Then again, maybe there are advantages. This way you don't know what you've been missing." His lips touched hers, just briefly, then moved on, touching, tasting, caressing.

"Let me up, Dillon," she said again, not bothering to sound strong. "Please."

His mouth didn't slow its lazy voyage down the side of her neck. She didn't touch him, didn't try to push him away. She simply lay beneath him, trapped, her arms beside her, hands flat on the table, every muscle rigid, her eyes squeezed shut. It would end, sooner or later, and she'd survive. She could endure anything if she had to.

His lips touched the corner of her mouth again, and she couldn't keep the tiny whimper from escaping. "Open your eyes, Jamie," he whispered.

She had no intention of doing any such thing. But her body had other ideas, and she slowly looked up into his face, into the deep, hypnotic blue of his eyes.

"That's better," he said. "If you want me to let you up you just have to do one thing."

"No!"

"Get your mind out of the gutter, Jamie. You just have to kiss me."

"You're drunk," she said. "Or stoned, or something."

"You know I'm not drunk. You just about choked on my iced tea. And frankly, the only thing affecting my judgment right now is you."

"Not for the better."

He smiled wryly. "I never said you had a very good effect on me or my judgment. But it's a strong one. So what are we going to do about it?"

"It's your problem. I'm not going to do a damned thing."

"You see—you're already feeling better. You've stopped shivering, and you're pissed as hell. That's progress."

She had stopped shaking, she realized. And her anger had just about wiped out her panic, and the fact that he'd noticed before she did made her even madder.

"Let me the hell up or you'll wish you had," she said, shifting slightly. She could bring her knee up, hard, into his groin. Not that she'd ever done such a thing, but it seemed easy enough, given their proximity.

"Don't even think it, baby girl," he said, pressing his hips down against her, effectively pinning her to the hard oak surface. There was no way she could move her leg, no way she could fight back, and she was so frustrated that she didn't even notice what he'd call her.

"I'll ask you one last time..." she growled.

"And I'll tell you one last time. All you have to do is kiss me and you can go safely back to bed. I won't even touch your breasts. But you really should think twice before coming around here without a bra. There's only so much a man can resist. You're a sore trial to my self-control.''

''You don't seem to be trying to control yourself at all.''

His laugh was low, running down her spine. ''You have no idea what I'd be doing to you if I gave in to temptation. Be glad I have scruples.''

''You don't have an ounce of scruples.''

''Well, then, be glad I'm going to let you go. After you kiss me. It's your fault, you know. You should have run while you could.''

''I didn't notice there was a time when I could run.''

''The race goes to the swift. I'm happy to spend all night like this. As a matter of fact, even if you refuse to kiss me I could have a whole lot of fun just rubbing against you. It might get a little messy, but I don't mind if you don't.''

''You're disgusting.''

''Just healthy, Jamie.'' He rocked against her, slowly, his erection fitting in the cradle of her thighs, and she felt an odd shiver at the feel of it. The disturbing pressure.

Her eyes met his with sudden shock, as the remembered feeling swept over her. The first faint tremors of arousal. And he knew it.

It was the cruelest trick of all. That she should go twelve years, trying to feel something for a man, only to have it be this man. This man, who was immoral, dangerous, heartless and cruel. And just plain wrong. But he rocked against her again, his eyes glittering as he gauged her reaction, and she could feel the heat build, no matter how hard she tried to fight it.

She had to get up, away from him. And there was only one way to do it, the least of many evils. "All right," she said, and quickly kissed him on the mouth.

He was noticeably unimpressed. "I don't think so."

"You told me if I kissed you you'd let me up."

"Use your tongue." Another bump of his hips against her, and the heat began to spread. It was getting to the point where all he had to do was touch her and she'd climax, and that was something she could never let happen.

She picked her arm up from the table, put her hand behind his neck beneath his long hair and pulled him down to her, pressing her open mouth against his. Using her tongue.

She felt his hands cup the sides of her face, his mouth slant over hers as he took her inside, tongue against tongue, lips and teeth and heat, and she tried to hold on, tried to stop the reactions that were sweeping over her, and then it was too late, and she surrendered to it, to him, to his mouth, kissing him with her body, her heart and her soul.

She'd probably forgotten to breathe. He was the one to break the kiss, to look down at her in astonishment, his mouth wet from hers, his eyes glazed. "God damn," he whispered. "That was a very bad idea."

The dreamy, half-erotic, half-fearful haze vanished, and she shoved at him. This time he moved, off the table, backing away from her into the shadows of the old kitchen, shaking his head.

She couldn't even begin to guess what he was thinking, and she didn't want to know. All that mattered was that he'd changed his mind and was letting her go. That was when she suddenly wondered whether she wanted to escape after all.

She scrambled off the table, trying to disguise the shakiness in her legs. "A very bad idea," she echoed. "I don't know why you did that, but you certainly weren't inspired by unbridled lust. I'm not your type, and you've always known that. Now, if you don't mind I'll just go on up to bed and we'll forget this ever happened."

He laughed, destroying her dignified reaction. "You sound just like the Duchess," he said. He moved out of the shadows into the light. "Take a good long look at me, Jamie, and tell me unbridled lust doesn't have something to do with it."

There was no missing the very visible evidence. "It's a normal biological response—" she began, but he stopped her.

"If I were you I'd get the hell out of here before I decide to show you what my type is." His voice was mild, the threat was not.

She ran.

She ran so fast she didn't even bother to slam the door behind her. He heard her stumble on the stairs, and if he weren't in such an unexpectedly savage mood he would have laughed. She'd break her neck trying to get away from him. Jump out a window. It was a good thing he wasn't burdened with an inferiority complex, or he would have found Jamie Kincaid to be thoroughly demoralizing.

Except for the way she kissed him. She tasted the same—innocence and eagerness and sex that was buried so deep inside her it would take a bulldozer to get at it. Or a very determined man.

And he was nothing if not determined.

He had to admit it had shaken him. It was one thing to have the hots for your best friend's little sister, and not even that unlikely to act on it. But the feel of her beneath him, shivering, the look of panic in her eyes, the taste of her tongue were more powerful than he'd ever expected. And it scared the hell out of him.

Maybe he'd listen to his conscience, to Mouser's arguments, and let her go. Make a miraculous recovery of her purse, spend half an hour beneath the hood of her Volvo and she'd be good to go. It was sitting under a tarp in the corner of the garage— he'd been in no hurry to let her escape. Once she left he'd never see her again—there'd be no reason. Nate was the only thing that connected the two of them, and it was a pathetic excuse for a tie. Time he broke it, kicked her out and went on with his life.

The only question that remained was whether he was going to screw the living daylights out of her first. Or resist temptation.

He knew the answer. Fucking Nate Kincaid's little cousin would have driven his old friend crazy. And if for no other reason than that, he was going to have her.

And there were many more reasons than that. It would be a spit in the eye to the overbearing Duchess, not to mention finishing something that had been started more than twelve years ago. He'd always liked a sense of closure in his life.

And besides, if it hadn't been for her he'd have had another eighteen months of his life. He figured she owed him. She'd be giving it up to someone, sooner or later. It might as well be him.

A million reasons, all of them good ones. And none of them the one that really mattered. The simple fact that he wanted her, so badly it made his bones ache.

And it didn't matter how scared she was. He was going to take her.

10

Nate wasn't quite sure when he decided to kill Jamie. Was it when he'd first seen her trudging down the snow-covered road to Dillon's garage? He told himself she'd come for revenge, but he knew better than that. Jamie was incapable of anything as elemental as revenge, as passionate as murder. Besides, she'd had a crush on Dillon from the time she was an impressionable teenager. She'd thought Nate hadn't noticed, but he had. And enjoyed throwing the two of them together, just to watch them squirm. It had been one of his favorite pastimes back then.

He'd thought about killing her the night of her prom. She looked like hell once Paul got through with her, sobbing uncontrollably, and he hated to think what Aunt Isobel and Uncle Victor would say. Aunt Isobel would turn a blind eye, of course. She adored him, for all the wrong reasons, and she wouldn't hear a word against him. It amused him to see how far he could go without Uncle Victor exploding.

That night he'd probably gone *too* far. Uncle Victor was protective of sweet little Jamie, and he'd have held Nate responsible for not looking out for her.

A tragic car accident would have put a stop to that. It would have been easy enough—he could have broken her neck and then run the car off the road, giving himself a few colorful bumps and bruises. Uncle Victor would have been devastated. Aunt Isobel would only be thinking of Nate.

Even better, Dillon would have hated it.

But he didn't do it. The police had picked them up for speeding before he could make up his mind, and in the short run it had worked out well.

Still, he'd forgotten how Dillon felt. Stupid of him to have overlooked that little fact, but it had been so long since Dillon had seen Jamie he thought his friend would have gotten over it. Particularly since he'd never admitted it in the first place.

But he'd heard it in Dillon's voice as he floated overhead, listening. Seen it in the way Jamie moved in her sleep, thrashing around. They were within days, hours, moments of having sex, and he was going to have to kill her.

It wasn't anything personal. He'd always been

fond of his little cousin, and she'd adored him. She'd never been a threat—even Uncle Victor had loved him more, although he was more observant than Aunt Isobel. And when Dillon had to choose between Nate and his innocent little cousin there'd been no question.

Maybe it was Jamie's very innocence that made him crazy, Nate thought. Her blind, stupid trust, when he knew she was much too smart for her own good. Just not smart in judging character.

He'd listened to them in the kitchen, the crash of glasses, the muffled conversation followed by long silences, and he could just imagine what they were doing. What they were going to do if he didn't put a stop to it.

He'd been waiting here for a chance to kill Dillon. Killing them both at the same time would simplify matters, but he wasn't going to give them that much. They'd die separately, alone, in pain, frightened. Dillon Gaynor would be a hard man to frighten, but then, he'd never come face-to-face with a ghost before.

He'd start with Jamie. She'd outlived her usefulness, and finding her dead would bother Gaynor. Bother him a lot.

The only question left was how to do it. How could a ghost kill?

* * *

Jamie huddled in the corner of her room, shivering, the comforter pulled tight around her. Sometime during the night the heat stopped working. She was freezing, and she was damned well going to freeze to death before she set foot outside her room.

She'd stolen the skeleton key from the bathroom in her panicked flight, and her door was locked, a chair propped under the doorknob for good measure. It wouldn't stop Dillon if he was determined, of course. But she really didn't think he was the slightest bit determined.

He'd stretched her across the big oak table in the kitchen with no other purpose than to intimidate her. She couldn't figure out why he would care. If he wanted to get rid of her all he had to do was give her the money. She'd pay him back and he knew it. The Kincaids had always had money, and Dillon Gaynor had none, even if he seemed to have mysteriously acquired that huge old garage. Probably bought it on drug money. And if he hadn't killed Nate then it was probably one of his Colombian drug lord friends who'd made a mistake, killing an innocent man rather than Dillon.

Though even the most forgiving of cousins couldn't really consider Nate an innocent. He was charming, sweet-natured and generous, but he was far from a good boy. And Jamie had never known for certain who was the leader and who was the follower with Nate and Dillon.

It didn't matter any longer. Nate was dead, and she was never going to see Dillon again. As soon as the sun was up she was going to put on every piece of clothing she could find and walk straight out into the snow, keep walking until she came to someone who could help. Hell, there was Triple A. She had no cards, no proof, but computers kept all that information. They could trace her records and send someone to fetch and fix her car. Isn't that what she paid money for?

The police would help. After all, her purse had been stolen, and she was stranded in a strange town. Even a homeless shelter was preferable to sleeping under Dillon's roof for one more night. Safer.

The wind had picked up, howling around the old building like a banshee. What the hell was a banshee? she wondered. Some Irish ghost? A harbinger of death? Death didn't need any harbingers—it had already come and taken what it wanted.

She waited, huddled in the corner of the room, until the first tendrils of light began to slide over the peeling windowsill. And then she stood up, looking around for her shoes.

She was already wearing most of her clothing as a paltry defense against the chill in the room. In the shadowy predawn light she couldn't see her shoes at first, so she switched on the light, still shivering slightly.

There were no shoes. No leather running shoes that could withstand tramping through snow, at least for a bit. And no suede heels that would be ruined after she took one step, shoes that would likely send her sprawling but that would still get her out of this place. There were no shoes at all.

Maybe she'd left them downstairs. But that was unlikely—she wasn't comfortable enough with Dillon that she'd kick off her shoes in his presence. She always had the unconscious need to run when she was around him, and taking off her shoes would only hinder her escape.

The bathroom? Possible, but not probable. The last time she'd seen her shoes they'd been neatly arranged at the foot of her mattress. And now they were gone, just like her purse.

She would have blamed Dillon if she could, but Dillon didn't want her there. She sat back down on the mattress and shivered in the icy room. It was cold enough that she could see her breath, and she suddenly had an even more unnerving thought.

Maybe the heat hadn't gone off at all. Maybe the room was icy cold because she wasn't alone in there. She'd seen enough movies—the temperature dropped when a ghost was there. And she'd felt as if someone was watching her ever since she set foot inside the garage.

"Nate?" she whispered in a soft voice. "Are you here?"

No answer, of course, and she wondered if she could feel any more stupid. But she persevered. "I don't believe in ghosts, but if you'd be anywhere I guess you'd be here, where you died such a violent death. Are you here to warn me about something?"

Silence. Jamie took a deep breath. "I'm not afraid of you, Nate. You'd never hurt me in life, and you certainly wouldn't in death. Do you want me to be here? Do you want me to find out what really happened to you? Did you take my purse and shoes? Do you know where the hell they are?"

It was a stupid question and she didn't expect an answer. "I need to get out of here, Nate," she said, trying one last time. "I need to get away from Dillon. You should understand that. You knew what I was feeling, even when I didn't. I need to get out of here."

There was a sudden clanking sound, followed by a thud and the screech of metal against metal, and she jumped. A moment later the heat duct behind her spewed out a wave of blessed heat, and Jamie just stared at the register in shock.

"If that's a sign I'm not sure what it means. But I'm going downstairs to find a pair of Dillon's shoes and get the hell out of here. I'm sorry, Nate."

The heat was filling the room as quickly as the early morning light, and Jamie pushed herself off the mattress and went to the door, removing the chair as quietly as she could. Dillon had to be in bed—she'd sat there huddled in the corner, listening to the sounds of his footsteps hours after she'd run from him. He hadn't even hesitated as he passed her door.

The key in the lock made a faint rusty noise, but the sound of the furnace was noisy enough to muffle it. Besides, Dillon's bedroom was at the end of the hallway—he wouldn't have heard her.

The floor creaked beneath her feet, every step she took, and she cursed under her breath. But she didn't hesitate.

The hallway was shrouded in darkness, but she didn't dare turn on the light. She made her way down by instinct, trying not to remember the feel of the dead rat beneath her bare feet. It couldn't happen two days in a row.

She pushed open the kitchen door, expecting the chaos of the night before. He'd swept everything off the table, onto the floor, when he'd lifted her on there, and she'd heard the sound of breaking glass as he pushed her down on the wood. She'd have to be careful where she stepped.

The kitchen was spotless. The dishes were washed, the empty beer bottles had disappeared, the floor was swept clean. Even the omnipresent ashtrays were empty.

Either Dillon was neater than he'd first appeared, or he'd been restless last night. Unable to sleep, just like Jamie.

There were no shoes. The row of pegs still held sweaters and jackets, but there were no boots or shoes underneath. She couldn't remember if there had been before.

She opened the door onto the alleyway and stared out into the snowy landscape. Why had she never realized how much it snowed in Wisconsin? Of course, she'd never had any reason to know much about the Midwest in the first place, and she would have been deliriously happy never to have had a reason to learn.

She closed the door again. She couldn't go out there barefoot, no matter how desperate she was. There were shoes in this place, and she'd find them, or end up binding her feet in rags. Anything to get away.

She eyed the door to the garage doubtfully. She knew for a fact that Dillon had to be upstairs in bed

at this early hour—she would have heard his footsteps in the hall if he'd left his room. The outside
door had been locked—she wasn't going to run into
anything she didn't want to. Anyone, she amended.

She half expected the garage door to be locked,
but it opened easily beneath her hand. The cavernous room was cloaked in shadows, and there was
no light switch by the door. None that she could
see anywhere.

The Duesenberg sat in the middle of the huge
room, its hood open, engine gleaming beneath. The
concrete was cold and rough beneath her feet, but
she moved deeper into the garage, drawn to the one
place she shouldn't have been. The bright yellow
Cadillac convertible.

He'd pulled the cover off it completely, and it sat
there in pristine glory. In fact, apart from the new
leather seats, it looked the same. Dillon had always
put huge pride into his car, and the car had showed
it. Back then the rips in the leather seat had been
covered with duct tape—at nineteen Dillon hadn't
been able to afford new leather. He could now.

She put her hands on the side of the car, forcing
herself to look down. She couldn't remember why
she'd been fool enough to get into the back seat
with Paul in the first place. There'd been the tequila,
of course. And the fact that Paul was the most

sought-after boy at the Marshfield School, and for some reason he wanted her.

But those weren't the reasons. It was that Dillon Gaynor had finally kissed her, touched her, then abandoned her the moment another girl had come along. Passed her along to Paul like a prize in a turkey shoot.

She began to shiver, and when the door to the garage opened she didn't turn.

"Why did you do it?" she asked in a quiet voice, so quiet that she doubted he could hear her.

But he could. "Do what?"

"Hand me over to Paul Jameson."

He didn't deny it, when she'd been hoping he would. "I thought he'd be love's young dream. The perfect boy for an innocent like you. Quarterback on the football team, senior class president, voted most likely to succeed and all that crap. I thought he'd be the prince for an innocent princess like you. And Nate told me you always had a crush on him."

That made her jerk her head around to stare at him. Mistake. He was shirtless, shoeless, his jeans zipped but unbuttoned. Even in the shadowy darkness she could remember why she'd always longed for him, daydreamed about him. His beauty was unmistakable.

"I don't know why Nate would have said something like that. It wasn't Paul I had the crush on, and I was pretty sure he knew it.''

"Who did you have a crush on?''

Dangerous territory, and she wasn't going to go there. "Why would Nate—'' she persisted, but Dillon interrupted her.

"Screw Nate. He'd lie any chance he had if he thought it would be to his advantage.''

"Why would me having rough sex be to his advantage?''

"It wasn't just rough sex, Jamie. It was rape.''

She didn't want to hear that word, the one she'd avoided for twelve years. "No, it wasn't. I got in this car with him on my own accord. It was my fault.''

"Bullshit. You were drunk, and Paul thought he was God's gift to womanhood. He wouldn't have listened if you said no. And you did say no, didn't you?''

"Yes,'' she said in a small voice. He'd moved closer, and she hadn't heard him advance. Too close, blocking the only doorway. She quickly looked back at the car. "I don't see why you'd remember it all so clearly. You had to have been drunk as well.''

"I was. I could hold my liquor better than that little pissant.''

Oddly enough she almost smiled at that. She'd always thought of Paul in such huge, frightening terms. *Pissant* was a good way to cut him down to size.

"Well, drunk or not, you were too busy trying to beat someone to death and getting arrested for it to remember what went on that night. Weren't you?"

"Yes."

Something in his voice stopped her. His single-word answer had been matter of fact—there was no reason why she should have thought twice about it. But she did.

She turned around, all the way around, and leaned her back up against the cold metal of the Cadillac. "Who did you beat up? So badly that you went to jail for it?"

"I'm sure Nate told you something," he said lazily. "Don't you believe your cousin's every word?"

"He said it was over a drug deal gone sour."

"You think the police and the courts would care that much over two drug dealers fighting?"

"Two?"

"I dealt drugs, Jamie, and you know it. Just weed and the occasional percs, but I did it. And I almost killed a man with my bare hands. No wonder they put me away for a year and a half."

"What man?"

"Boy, really."

"What boy?"

His smile was faintly mocking. "You know what boy. It's just taken you twelve years to figure it out."

"Paul."

"I broke his jaw, his cheekbone, cracked three ribs, broke several bones in his right hand and bruised his spleen. As I remember he had a concussion and he was pissing blood for a month. I probably would have killed him if people hadn't pulled me off him. Fortunately a car accident took care of that little detail a few years later."

"You didn't have anything to do with that?" she asked in sudden panic.

He shook his head. "I haven't killed anyone. Not directly. Not yet."

She swallowed. "That's doesn't sound very encouraging."

"It wasn't meant to."

"There had to have been something else going on," she said. "You couldn't have been sent to jail for just being in a fight."

"It wasn't just a fight, princess. I was trying my best to kill the little bastard. Unfortunately his parents doted on their son, and they had the political clout to make sure I got punished. I would have been locked away for the rest of my life if they'd had their way, but it only ended up a little over a year.''

''That isn't that long,'' she said, still reeling.

''Try spending it in a state prison and you'll see how long it is. The days crawl along at a snail's pace. And I spent all that time figuring you were blown away by my heroic defense of your honor. My mistake.''

''I didn't ask you to.''

''No, you didn't.''

''I didn't know.''

''That's also true. In the end it doesn't make any difference. The bottom line is I gave up a year and a half of my life for you, Jamie Kincaid. I think it's about time I got something back for my sacrifice, don't you? I've waited long enough.''

''Long enough for what?''

''For you, Jamie. You can start by taking off your clothes.''

11

For a moment she wasn't sure she'd heard him
right. The garage was still shrouded in darkness,
and he hadn't bothered to turn on a light when he'd
approached her, but she could see him quite clearly.
Blocking the way to the door.

It didn't mean she wouldn't run. There was always the element of surprise, and since she was
smaller there was a good chance that she was faster.
Running barefoot through ankle-deep snow was beginning to sound far more appealing than to have
him put his hands on her. She could still feel the
weight of him on top of her, the taste of his mouth
from the night before. She couldn't let that happen
again. She couldn't.

"No," she said in a flat voice.

If she'd hoped to get the advantage of surprise
she lost it when he took another step, so close that
his bare feet almost touched hers, so close that she
could feel his body heat. He was shirtless, radiating

warmth, she was wrapped in layers of clothing and shivering uncontrollably.

"Yeah, right," he drawled. "I knew about the crush, Jamie. Nate used to tell me all the details. I'm just planning to fulfill your fantasies after twelve years of foreplay."

"I don't want you touching me. You're as bad as Paul." Her voice shook, but there was nothing she could do about it.

His smile was faint. "Now, that's where you're wrong. I'm a hell of a lot better than Paul ever was, and I'm prepared to demonstrate. Just start unbuttoning that sweater. You're wearing enough clothes that it's going to take a good, long time, so you may as well begin."

"We're not doing anything. You're going to step away from me and I'm going to leave this place. I'm going to get my shoes or your shoes or any damned pair of shoes I can find and walk straight out the door and not ever come back."

"No, you aren't. You'd have to get around me to leave, and I'm not ready to move."

"So you're going to force me?" Her voice shook, just slightly. He'd think it was from the cold. Maybe it was.

He shook his head. "Don't have to," he murmured. "Do I?"

He reached out for the top button of her sweater. The layers of clothing kept his hands far away from her flesh, and she simply stood there, frozen, hands at her sides, and let him unbutton the long cardigan. Let him pull it off her shoulders, down her arms and onto the floor. Then he reached for the hem of her sweatshirt, pulling it, and she had no choice but to raise her arms and let him pull it over her head. It fell on top of the cardigan, at her bare feet.

She was half blind with fear, but she wasn't going to cry. Not for some damned man, not ever again. "This time I'd press charges," she said in an even voice. "You think I wouldn't? I'm older and smarter now, and I'm saying no. I'm saying get your goddamn hands off me."

"I'm not touching you," he said absently, taking the hem of her outer T-shirt and pulling it over her head. One more T-shirt to go, then a camisole and bra. And then skin. "I can't even figure out why I want to bother. It's not like I can't have all the ass I want, when I want it. It's always been that way. Women like me."

"Terrific. Go find one that does." He was pulling the last T-shirt off, and she considered locking her elbows to keep him from pulling it over her head. But then he might touch her, and she couldn't bear it if he did.

"Most of the women I know would be asleep at this hour. You'll have to do." He stepped back a fraction of an inch, just to look at her. The lavender silk camisole had been a secret indulgence, not meant for anyone's eyes but her own. The skimpy bra beneath it was even worse. She'd thought that if she ever were tempted, ever found a man attractive enough to risk everything, then she'd wear the lavender silk from Victoria's Secret. So why the hell did she bring it along with her on this trip to see Dillon Gaynor?

"Nice," he murmured. He leaned forward, his voice at her ear. "You smell like cinnamon."

"You smell like axle grease," she shot back.

"It has all sorts of uses, if you want to try it that way."

There was no way she could disguise her utter horror. It didn't help when he laughed. "You should see your expression, princess. I was kidding." He waited long enough for her to relax, marginally, before he added, "Besides, I've got much better stuff upstairs."

She'd thought she was as far back from him as she could go, but at that moment she slammed up against the side of the Cadillac.

He reached down for the waistband of her skirt, unfastened the zipper and let it drop around her feet.

She was still wearing a pair of jeans, but it wasn't enough. She could have worn a HazMat suit and it wouldn't be enough.

He leaned down and blew, ever so gently, on her stomach, his breath warm and moist. In another place, at another time, it might have been erotic. It almost was, even in these horrible circumstances.

He straightened up and put his hands on either side of her waist, holding her. "Now I'm touching you," he said. "You knew I would sooner or later. Tell me no again."

"No. Again."

He slid his fingers inside the top of the waistband, then slid them around to the front button. "I don't know why I bother," he said, half to himself. The button flicked open almost by itself, and she stared down at his hands, fascinated. Waiting for him to reach for the zipper. "Virgins were never my thing. Probably why I kept my hands off you, years ago, when you were so fucking tempting."

"I'm not a virgin anymore," she said bitterly. Then could have bit her lip.

"Was that supposed to be encouraging? I thought you were saying no?" He began to pull the zipper down, slowly, almost lazily.

"I am saying no. I'm just saying I'm not a virgin anymore. Thanks to you."

"If only." His rueful smile should have been in-furiating. "And it doesn't matter how many men you've fucked since Paul got you in the back of the Cadillac, you're still a virgin at heart. Untouched, inviolate. You probably lie back and close your eyes and think you're supposed to like it. When you don't, really."

His deep, insinuating voice was driving her mad, just as the feel of his long fingers against her skin burned her cold flesh. "Shut up."

She was wearing very skimpy bikini panties be-neath the jeans, ones that matched the lavender bra and camisole. She hadn't gone for the thong, though she'd been tempted. The bikini was indecent enough, but no one was supposed to see it. And if she didn't do something to stop him, Dillon—the last person in the world she wanted—would be the one to see it.

The jeans were unzipped, but he didn't seem in any hurry to pull them down. She'd fight him when he tried, she knew she would. She had to.

"You must make men jump through hoops," he said, brushing his mouth against the side of her neck, so softly it was like the brush of a feather. "What do they have to do—submit a blood test and a family pedigree? I expect the Duchess would be more interested in the class issue than any health concerns.''

''Is this your subtle way of asking me if I'm HIV positive? Because I am. You should get as far away from me as you can.''

''Don't waste your time, baby girl. You never were a very good liar, and I could always see through you. Just as I can right now. Tell me you don't want me.''

''Are you insane? I've been trying to tell you that for the last half hour! Leave me alone.''

''Then walk away.''

''What?''

''You heard me.'' His patience was paper thin. ''If you don't want me putting my hands on you, then push me away and walk. You think I'd chase after you, drag you down on the cement floor and ravish you? Not my style.''

''I'm not your style,'' she said, putting her hand in the center of his chest. His hot, sleek chest. She hesitated for a bare moment, then pushed, and he fell back with seemingly no effort at all. She could run now, except that she was wearing nothing but her bra and camisole on top, and her jeans were unzipped and falling down around her hips.

He seemed untroubled. ''If I didn't know better I'd say you were even more of an innocent now than you were before Paul got his hands on you. What's wrong with the men in Rhode Island? Don't they know anything about sex?''

"I wouldn't know," she said bitterly, reaching for the zipper of her jeans.

Wrong answer. He'd stepped back, seemingly willing to let her go, but her words stopped him.

"You wouldn't know?" he echoed. "Just how many lovers have you had since that night with Paul?''

"None.''

"Okay, let me rephrase that. How many men have you gone to bed with since that night?''

It was too late to change her mind. Besides, she was too angry, too panicked to be able to keep her mouth shut at this point. Besides, the truth was more likely to keep him away from her. "None.''

"Boys?''

"None.''

"Women?''

He was trying to shock her, but she was past the point of worrying about it. "None.''

"Well, at least that simplifies matters," he murmured. "So clearly you've been saving yourself for me.''

It was such an outrageous statement that she

couldn't come up with a response. She could only stare at him in amazement.

"I've been keeping myself safe," she snapped.

"Safety is an overrated commodity. I think it's time we finished what we started that night."

"I don't."

"Let me convince you."

It was her last chance. She'd already told him more than she wanted to, she'd stood there and let him undress her, and he'd given her plenty of chance to run. She hadn't moved.

"I could count to ten. Give you a head start," he mocked her. "But I'm not sure you really want to get away."

She still didn't move. She wanted to. Needed to. But for some reason her body wasn't responding to her demands. It seemed to know her better than her mind.

"Last chance, princess. I'm going to put my hands on you again, and this time I'm not going to let go."

At the last minute she pushed away from the Cadillac, almost weak with relief. He hadn't moved that far out of the way, and as she leaned down to pick up her discarded clothes her jeans began to sag. Her hands were full of clothing, so she couldn't refasten them, but if she ran really fast then maybe she could keep them up. Why the hell did she wear such baggy jeans? If she wore form-fitting ones like most people they wouldn't be sagging. But she already knew the answer to that. She wore baggy clothes to hide her body. Not that there was that much to hide.

Dillon was watching her, an enigmatic expression on his face. As if her eventual decision was no more important than what to have for breakfast.

"I'll go now," she said, her clothes clasped to her chest. Not moving.

"Sure you will. I think we've talked long enough. Come here."

He had to be crazy. She was halfway to the door, hugging her clothes against her, and he expected her to come to him.

"Come here, Jamie," he said again, soft, beguiling. "You've been running long enough. Let's just get it over with."

If she ran she'd panic, and she was already frightened enough. Frightened by the inevitability of it. He was inexorable, determined, and he wouldn't stop. Because in the end she really didn't want him to stop.

She stood there, frozen, as he came toward her, lean and smooth and very dangerous. He took the clothes out of her arms and dumped them on the cement floor. They'd get oil stains, she thought, trying to concentrate on trivialities. Her mother would be horrified. She should pick them up.

He pushed her jeans down her hips and she let him. They pooled at her ankles, and when he took her hand she stepped out of them.

He didn't let go of her hand, and she didn't try to pull away. She couldn't fight him with her body, but she could fight him with her words. "Don't do this," she whispered.

He didn't say anything, simply pulled her into the shadows of the huge garage. There was an old sagging sofa back there, a hideous shade of green with the stuffing coming out of the cushions. She didn't want to go there. And he wasn't giving her a choice.

"I think we better do this fast," he said, pushing her down on the sofa with deceptive gentleness. Deceptive, when she knew how violent he could be. He'd never turned that violence on her, but that didn't mean he wouldn't if she pushed him far enough. As she'd been trying to, ever since she got there. "I don't want you to panic and change your mind."

"I never said..." Her voice caught in a gasp as he pulled the skimpy panties down her legs with the ease of long experience.

"You didn't need to," he said, kneeling down on the sofa beside her, pushing her back against the lumpy cushions. "You can't spend your life running away. I never thought you'd be a coward, Jamie Kincaid."

"I am," she said. "A sniveling, desperate coward." He'd pushed the camisole up and flicked open the front clasp of her bra, but he didn't bother pulling it off her. It lay beneath her on the sofa, and the lacy straps and the camisole were halfway down her arms, limiting her movement.

He reached for the snap of his jeans, and she shut her eyes. She heard the rasp of his zipper, she could feel the shudders of panic wash over her body. He moved between her legs, and she tensed, waiting for him to touch her.

"I'm not going to help you," she said in a low voice. "Paul made me help him. He was too drunk, and he hit me, and he made me—"

"I don't need any help."

She heard the sound of paper tearing, and she almost opened her eyes. A condom, she realized. He was going to use a condom.

She made one last attempt. "You're wasting your time. I tried to get over this once. I even got this far, but he couldn't...I was too..." There was no way she was going to explain it, and now she was sorry she'd started.

"You were too dry," he said in a prosaic voice. "And too tight. And you didn't really want him."

"I thought I did...." Her voice disappeared in a little squeak as he put his hand between her legs. His long fingers touching her, sliding inside her, that fast.

"Well, you're not dry now. And you want me, whether you admit it or not. And I'm not going to give you a chance to change your mind."

She started to tell him she'd never said yes in the first place, but it was too late. She'd expected kisses, caresses, practiced attempts to still her fears. Instead he'd moved between her legs, pressing against her, and before she could protest he was inside her, pushing deeper, holding himself above her as he slowly invaded her body.

He was too big, but there was nothing she could do about it. This time her body didn't stop him, and then it began to betray her, letting him in, until she could feel the whole length of him inside her, her hips cradling his as her fingers dug into the torn cushions beneath her.

"Breathe, Jamie," he said in a tight voice. "It's not going to kill you."

Because she didn't have much choice she took a breath, and somehow he moved even deeper inside her, when she hadn't thought he could.

He was holding himself above her, only the weight of him inside her, and she felt him lean down, bring his head toward hers, and she knew he was going to kiss her. And she couldn't stand it. She jerked her head away, so that he couldn't reach her mouth, and she bit her lip.

"All right," he said, and she could hear the iron tension in his voice. "Do you want this fast or slow?"

"Fast. Get it over with."

"You don't know what you're asking for, baby girl." He started to pull out, and she let out her breath again in momentary relief. Until he pushed inside her again, deeper than ever. Again and again and again, and there was nothing she could do but shiver and find that dark spot inside herself where she could hide.

But that dark spot was filled with sparkling lights, and he was in there, too, in every part of her, and there was no escape, and she could feel the heat spreading through her, rich and languorous, and the more she tried to fight it, the more it spread through her body like a warm, sweet poison.

And he knew it. He could feel it. "Open your eyes, Jamie," he said. "I want to watch you."

She could no more resist than she could stop her

heart beating. Her eyelids fluttered open, and she stared up into his face, half dazed.

"We're going to do this again," he whispered. "And again. And again." Each word was punctuated with his body rocking against hers. "Every way I can think of, every place, every time of day. You'll be thinking and breathing and tasting me. And I'll be thinking and breathing and tasting you."

She was shivering, inside and out, but she wouldn't touch him. Her fingers dug into the sofa, her hips cradled him, and he thrust hard, deep inside her, over and over again, until she felt his body go rigid, saw his eyes close, heard his voice let out a strangled curse as he caught her hips in his hands and pulled her up even tighter against him.

She watched him almost from a distance, and for a moment she felt almost serene. It was a strange kind of power, to feel him climax inside her, to feel his total loss of control, when she was the one who always felt powerless.

And then he collapsed on top of her, sweat-slick, panting, his heart hammering against hers. She noted all these things with detached interest. It was a kind of revelation. She hadn't hated it. Hadn't hated it at all. There was even a moment when she'd begun to feel something almost like...

He rolled off her, off the narrow sofa and onto

the floor, where he sat, cursing. "Shit," he said after a moment. "That was a fucking disaster. That wasn't what I had in mind at all." He turned his head to look at her. "Stay put," he growled. "I have to go clean up, and then I'll be back."

She closed her eyes, shutting him out, until she heard the door close, the water running. And then she sat up.

A disaster was something not to be repeated. To be talked about. The inevitable had happened, and somehow she'd known it would. But now she was getting out of here, as fast as she could go.

Mouser was the last person he expected to see when he emerged from the bathroom. He was so damned pissed at himself his savage mood spilled over onto the world in general. He'd planned to make her come, over and over again, until there was no way she could hide away in that pseudo-virgin body of hers. No way she could hide away from him.

And instead he'd lost control like a teenage boy and shot his load before he'd given her no more than the first taste of arousal.

He'd been planning to take care of that the moment he got back to her. But she was gone, and instead Mouser was standing there looking at him like he'd murdered a kitten.

"What the hell do you think you're doing, Killer?" he demanded.

Dillon managed a grim smile. "I'm about to cut your throat. I happen to be busy. Go away."

"I don't think so. It doesn't take a rocket scientist to figure out what's been going on here. Why don't you leave the poor girl alone? You don't need her. You'll only hurt her, and no matter how much Nate fucked you over you shouldn't take it out on his cousin."

"It has nothing to do with Nate. I spent a year and a half in jail because of that woman. Don't you figure she owes me?"

"No. Any time you spent in jail was long overdue and you know it. That's no excuse, and you don't even believe it yourself. I figure you've got a major jones for that woman and it ain't her fault. Send her home, man."

"Not yet."

"You're a stubborn son of a bitch, you know that? Don't blame her for Nate. Any score you had to settle with him has already been paid in full, don't you think? You've never been a cold-blooded bastard, Killer."

"That's where you're wrong. I've had lots of experience being a cold-blooded bastard, and that's what she expects from me. I wouldn't want to disappoint her.'' He leaned down and picked up the T-shirt she'd dropped in her escape. He'd had her. A good solid taste of her after God knew how many years of waiting. And it had just whetted his appetite.

Cinnamon. The T-shirt smelled of cinnamon. He couldn't let her go. Not yet. Even though he'd done his damnedest to atone for a lifetime of sins, there was a limit to his good behavior. And that limit was Jamie Kincaid.

''Get the fuck out of here, Mouser. We've had this argument before and it's just a waste of time. I'll do what I want with her, and she's not going to object. And next time knock before you walk in.''

''She probably doesn't know how to object. You're the experienced one. You could let her go.''

''I'm not going to. Lock the door behind you.''

''You're a bastard, Dillon. I love you, anyway, but sometimes you make it real tough,'' Mouser said sternly. ''Think twice before you hurt that girl again. You'll only end up hating yourself even more than you do now.''

''Go fuck yourself, Mouser.''

Dillon made no noise as he walked up the creaky stairs. Mouser was gone, the door locked behind him, and no one was going to stop him this time. He wouldn't be able to start where he left off, but it wouldn't take long to get her back to the point of trembling surrender again. This time he'd do a better job of it. And to hell with Mouser and any trace of conscience that was bothering him.

He almost had his hand on the doorknob when he heard her. It took him a moment to figure out what the choking sound was. She was crying, and trying to stifle the sound against something. The pillow, the mattress, her fist. It didn't matter. She was trying not to make a sound, and it made it all the worse. She was probably huddled in some corner, waiting for him to come get her.

He'd never been susceptible to a woman's tears. He'd had more than his share cried over him, at him. Women trying to manipulate him, make him feel guilty. And Jamie Kincaid was the kind of woman who cried at the drop of a hat. Hell, she was probably just frustrated by his rushed attempt at fucking her and didn't know it. If she wouldn't open the door he could kick it down without any difficulty, and finish taking care of her as she needed to be taken care of.

And he knew he wasn't going to do it. Some latent sense of decency had cropped up at the sound of her crying. He was a fool and a half, when he finally had gotten her where he'd wanted her for far too long. Shaken, trembling and willing, and it wouldn't take much to get her that way again. And he wasn't going to do it.

He was about to hang the discarded T-shirt on the doorknob, but he hesitated, bringing it to his face, breathing in the scent of her. And he moved down the hall, the shirt still in his hand.

Mouser shook his head ruefully. Killer had it bad, and he didn't even realize it. Far be it for his old friend Mouser to point out that the poor bastard was in love. Killer didn't believe in love, certainly not the romantic kind. He'd chalk it up to simple lust. But Dillon was way past anything as simple as lust when it came to Nate's cousin.

She was bringing out the worst in him, that was for sure. Dillon could be utterly ruthless, but he didn't usually take it out on the helpless. It wasn't like him, and he'd hate himself for doing it.

The best thing a friend could do for him was to get the woman out, before Dillon made a mistake that he couldn't fix. A light snow was falling, and Dillon had locked the door after shoving Mouser out into the snow. But the door to the alleyway didn't have a lock. He figured he'd managed to ruin the mood for at least the time being, long enough to get Jamie out of there. But he couldn't afford to wait.

The grim alleyway looked almost pretty beneath the thin layer of snow. Only a trail of footsteps marred the pristine white, and he frowned, trying to figure out who the hell had come in the back entrance. The prints were too small to be Dillon's feet, too big to be Jamie's.

He opened the door. The hallway was warm and shadowy, and he closed the door behind him, moving into the darkness.

And then he stopped, staring into the shadows in disbelief. "You're dead," he said in a choked voice.

"No. You are."

12

It took her too damned long to stop crying. All she could do was thank God he'd left her alone for a moment, so she could run. Because if she'd stayed, it would have been even worse. She might have grown to like it.

There was rape and there was rape. Dillon Gaynor could force her just by looking at her. For twelve years she'd kept her distance from men, only to come face-to-face with the worst of all of them. The only one who could get through to her.

She thought she'd been safe. He'd touched her. Kissed her. Slid his hands beneath her clothing and felt her breasts, he'd stretched her across the kitchen table and covered her body with his. He'd done almost everything she'd been terrified of, and she'd survived.

Until this afternoon, when he'd pushed her down on the battered old sofa and came inside her. He hadn't kissed her, caressed her, barely touched her. And he still almost made her want it.

She could hear the noise of his infernal music beneath her, the rumble of a car engine and the metal sound of tools. She needed to get clean, to get the feel of his hands, his body, off her, and then she needed to get the hell out of there. She sprinted down the hall, taking the fastest shower imaginable, but when she emerged the noise was still coming from beneath her.

His bedroom door stood ajar—at least, she assumed it was his. She pushed it open—if she could find anything at all to put on her feet she could get out of there before he even realized she was gone.

There wasn't much in the room. A big bed, unmade, sheets in a tangle. She stared at it a long moment, unnerved. She couldn't really look at that bed without thinking of Dillon. Lying in it. And her. Beneath him.

There was a splash of color against the white sheets, and she recognized one of the T-shirts she'd put on earlier. She must have dropped it in her flight. Typical of him to have taken it. If she was around for much longer she'd end up with nothing at all.

She grabbed the T-shirt and headed for the closet. No shoes, no boots, nothing she could put on her feet. She turned back to the room in frustration. There was a large-screen TV on the dresser opposite the bed, and on impulse she pulled open the drawers. It was more than likely he'd taken her purse and shoes in the first place, and this would be an obvious spot to stash them. But the drawers held nothing but clothes—T-shirts and jeans and socks. No underwear, though. She wasn't surprised.

Until she saw the scrap of red and pink, wedged into a corner, tucked away underneath the T-shirts. She pulled it out, and she felt a weird clenching in her heart as she recognized it.

She hadn't seen it in thirteen years, but she would have recognized it anywhere. She'd gone out with her friend, Carly, the one her mother had always referred to as white trash, and she'd found it on a sale rack at Macy's. It was a dress made of a lacy pink-and-red-striped knit. The sleeves were long, with an uneven ruffle at the end, the skirt was short, and the neckline much too low. At fifteen she'd been flat-chested enough to get away with it—her now respectable 34B would make it as indecent as her mother had insisted it was.

Of course, there'd always been the little problem that the dress was see-through. It wasn't as if Jamie hadn't worn a full slip underneath, so that nothing showed. Carly wore things a hundred times more revealing, and Jamie had loved that dress. For the first time she'd felt beautiful. Even desirable. Back when desire was a good thing. She'd put the dress on and felt like a sexy, sultry creature, and she'd reveled in it.

Her mother had taken it, of course. Ripped it and thrown it in the trash where it belonged, Isobel had told her, and proceeded to buy her a complete new sweater outfit that made her feel like a Catholic schoolgirl.

She shook out the dress and looked at it. Maybe it was a little tacky, in retrospect, but she'd loved it. The ruffle at the neckline was ripped, but even Isobel's strong hands hadn't been able to do much damage to virgin polyester. She held it up to her face, breathing in the past.

It smelled like the perfume she used to wear. Just a trace of it, something light and virginal that she'd gotten for Christmas. And the faint trace of gasoline and cigarettes. Dillon.

Why in hell did he have it? Why in the first place, and why after all these years? It was crazy—he hadn't even been aware of her when she was fifteen and had worn this dress.

If she were really honest with herself she'd admit the truth about who she'd wanted to impress with this dress. There was only one person she'd wanted to notice her, only one boy she wanted to realize she was a grown woman. At fifteen, she thought ruefully.

And that boy was Nate's oblivious best friend, the wicked Dillon Gaynor from the wrong side of the tracks.

She'd never understood why her mother had let Nate continue his relationship with someone as problematic as Dillon, the baddest of the bad boys, and yet had ruthlessly cut off Jamie's relationship with Carly, whose only crime was a lesser pedigree. But then, Jamie knew the answer. Nate could talk his aunt Isobel into anything, and Isobel had gritted her teeth and bore it for Nate's sake.

She didn't even want to begin to think about how the torn dress had gotten into Dillon's possession. All she knew was she wasn't going to leave it with him.

It was past time she began to stand up to the people she loved. Past time she stood up to Isobel, with her plaintive demands and her disapproval. Hell, maybe she'd even wear the damned dress when she got back.

She wasn't going to let Dillon touch her again. The moment she heard him come up to bed she was going downstairs, climbing into the damned yellow Cadillac and driving out of there, even if she had to go straight through the wooden garage doors. She wasn't going to be a victim to the people she cared about....

Well, not that she cared about Dillon. She despised him, always had, since the night when Paul Jameson had raped her in the back of Dillon's car.

But then, she'd never known what had happened afterward. Never known that Dillon had beaten him half to death. And now, staring down at the dress in her hand, the dress he'd kept for more than a decade, she realized she didn't know anything at all.

The Volvo took Dillon longer than he expected, but by late afternoon it was running better than it probably had in years. There'd been no sign of Jamie—she hadn't emerged from her fortress to eat or even to pee, as far as he could tell. Though he'd been blasting Nirvana again and it would have covered any noise.

She was still up there, he had no doubt of that. He could feel her there, underneath his skin. Like poison ivy, he thought savagely.

Mouser was right. Mouser was always right, damn him. He was like Jiminy Cricket, his fucking conscience. Friends you could trust were a hell of a lot more important than even the most longed-for piece of ass—he'd learned that the hard way.

He was going to let her go.

He backed the old Volvo out of the garage, feeling a trace of satisfaction in the sweet purr of the engine. The snow had almost stopped, the streetlights that were still in working order had come on, and the late-afternoon air was fresh and crisp. She had credit cards and a couple of hundred dollars in cash in her purse—she'd have no trouble finding a hotel room once she got away from here. He'd been prepared to put more money in her wallet if need be, but she probably would have noticed and had a fit.

He pulled the Volvo in front of the garage and cut the motor. He considered leaving it running. She was going to leave like a bat out of hell, and the gentlemanly thing would have been to warm it up for her.

But fuck it, he was no gentleman, and he was already being a revoltingly decent guy. Mouser was going to owe him, big time.

Except that Mouser would tease him, mercilessly. He always insisted that Dillon was a better person than he knew he was. And this would just give him more ammunition.

Couldn't be helped this time. He never drove the Cadillac without thinking of Jamie, and that wasn't likely to change. But he'd lived with it for twelve years—he could live with it for another twelve. Besides, he had other things to feel guilty about. Like Nate's bloody death.

At least he'd managed to keep Jamie from seeing the room. There'd been no way to get all the blood out of the old wood, not without ripping out the floors and replastering the place. And he couldn't be bothered. Once the police had removed Nate's bloody corpse, once the yellow tape had been taken down, he'd dumped all of Nate's possessions in there and locked it. He should have sent the stuff back to the Duchess, but he'd never gotten around to it, telling himself he owed the old bitch nothing.

But he knew the real reason. He was hoping Jamie would come to find it. Find him.

She had, and now he was wishing to hell he hadn't done anything so fucking stupid. But he was making up for it, salvaging things before they exploded in his face.

The room still smelled like death, even three months later. The brown stains covered the floor and the walls, visible in the twilight, and he could see it all over again. The lifeless, battered figure, the face smashed in, the clothes soaked with blood. He'd seen a lot in his life, but that was something he wouldn't soon forget. He had sat downstairs at the kitchen table and listened to the distant sounds of his former best friend being beaten to death. And done nothing to stop it.

He told himself he didn't feel guilt or regret. If he had to do it over again, he would, without hesitation. He simply had to live with the consequences. And he'd never complained about the price he had to pay.

He dumped the two cardboard boxes into the trunk of Jamie's car. She was as neat as she'd always been—no extraneous books or packages rattling around back there. It was as empty as her life.

And who was he to judge? His life consisted of his work, a couple of friends, and getting laid when he was in the mood for it.

That and meetings.

He would have killed for a drink right then. The moment she was out of there he'd find a meeting. Hell, there were at least three in the city on a Sunday night, and he hadn't needed one so much since he'd gotten sober. He should have known Jamie would put five years of solid sobriety in jeopardy. No woman was worth that.

He grabbed her purse and her shoes from the safe. It was already growing dark, but he didn't turn on the lights.

He didn't bother muffling his footsteps as he climbed the stairs—this time he wanted her to know he was coming. Give her enough time to hide. If there was one thing he knew, it was that he absolutely never wanted to see Jamie Kincaid again. For some reason he couldn't see her without touching her, and he couldn't allow himself that kind of weakness. All he did was hurt her, anyway—the sooner she was out of here, the better. After all those years he was finally ready to put that part of his life behind him.

The door was still tightly shut, but there was no sound of tears from behind the thin pine. No sound at all.

Maybe she'd already left, but he didn't believe it for a minute. He'd developed a sixth sense about her, and he knew she was just on the other side, holding her breath, probably closing her eyes and praying for him to move on.

Which he would, in just a moment. He rapped on the door, loudly.

"Go away!" Her voice was still husky with tears, and he found he could smile. Fighting to the end. What would it feel like to finally be done with her? Liberating? Or empty?

He set the bundle down on the floor outside the door. "Your purse and shoes are here," he said. "The Volvo's parked out front, with Nate's things in the trunk. Just a little word to the wise—if you're going to drive such an old car you might at least keep up the maintenance on it. Your plugs and points hadn't been changed in years. You should have no trouble getting back to Rhode Island in one piece—it's running better than it has in a long time.''

No answer from the other side of the door, but he hadn't expected it. ''If you need any more cash you'll find it in the safe in the garage. I left it open for you. And don't worry about having to see me again. I'll keep out of your way until you're gone.''

Nothing. He hadn't really expected a word, and God help him if she opened the door.

He walked the rest of the way down the hall, noisily, and closed his bedroom door behind him.

Jamie sat cross-legged on the thin mattress. The sound of his footsteps in the hall, his voice outside her door, only made things more complicated. She heard the thump of her shoes and purse on the floor, the sound of his door slamming, and then everything was silent.

She stared at the door in disbelief. It had to be a trick, but she'd heard him walk away, heard the sound of the slamming door.

Just when she thought she'd begun to understand him he'd thrown her a curve. She opened the door cautiously, half expecting him to be lying in wait for her, but the hall was dark and empty. And at her feet were her shoes and purse.

She scooped them up before he could change his mind and shut the door behind her, scarcely believing her luck. He was letting her go, and nothing on God's green earth would make her ever see him again.

Except that God's earth was white with early December snow, not green at all, as she peered out her window. The Volvo was sitting in the alleyway, just lightly dusted with snow, and if she hurried she'd get away from there before it was completely dark, before the snow came down harder, before she changed her mind....

How could she possibly change her mind? Dillon Gaynor was the most dangerous thing in the world as far as she was concerned. He ruined her defenses, he didn't take no for an answer, he terrified her, stole from her, lied to her. Why wasn't she shoving her feet into her shoes and running out of there as fast as she could?

If only Mouser were around, she could talk to him. Not that she had the faintest idea what she'd say. Tell him to watch over Dillon, maybe. Take care of him.

Not that she cared. Not that it mattered. Not that

she was going anywhere that night—she knew it with a sinking feeling. Nowhere but down the hall to his bedroom, to the rumpled white sheets. She was tired of being afraid.

It was easy enough to turn off her brain, to move on autopilot. What she was doing made no sense, therefore she didn't have to think about it. She stripped off the clothes she'd put on after her hasty shower—the jeans and T-shirt, the plain white cotton underwear.

Maybe she'd known ahead of time. The pink silk bra and panties were tucked in a corner of her suitcase. They were even more risqué than the lavender ensemble she wore earlier—these consisted of nothing more than a few strategic scraps of cloth and silk ribbon.

The dress still fit, though it hugged her riper curves more tightly than it had her coltish fifteen-year-old body. There was no mirror in her room, but she didn't want one. She knew what she looked like. Too pale, tangled hair, eyes too big in her face. All the strain and exhaustion of the last few days coming due. If she saw herself she'd probably chicken out. And this was her last chance.

If she was going to sleep with anyone on this earth it would be Dillon Gaynor. He wanted her— there was no question of that any longer. He wouldn't have held on to her dress, wouldn't have kept her trapped there. Hell, he wouldn't have kissed her, wouldn't have pushed her down on the sofa and had sex with her if he didn't want her. Unless it was some twisted score he had to settle against Nate. And against her.

It didn't matter. Nothing mattered anymore, but finishing what he'd started. Walking down that hallway and opening the door.

The bedroom was dark, lit only by the flicker of the television screen. He was stretched out on the bed, wearing jeans and a white T-shirt, and he turned his head to look at her. At the dress she was wearing.

He was very still. He moved his arm, and she realized he'd muted the noise of the television, so that there was only silence in the room. She licked her lips, nervous.

"I thought you wanted to leave."

"I did."

"I thought you were afraid of me."

"I am," she said. He made no move to come toward her, to get off the bed. He simply lay back against the pillows, his smooth skin against the whiteness of the sheets, and watched her.

"So what are you doing here?" There was no sultry welcome in his voice. Just cool suspicion, enough to make her want to turn around and run. Instead she closed the door, leaning against it. Her hand behind her back, still on the old iron door handle if she had to run.

"You said we should finish what we started." Her voice came out a little shaky, and she cleared her throat. "I'm not sure if I consider that a proper finish. If it was that disastrous you ought to give me a chance to improve." She couldn't believe she'd just said that. She couldn't believe she was here in the darkened bedroom with him.

There was only a flicker of reaction on his shadowed face. "You weren't the one who was a disaster. Besides, you've never paid attention to what I've said before. Why now?"

She let go of the doorknob. He didn't seem the slightest bit interested in keeping her there—escape would be easy. And probably a very good idea.

"I thought you wanted me. Apparently you've changed your mind, seen the error of your ways. Maybe once was enough. Too bad Nate isn't around to see it—he'd be proud of you."

"Nate would never be proud of a noble gesture." The reflection of the TV screen flickered over his chest. He was just as beautiful as he'd been twelve years ago, just as far out of reach.

"All right," she said. "Maybe I've just come to say goodbye."

He hesitated for just a moment, and then he seemed to come to a decision. "Then you ought to do it properly. Come here, Jamie."

"No."

The tiny smile at the corner of his mouth was the first expression to break through his distant, enigmatic look. "You started this. You came this far. Come over here and get on the bed."

For a moment she didn't move, paralyzed. And then she took a step toward him.

13

He probably expected her to run. She probably should run. Instead she took the first step toward the bed.

The wood floor was cold beneath her bare feet. Dillon obviously didn't believe in rugs, Jamie thought.

He sat up in the bed, watching her approach, making no move to touch her. He could be making this so much easier—just put his hands on her and take the decision away from her as he had earlier. But he just looked at her.

She took another step. There wasn't that great a distance between the door and the bed, and it wasn't going to take long for her to reach it. Maybe she could take smaller steps.

"Where'd you get the dress?" he asked.

She'd forgotten she was wearing it. "In your middle drawer. I was looking for my things."

"They were in the safe in the garage. Not that that isn't yours, as well."

"I know." Another step. Too damned close, and her heart was slamming against her chest. "Why did you have it?"

"I could tell you Nate had it, and he left it behind. Maybe he carried it with him wherever he went, maybe he had a sick fascination for you."

She halted, horrified, and he laughed.

"And you might be naive enough to believe me," he continued. "But the truth is, I stole it from the trash can that your mother stuffed it into. In memory of the most luscious piece of jailbait I'd ever seen."

"You expect me to believe that? You didn't even know I was around."

"I knew. And you look even better now, though I wouldn't have thought it was possible. Stop stalling, Jamie. You're the one who chose to come in here. Time to find out what you've been missing. What we've both been missing."

She took another step and came up against the side of the bed. It was a high, big bed, and the top of the mattress came halfway up her thighs. Her eyes met his, the same eyes that gave nothing away as he watched her. And she climbed up onto the bed, pulling her skirt around her, and sat back on her knees.

She could feel her stomach twist. He reached for

the hem of his T-shirt and pulled it over his head, tossing it on the floor beside the bed.

"Take off your panties."

She let out a little sound of protest, but he ignored it. "They're coming off sooner or later, and I know from experience they're a bitch and a half to rip off no matter how appealing it may sound. Take them off, Jamie."

She reached under her short skirt and caught the thin bands of lace, sliding them down her hips. Getting out of them was tricky while she was kneeling, and she had no choice but to sit back on the bed and pull the tiny scrap of peach silk over her ankles. She was about to toss them on the far side of the bed when he stopped her, filching the panties out of her hand.

"They're too small for you," she said in a caustic voice.

"That's not what I wanted them for," he said amiably. "Now the bra."

"This dress is see-through."

"That's the idea."

She stopped protesting. Instead she turned her back to him, pulling the knit dress down far enough to take off the bra.

"You're wasting your time trying to be modest," he said, but she'd already pulled her dress back up over her bare breasts, and she turned back to face him.

"I suppose you want this as a souvenir, too," she said, dangling the bra from one finger.

He took it from her, tossing it to his side of the bed. The bed, she thought in sudden horror. She was on a bed with Dillon Gaynor, one thin, semitransparent layer away from being naked.

"Now, climb on top of me."

She couldn't help it—she looked at his crotch in sudden panic. There was no mistaking the way his erection pressed against his zipper, but he hadn't even unsnapped the button of his jeans.

"No, we're not going there yet," he said, reading her mind. "Since I'm taking the role of your sex therapist you're going to have to go at my pace and do what I tell you to do."

"And if I don't want to?"

"Then you can leave. I won't stop you. But if you're staying you need to climb on top of me."

Point of no return. She bit her lip and straddled his hips very carefully, arranging her skirt around her. And she looked into his deep blue eyes.

He slid his hands under her skirt, up to her hips, settling her back, so that now she rested against his erection. He felt harder, bigger than she'd realized.

He slid his hands down her thighs, then up the

backs of them. "This is how we'll do it," he said in a low, silky voice. "You can be in control, go as fast or as slow as you want. It's all up to you. Hell, you can even tie me up if it makes you feel safer. I have nothing against a little friendly bondage."

"You're disgusting."

"Then why are you here?"

She bit her lip. "I don't know."

"I do. You want to be here. Or you'd be long gone into the Wisconsin night, running straight back to the Duchess with your tail between your legs. Except that's not what you want between your legs."

She wasn't expecting his sudden move. In one moment she was nervously straddling him, staring down into his eyes. The next she was lying on her back on the rumpled bed and he was on top of her, her legs pulled around him. In the darkened room the flickers from the muted television played across his face, making him look almost brutal.

And then he kissed her. Put his mouth on hers, and she opened for him, so that she tasted his tongue and his desire, kissing him back.

There was a stifled moan of pleasure, and she realized that it had come from her. It shouldn't have shocked her. It was past time to admit that kissing

Dillon had been the central fantasy of her teenage years. And the hidden, unacknowledged fantasy of her twenties. The only carnal one she'd ever had.

His hands cupped her face, and he seemed ready to take all the time in the world, nibbling on her lower lip, brushing his mouth across her eyelids before he returned to her mouth. She was almost afraid to touch him, but she slid her arms up around him, anyway, against his hot, sleek skin, her fingers running across the shape of his back, the sinew and muscle, bone and flesh of him.

He broke the kiss, his blue eyes almost black in the darkness. "I got ahead of you earlier today. Time to catch up." He pulled out of her arms, moving down on her body, pushing her skirt out of the way as he put his hand between her legs.

She let out a muffled cry, but he ignored it, pushing her skirt up higher. "Come on, Jamie, you remember this. You liked it. You can't tell me you didn't." And he let his long fingers slide against her, so that her body arched instinctively, wanting his touch. He did it again, a little harder this time, and she made a small whimpering sound of need.

"See, I told you you liked this," he said, and he leaned down and kissed her stomach, his mouth hot against her flesh. "You'll like this even better." And he put his mouth between her legs.

She panicked, pushing at his shoulders, but he ignored her, cradling her hips in his hands as he used his mouth, his tongue, even his teeth on her. She began to shake, but this time it wasn't fear. The heat began between her legs and spread outward, upward, in a spiral of pleasure that almost shamed her.

It was too fast, too much. She tried to pull back from that dangerous place, but she was already too far gone. She could feel her body begin to convulse, and she panicked, afraid, only to have Dillon slide his fingers deep inside her at the last moment, and she was lost. Wave after wave of hot, wild pleasure suffused her body, and she had no choice but to let go, surrender to it, and he moved up her body, covering her cry with his mouth.

Slowly, slowly her heart began to slow its pace, and she opened her eyes to see him leaning over her, a smug expression on his face. She would have slapped it if she'd had any strength left in her body.

"That's better," he murmured. "Now, let's get this dress off you. Sexy as it is, it's ready to go. Or I might rip it off you."

She was beyond the point of making any protest, and she let him pull the dress over her head. She didn't bother to look where he tossed it—it no longer mattered.

She lay back on the bed, naked, and he looked down at her out of sober eyes. "Damn," he said in a soft voice.

"Damn what?" Her own voice was no more than a cracked whisper, something that shouldn't have surprised her.

"Just damn." He kissed her mouth, hard and deep, and she could taste herself on his lips. He pulled her into his arms so that her bare breasts were up against his hot skin. "Time to get bolder," he murmured against her mouth, and taking her hand, he put it on his zipper. On the steel-hard rod of flesh beneath it.

She didn't pull away. The feel, the shape of him beneath the jeans was something mysterious and powerful, and his quiet sound of pleasure made her burn hotter.

He rolled onto his back. "That's right, baby girl," he said. "Go ahead," And he took her hand again and put it inside his jeans, to touch him.

She tried to pull away at that, but he was too strong, holding her hand against his silken skin as he unzipped his jeans with the other, shoving them down his hips and kicking them out of the way.

He reached for something from the table beside him, and she realized it was a condom. She was getting used to the feel of him, the silky skin, the hardness beneath, the dampness, but he took her hand away and she heard the ripping of foil.

"Playtime's over, baby girl. Time to get serious."

"We weren't serious before?" she murmured dazedly.

"I want to make you come when I'm inside you."

His words burned her, but she shook her head. "It won't work—"

"It did before, and this time you're wet." He lifted her up, seemingly effortlessly, back to her position astride his body. Except that this time they were both naked, and he held her by her hips, just above his body.

She could feel him between her legs, hard and solid, just waiting. "It's up to you now, Jamie," he said in a tight voice. "If you want me there you have to take me."

She could feel him, the head of his sheathed erection pressing against her. Waiting for her to make her move. She held her breath, and then began to take him, feeling him slowly fill her, inch by inch, until she had all of him deep inside her.

She was shaking, covered with sweat. It made no sense that the invasion of his body would have such a powerful effect on her. He was big inside her, thick and hard, but there was no pain, and she rocked forward a little, then back again, and the pleasure was astonishing. And she needed more.

"I can't," she said in a strangled voice.

He put his hands on her hips, cradling them. "Let me get you started," he whispered, and he moved her, up and down, a slow, steady pace of advance, retreat, empty and fulfilled. But there was nothing relaxed about it—each time she took him inside her she wanted more, needed more, and she unconsciously quickened her pace.

"Are we in a hurry?" His voice sounded almost lazy, but she could feel the tension in his body, the feel of him inside her, and she knew he was feeling it, too, that inner trembling that shook her.

Faster, harder, and she was sliding against him, her body slick with sweat, and she shook, frustrated, pleading. "No," she said in a choked voice. "I can't do this. Help me."

"You just have to ask." He rolled her beneath him, and all she could do was wrap her legs tight around him, feeling the fierce knot of pleasure expand and build.

"Me inside you," he whispered in her ear. He put his hand between their sweat-damp bodies and touched her, hard, as he slammed his body deep inside her.

She could feel him. Feel his sheathed cock begin to expand and jerk as his orgasm hit him, and then she couldn't think or feel anything but the dark, unspeakable pleasure that felt somehow like death.

It was a long time before he pulled away from her, and she was too dazed to do anything but lie still as stray shivers danced across her body.

She felt his fingers on her cheek, brushing the tears away, but she didn't open her eyes. "Poor baby girl," he murmured, his voice slightly shaken. "I should have just dumped Nate at that party and driven off with you. That's what I wanted to do, you know. Take you back to my place and fuck your brains out. I knew the Duchess would have my ass in jail, but I was going to end up there sooner or later. It would have been worth it if I'd gone for this."

He let his hand slide down her neck, her throat, to brush against her breast, and she let out a gasp.

He laughed. "We haven't even gotten to your breasts yet," he said, his fingers glancing against the tip of her breast, and her nipples tightened with almost painful longing. "Or your ass, or your mouth. I wonder how long it's going to take to convince you to go down on me."

She let out a little whimper.

"Thirteen years, Jamie," he whispered. "And we've only just gotten started."

He was gone then, the door closing behind him, and Jamie lay in the dark, her body leaden, unable to move.

And she shivered.

Nate could smell it. The sex, permeating the building, reeking of it. Could ghosts smell? Could ghosts see through walls? He only knew that he could. His hearing was just as acute—he'd listened to Jamie's soft little whimpers, the sound of skin against skin, the slap of flesh, the muffled grunt. He knew when Dillon came. He'd watched him often enough over the years, so that he knew him better than the women he fucked. He knew the sound he made, a growling choke in the back of his throat. And he knew the climax he had inside his cousin's little pussy was one of the best he'd ever had.

It should have annoyed him. He never liked it when Dillon took lovers. Dillon didn't like to hurt them, and sex without pain was boring. It didn't matter. None of them mattered—he didn't care about anyone. He didn't really care about anyone but his best friend Nate.

Until he'd sent him to his death.

Revenge was a bitch. But watching Dillon Gaynor fuck his sweet little cousin almost made it worthwhile. Especially since he knew he was going to kill Jamie for it.

And the best thing about it was how it was going to make Killer suffer the torments of the damned. Before the ghost of Nate Kincaid killed him, too.

14

Dillon stood in the shower a long time, so long that his usually abundant supply of hot water turned cold. He pressed his hands up against the wall of the stall and let the water beat down on him, and he closed his eyes, turning his face up to the pelting stream. He didn't feel guilty. There was nothing to feel guilty about. He'd just done what she'd asked, and this time he'd done it well. And he was going to do it again, as soon as he thought she was up to it. Again and again and again, until they'd had enough of each other.

Jamie was absolutely clueless about what was between them, he thought, ducking his head under the rapidly cooling water. The poor fragile semivirgin, whose only experience with sex was at the hands of a punk kid who'd raped her. She didn't realize how unexpected her response to him was. He thought it would take days to get her to come, and in the end it had been simple enough. It shouldn't have surprised him—she'd always had a crush on him, and getting a teenage fantasy fulfilled went a long way. And he knew more than his share about sex—he knew how to do it, and do it well, and never had any doubt he could bring her off eventually. In the end it hadn't taken much at all.

He was trying to kill some time. She needed sleep, she needed time to recover. Hell, he was hard as a rock just thinking about her, ready to go again, but he knew she'd probably be uncomfortable. If he went back in there there was no way he wouldn't be inside her, and he didn't want to hurt her. He needed her to keep liking it. For as long as he wanted her.

It wouldn't be forever. It never was—sooner or later even the most adept of his lovers began to pall, and he didn't like emotional demands. Jamie used to think she was in love with him—one good orgasm and she'd probably be convinced again. And he'd given her at least two.

She'd be disillusioned after a while. He was still Dillon, still the Killer. A man whose one gift had been for friendship, and he'd turned around and betrayed the man who'd been closest to him for most of his life.

No, there wasn't any future for the two of them— there wasn't any future for him with anyone. But who gave a rat's ass about the future? Right now was what mattered, and right now a woman lay in his bed. A woman he needed. And in the end, that was the only thing that was important.

He finally turned off the water and dressed. He shaved—he usually didn't bother, but he didn't like the idea of his evening stubble abrading Jamie's face. Or her thighs, he thought with a grin. He didn't meet his eyes in the mirror as he concentrated on shaving. He wasn't a man to lie to himself, and he didn't want to risk seeing something in his face that he didn't want to see.

He dressed quickly, then peeked in the bedroom door before heading downstairs. She was asleep, lying facedown on his bed, her pale hair tangled around her face, his white sheets tangled around her hips. He closed the door silently and headed down to the garage.

He had no idea whether or not she'd try to run again. There was a good chance she would—she'd have a hard time looking him in the face after the last few hours they'd spent. But the snow was piling up, and her venerable Volvo didn't have snow tires, only slightly balding all-season radials, which weren't worth a damn in a Wisconsin winter. He headed out into the snowy night, turning the ignition of the old car and listened to it purr to life. He backed it up, then drove it into the garage, closing the door behind him. There was a patch of dark in the snow where the Volvo had sat parked, and he paused for a moment. Nothing should be leaking— not the oil or antifreeze or anything else—he'd gone over the engine with his usual obsessive attention to detail. At least, when it came to cars he was obsessive. He couldn't give a damn about the rest of his life.

He parked the car in the middle of the garage and opened the hood. Everything seemed to be fine— no leaking hoses, every reservoir safely filled. He glanced at the back, but if whatever had darkened the snow had come from the Volvo, it was no longer draining.

He'd check the underside in the morning, just to make certain. But in the meantime he had the per- fect excuse to keep her longer. Not that he needed an excuse. But she would. She couldn't very well admit that she wanted to blow off her controlling mother, her job and her neatly ordered life for a few days, a few weeks, a few months of hot sex. Even if she did. He'd given her a taste, and she'd want more. But his instincts told him she'd still want to run.

At least the car would give her an excuse to stay. And he could always continue to make it an excuse easily enough. But he didn't think he would. In the end, she was going to have to admit it. That for some reason, some twisted trick of fate, she wanted him just as much as he wanted her. And it was going to take a hell of a long time to burn that wanting out.

Jamie forced herself to relax as she listened to his footsteps outside the bedroom door. Her head was turned away, and she heard the door open. She held her breath, wondering if he was going to come back in there, if he was going to touch her again. And how she was going to say no when saying no was the last thing she wanted.

She had her purse back, with all her money and identification and credit cards. He told her she had her car back, but even if she didn't, she now had the wherewithal to rent a new one and get the hell out of there. He wouldn't try to stop her. Her question was, did she really want to run?

The door closed, and she heard him move down the stairs, and she let out a deep sigh of relief that had nothing to do with disappointment.

There was no hot water in the shower, but she was past caring. It was one way to punish herself for her stupidity, and it should certainly wipe away any lingering, errant lust. That's what it had been, pure and simple, right? Except she never would have thought herself capable of such a primal emotion.

It sure as hell wasn't love.

She wrapped the towel around her and ran down the darkened hallway to her room, closing the door quietly behind her. If he wanted to keep her old dress she was more than welcome to it, as well as the ill-advised racy underwear. She just needed her clothes and shoes to get the hell out of there.

She dressed quickly, throwing the rest of her clothes in her suitcase and slamming it shut. Her sneakers didn't really go with the sedate dress that her mother had bought for her, but that didn't matter. All that mattered was escape.

She couldn't find her watch. Not that the stupid thing would tell her what time it was—she hadn't wound it since she arrived. But it was an heirloom, given to her by her father when she was sixteen, and she treasured it.

It wasn't in her suitcase, wasn't anywhere around. Had Dillon taken that, as well, and then neglected to return it? It was the most valuable thing she'd brought with her, and if Dillon was the man she'd always thought him to be, he would have made off with it, looking for a fast buck.

But Dillon wasn't the man she'd always thought him to be. And she didn't want to consider exactly what kind of man he really was. All she wanted to do was escape.

She didn't know why she had to run, just that it was a deep moral imperative. She was over her head here, drowning, and her only hope was to get out before it was too late. She still had enough self-preservation to know that going into his room last night had been the most stupid thing she'd ever done, even worse than getting into the back seat of Dillon's Cadillac with Paul Jameson. In retrospect that had been nothing more than a physical assault. Dillon was fucking her body *and* her soul.

She reached out and grabbed the sleeping bag that covered the thin mattress, pulling it away to see if she'd left the watch in bed. And then she screamed.

She ran full into Dillon as he came racing up the stairs, and she slammed against him, adding to her breathlessness.

"What the hell's going on?"

"Dead..." she gasped. "On the mattress..." She shuddered. "There's blood."

He pushed past her, heading for her room. "Stay here," he ordered her.

She leaned against the wall, trying to control the shivers that ran through her body. She hated the hallway—she always felt as if someone was watching her, some pervert with graveyard breath and twisted thoughts. Silly, of course, when the only other person in the building was Dillon, and he was in her room, not watching her.

"It's a dead rat." He appeared in her doorway, his voice matter-of-fact. "I told you I get them all the time."

"The other one didn't have so much blood," she said faintly. "And what was it doing in my bed?"

"If it were a man I could think of any number of reasons, but since it's only a very large dead rat, then I have no idea. It must have gotten into the rat poison I've had lying around, and it dragged itself up to your room to die."

"Lucky me. Why the blood? The other rat wasn't bleeding. Until I stepped on it," she added with a reminiscent shudder.

Dillon shrugged, looking down at her. She was suddenly conscious of how very tall he was, how very strong. And they were alone in the hallway, and she'd just had sex with him. "Who knows? I could come up with all sorts of graphic suggestions, but I don't think you really want to hear them. Besides, what does it matter? You aren't going to be sleeping in there anymore."

"I'm not going to be sleeping here at all," she said.

His slow grin wasn't exactly the reaction she'd expected. "Well, no, sleeping wasn't what I had in mind, either. I'll stay awake as long as you will."

"I mean I'm leaving here. Okay? Accounts settled. We've done what we needed to do. You got your revenge for spending a year in prison, I got to fulfill a teenage fantasy and now I can get on with my life. Case closed. I'm leaving." She waited for him to explode in rage.

Instead he tilted his head to one side, unperturbed. "Oh, really?" he said. "And what makes you think that? Personally I haven't even begun to do what I've needed to do for the last twelve years."

For once he wasn't standing between her and escape. Her purse and her suitcase were in the room behind him, but as long as she had her shoes and her car she was ahead of the game.

"You can try and catch me," she said, trying to hide the edge of nervousness in her voice, "but it won't do any good. I'm faster—"

"I'm not going to run after you, Jamie," he said in a calm voice. "I told you, I'll let you go. If you want to leave, go ahead. I put your car back in the garage, but you won't have any trouble opening the doors. The keys are on the passenger seat."

She couldn't believe she'd heard him right. "You're letting me go?" she echoed, waiting for a burst of elation to replace the sinking feeling in the pit of her stomach. "Then would you hand me my purse and suitcase? I really don't want to go back into that room."

"Certainly." He disappeared into the bedroom, coming back with her possessions. "You want me to carry them down for you?"

Now, why in hell did she want to cry? "I can manage," she said, yanking them out of his hands. She spun around and started down the stairs, for once grateful for the darkness. She felt an odd stinging in her eyes, and the last thing in the world she wanted was for him to see them.

He followed her, of course, keeping a safe distance. She couldn't even remember if she'd brought a coat, but at least the heater in her car was a powerful one, built for Scandinavian winters. Once she got the car warmed up it would be fine.

The kitchen was as cosy as usual, a deceptively welcoming space, and she set her suitcase down, steeling herself for a polite goodbye. But Dillon walked right past her to the back door onto the alleyway, a red-streaked sheet in his hands, and she knew he carried the dead rat.

He tossed it out into the back alley, sheet and all, then stood there staring for a moment, down at the snow at his feet, at the alleyway that led out to the main street. And then he turned back, momentarily lost in thought, shutting the door behind him.

"The car's in the garage," he said absently. "Don't worry about closing the door after you drive out—I'll take care of it."

It had all taken on a tinge of unreality. She couldn't believe it could be that simple, that after all that had happened he'd simply let her take her car and drive away from here, without a word. It was exactly what she wanted, of course, but it felt almost surreal.

She plastered her best social smile on her face, the one that her mother had drilled into her. "Well..." she said.

"Well," he said finally, turning his attention back to her. "You've got that Duchess look on your face. Sorry you had to pick that up. Next thing I know you're going to want to shake hands with me and thank me for a lovely time."

Jamie dropped her hand surreptitiously behind her back. "Of course not," she said in a frosty voice.

"So what do you want to say?"

"That's easy enough. Goodbye." She picked up her suitcase and purse before he could and walked into the garage.

Her Volvo was there, all right, parked in a corner,

snow melting off the roof. It also had at least two flat tires.

She put her suitcase and purse down, just staring at it, as Dillon came up behind her. "What happened to the tires?"

"Beats me," he said, clearly untroubled by this latest development. "You must have run over something when you went off the road."

"And you didn't notice when you were working on it?"

"They hadn't gone flat when I was working on it."

She turned to look up at him. "Did you have anything to do with it?"

"I fixed your car."

"Anything to do with the flat tires. Did you let the air out of them?" It was a stupid thing to ask. Of course he hadn't—he was more than happy to get rid of her at this point.

"Yes."

"We could...yes?" she echoed in sudden shock, realizing what he'd said.

"Yes. I let the air out of your tires. All four of them, as a matter of fact. Just in case you got it in your mind to run away."

"I thought you were going to let me go."

"I should." He was trying to sound diffident, but

even she could tell he was uncomfortable with the admission.

"But you're not." It should have been anger, fear flooding her body. Not relief.

"No, I'm not."

She set down her things on the cement floor, then turned to look at him. He frightened her—there was no question about that. But he was also nothing more than human, a bad boy who'd gotten his way for too long.

"Then convince me to stay," she said, pushing her hair away from her face and watching him calmly.

Her face was pale, and she had circles under her beautiful gray eyes. And she was looking at him as if he were a cross between the devil incarnate and Prince Charming. He could have told her which one he was. He'd tried to convince her what a monster he was. For some reason he didn't want to try anymore.

The garage was warm—heat blasting from the corner fans. He still didn't know why he'd ended up sabotaging her car at the last minute. If she wanted to go he should let her. Let her get on with her life. Let them both get on with life. But in the end he couldn't do it. Maybe because it wasn't the end.

She was still looking at him, both hopeful and frightened. Those wide gray eyes of hers were absurd—no grown woman should look quite so vulnerable. She was a little too thin, but he could feed her up. She was a little too nervous, and he'd done everything he could to perpetuate that.

And she was a little too irresistible. He should have been doing everything he could to scare her away, push her away, drive her away. Instead he'd done just the opposite.

He walked past her, careful not to touch her, and headed toward the front wall of the garage. He knew exactly what he had in the CD changer, and he punched a couple of buttons. A second later music filled the room, like a blanket of sound that drowned out any possibility of conversation, and he turned back to her.

She'd turned even paler in the harsh light of the garage. It was a cheap shot, and he knew it, and he should have been ashamed of himself. But he wasn't.

U2 filled the room, and suddenly he was back twelve years ago, on a one-way path to disaster, with a trembling virgin in his arms. And that trembling virgin was looking at him right now, remembering that song.

He moved slowly, so as not to scare her, but she'd gotten brave in the last few hours. When he reached out for her she didn't flinch away, and when he pulled her into his arms she went without hesitation, putting her arms around his neck, resting her head against his shoulder, as they moved to the music.

He closed his eyes and danced with her, and he could see the old gym at the Marshfield School, tarted up with crepe paper and black lights. He should have taken her to that dance, should have had the balls to ask her. But then she'd been dating some purebred jock, a clone to Paul, and she never would have gone.

But right now she settled her body against his like a lazy kitten, and she let him move her to the music, slowly, rocking, barely dancing in the dimly lit garage.

He wanted her, craved her, more than coffee and cigarettes, more than the last drink he'd had five years ago, more than a free conscience. He needed her, and the more he fought it the stronger that need grew, until it threatened to destroy him.

He could drive her away from him—it would be easy enough. The song was almost over, another

CD would flip onto the changer, and then he'd tell her he loved her, and his life would be over.

He had one chance to save himself. One chance to drive her away before it was too late for him.

He stopped moving and put his hand under her chin, tilting her face up to his. Her eyes were bright in the darkness, and she had a soft, blissed-out look on her face. And he could come just from looking down at her.

But he had to get her out of there. Last-minute sanity reared its ugly head. So he said the one thing he knew would drive her away.

"Get in the back of the car."

He waited for her outrage, for her to shove him away and run off. It would take him five minutes to put the air back in her tires, and then he'd take off, so he wouldn't have to see her again, and he'd be safe.

She looked up at him, her face pale, her mouth, her gorgeous mouth, tremulous. She stepped back from him, out of his arms.

"Yes," she said.

15

Dillon couldn't believe his ears. But she turned and walked away from him, walked over to the old Cadillac, and she looked like she had when she was sixteen and he'd wanted her badly enough to risk going to jail. Wanted her badly enough to almost kill someone who hurt her. Wanted her badly enough right now that he was putting his entire way of life, peace of mind, in danger.

He was unbuttoning his old flannel shirt by the time he reached the side of the car, but she put her hands on his, stopping him. And then she began to unbutton them herself, head down, concentrating on the task.

She pushed it from his shoulders, her hands skimming his skin as the shirt slid to the floor. And then she leaned forward and put her mouth against his pounding heart, as her hands reached for his belt.

She touched him. Through the thick denim of his jeans, she put her hand over him, her fingers slowly stroking, and he let out a strangled moan.

"If we don't get in the car now we might not make it," he said in a rough voice.

She looked up at him. Her pale hair had fallen in her face, and her cheeks were flushed.

"We're already here," she said.

"And I'm ready to drag you down on the cement."

She looked down at the cement floor beneath them. "Looks uncomfortable," she said. She'd already unfastened the snap at the top of his jeans, and now she began to undo the zipper, her hands delicate, barely touching him, and the feel of her was more erotic than a practiced caress.

"Get in the goddamned car," he said in a choked voice.

"In a minute," she said. She pushed his jeans down his legs, and then sank to her knees in front of him, on the hard cement floor. And she put her mouth on him, just tasting him.

He let out a groan of agonized pleasure, but she pulled away, looking up at him out of wide eyes. "Did I hurt you?"

"No," he said. "God no." And threading his fingers through her hair, he gently brought her head, her mouth, back to him.

It was the most profoundly erotic experience of his life. She had absolutely no idea what she was doing, she simply experimented, touching, tasting, sucking. He didn't have to guide her, didn't have to say a word. He just leaned back against the old Caddy so his knees didn't buckle and let her bring him to the point of explosion with her sweet, un-tutored mouth. And he knew she wasn't ready for that. She was making soft whimpering sounds, and he realized that she was almost as turned-on as he was.

He pushed her back, gently, though her hands still clung to his hips. He picked her up, easily, and swung her into the open convertible, into the back seat. She lay back in the corner, breathless, waiting for him, as he kicked off his jeans and climbed into the car with her.

This time her underwear was the plain white cotton he knew she usually favored. And it was even more erotic than the stuff she'd been wearing before.

He slid the panties down her legs, and she leaned back to help him. The back seat of the Cadillac was so huge it was almost a bed, and even though he was tall he knew it could be managed. He started to push her back down, but she shook her head. Instead she simply moved over and straddled him as he leaned back against the old leather seat.

He reached under her damned skirt and touched her, and she was wet. Ready. Trembling.

"Show me how to do this," she whispered.

The condoms were in his jeans outside the car. And nothing in this world could have made him stop. He took his cock and placed it against her, just touching her, feeling her quiver in reaction. "Just move slowly. You don't want to hurt yourself, you don't want to hurt me. See what feels good—" she was slowly filling herself with him, and he could barely speak "—and then do it some more."

She took him at his word. Slowly, slowly she sank down on him, taking him inch by inch. She was so hot and damp there was nothing to stop her, but the agonizing slowness was unexpectedly powerful.

He was only halfway inside her when she let out a sudden cry, and he felt her body contract around him. It shocked her so much that she almost started to pull away, but it was too late for that.

Her dress was stupid, and he ripped it open, so that her breasts were free, and he covered them with his hands, his fingers touching her, caressing her, and he felt a second flutter of an orgasm tighten around his cock.

She whimpered again, but by now he recognized that sound as pure need, and she finally took all of him inside her, coming to rest on him with her forehead pressed against his shoulder.

She had exquisitely sensitive breasts, reacting to even his lightest touch. Her nipples were as hard as pebbles against his hands, and he wanted to put his mouth on them, needed to, when she moved her head and whispered in his ear.

"I wanted you to come in my mouth."

He almost came right then. His cock seemed to expand inside her, and she looked at him, her eyes open wide. "But not yet," she added. And she began to move.

He let her. Let her do what she wanted, no matter how much he wanted to take over, no matter how desperate he was. She was learning what she wanted, and he was willing to let her, even if he thought it might just possibly kill him.

And finally she began to move, faster, and he put his arms around her, pulling her against him, as he thrust up to meet her plunging hips, and she was breathless, sobbing, crying out, and he was gasping, beyond words, until they both reached it at the same time. She let out a soft, keening howl, and her body clamped down around him, and his last bit of control vanished. He filled her with thrust after thrust, and she held on, until they both shattered.

She was crying when she collapsed against him,

a rag doll of a woman, but he didn't make the mistake of thinking she was unhappy. He didn't have much breath left himself, but he put his hand on the back of her neck and turned her face to his and kissed her, a soft, deep, hungry kiss. And he felt one more contraction ripple through her body.

He left their clothes behind, scattered on the garage floor, kicking the door shut behind him. He carried her upstairs, up to his bed, and lay down with her, wrapping his body tight around her. And for the first time in his life, he slept with a woman.

When Jamie awoke it was morning and she was alone. She hadn't been alone all night—she knew that. She'd slept with his body wrapped around her, she'd wakened to him inside her. At one point they just lay there and kissed, endlessly. He knew how to kiss. He knew how to do everything.

She was cold, sticky, aching all over. She needed a shower, she needed clean clothes, she needed food. But most of all she needed Dillon.

There was no music pounding up from the garage. It was late morning—she couldn't believe how long she'd slept. But then, she'd had a very busy twenty-four hours. She climbed out of his bed, taking the sheet with her and wrapping it around her body. She had no idea why she was feeling modest, after last night. Maybe it was because of last night. And earlier this morning.

Damn, she hurt! A hot soak in the claw-footed bathtub would do wonders, though. Since she'd been in Wisconsin she'd taken the fastest possible showers she could, just to make sure she didn't run into Dillon. At this point, if he walked in on her in the tub, it could prove...interesting.

The bathroom was warm, heat pouring from the air duct on the floor. For once there seemed to be enough hot water, and she filled the tub as full as she could before dropping the sheet and slipping into the blissfully hot water. She let out a little moan of pleasure. How could she feel so battered and so good at the same time?

But she did. She rested her head against the cool edge of the cast-iron tub and closed her eyes, and she could feel a smile forming on her face. He'd told her he could make her scream, and he was right. He hadn't told her he could make her smile.

When she was ready to get out, she looked around. There was only one towel in the bathroom, and it was still damp. His. She brought it to her face, and she could smell the soap he used, the shampoo. She breathed it in, like a drug, and for the first time she understood why he'd kept her dress. If he sent her away, if she ran away, she'd steal this towel and take it with her. And sleep with it, like the lovesick adolescent she'd always been. And still was.

She wrapped the sheet around her again and headed back to her room. He'd brought her suitcase upstairs at some point, and she dressed quickly, in her jeans and an old cotton sweater. She kept listening for him, wondering if he was going to come back upstairs, wondering if she really wanted to get dressed, after all, when she heard a noise overhead. Just a faint creaking noise, like a ghost walking.

She froze, listening intently. And then another sound, like something being dragged across the floor. Dillon must be up there, though she couldn't imagine why.

If she had any brains at all she'd go downstairs and find something to eat and keep her distance from Dillon for as long as she could bear to. Her body needed time to recover, because if he put his hands on her she wouldn't be able to say no. Wouldn't want to.

But right then she didn't seem to have any brains at all. She was going up to the third floor to see what Dillon was doing, and if they ended up doing something else she'd manage to survive. Besides, there were other things she was interested in trying. In having him show her.

The stairs were cloaked in shadows—if there was a light anywhere it had burned out. The top of the stairs was dark, unwelcoming, and if she had an overactive imagination she'd think there were monsters up there, waiting for her. But she was a practical woman. Except where Dillon Gaynor was concerned.

The stairs creaked beneath her feet. But she stepped carefully, not willing to make contact with another mangled rodent. She had the oddest sense that someone, something was watching her. But it was too dark—she could barely see in front of her. Nothing on this earth would be able to see her in this darkness.

The hall at the top of the stairs was identical to the one beneath it. All the doors were tightly shut except one, halfway down on the left side. The place must have been some kind of boarding house, long ago. The room with the open door would have been two rooms down from her own austere cell.

The only light was coming from that room, the stark gray of snowlit daylight.

"Dillon?" she called out. Her voice was swallowed up by the darkness, and there was no answer. Just the sound of something moving in that room.

It wasn't the scrabbling feet of rats. It was something bigger, more forceful. She walked down the hall, the ancient wood beneath her creaking loudly, announcing her approach. "Dillon?" she called again. Still no answer.

She reached the door, but it was only partway open, just letting out a sliver of light into the hallway. She pushed it the rest of the way, but the room was empty. Not a living soul in sight.

She stood motionless as her eyes adjusted to the dim light. The room was a twin to her own, except there was nothing inside—no mattress on the floor, no light. The walls and bare wood floor were covered with dark stains, and the plaster had been crushed in several places, as if someone had smashed something into the wall. The stains were darkest there.

She could feel it, like an icy blanket draping around her. The pain. And the evil. And she knew this was where Nate had died. The stains were the marks of his blood soaking into the walls and the floor of this old building.

The heat didn't reach up to this floor. Or if it did, she was beyond feeling it. Beyond feeling anything but the pain and horror that had filled this room only three months ago. And still lived within the walls like a ghost yearning for revenge.

She could feel him behind her, and a crawling sense of horror began to snake up her spine. There was no one there—she knew that with every practical bone in her body. She didn't hear anyone, the air wasn't disturbed around her, there was no body heat radiating off another soul. But she wasn't alone any longer, and she didn't dare turn around and look, suddenly terrified at what she might see. She simply froze, staring blindly ahead of her at the room covered in dried blood.

In the end it didn't matter. The push was as insubstantial as a puff of wind, as hard as an angry shove, and she fell forward, into the room. The floor gave way beneath her feet, and she went crashing through the splintering wood that seemed to dissolve beneath her feet.

She must have screamed. She was trapped in the rotting floorboards, up to her knees, and when she twisted around to look the doorway was empty.

The wood had collapsed around her, and every time she tried to pull free it simply crumbled beneath her. She was trapped, almost up to her hips, and she had a suddenly, irrational terror that ghostly hands would reach from underneath and pull her down, down into some inexplicable hell, and she screamed again, this time for Dillon.

She heard the thundering sound of his footsteps, and she closed her eyes in relief. There hadn't been time for him to have pushed her, disappeared and then come back up. There couldn't have been.

He reached under her arms and hauled her up, the wood splintering as he pulled her through, and she let out a cry of pain. He set her down in the hallway, ungently, and she leaned against the wall, her legs weak beneath her, and watched as he slammed the door, plunging them into darkness. And then locked it, locking away the evil, locking away the truth.

"What the fuck were you doing in there?"

She was glad she didn't have to see the fury in his face. Her left leg was beginning to throb, and her entire body was trembling with the aftermath of shock.

"That was where he died, isn't it?" Her voice was low, strained. "That's where Nate was murdered. That's his blood all over the place. For God's sake, couldn't you have at least cleaned up the blood?" she cried.

Silence. She could barely see his shadow in the darkened hallway—his expression was beyond reading. "I didn't expect you to go nosing around where you didn't belong."

"Hell, I don't belong here, anywhere here, and we both know it! I certainly don't belong in your bed."

"Or in the back seat of my car. Or on the floor of the garage. Or on the kitchen table, or anywhere else we end up doing it. Whether you belong or not is beside the point. It's where you want to be."

The pain in her leg was nothing compared to the harshness in his voice. "Go to hell," she said. She pushed away from the wall, but her leg buckled beneath her. It should have been too dark for him to see, but she should never have underestimated the Killer.

He picked her up, and she hit him, trying to squirm out of his arms. He was much stronger, of course, and it only took him a moment to pinion her arms between them. "Stop fighting me," he said gruffly. "It puts me in a bad mood, and you don't want to see me in a bad mood. You're hurt, you can't walk, so you might as well shut up and let me help."

"I could crawl," she snapped.

"A lovely thought, but we'll wait till I'm not so pissed at you to play those games."

"You're disgusting."

"By your standards, yes." He was totally un-moved by her struggles or her fury, and she could tell by the strength and tension in his body that he was just as angry with her.

He carried her down the stairs. Down two flights

of stairs, thank God, not stopping at the floor with
the bedrooms. The kitchen was filled with warmth
and light—a shocking contrast to the bleakness of
the third floor, and she could smell something cooking. Something wonderful, and her empty stomach
growled in sudden hunger.

He set her down on the oak table, and she immediately tried to jump down.

"Don't waste your time, and don't piss me off
more than I already am," he growled. "You
screwed up your leg big time, and I don't want you
turning around and suing me. I don't have any kind
of insurance, and while I know you'd like nothing
better than to take this place away from me and
burn it to the ground as a tribute to your darling
Nate, I've worked hard for it and I'm not about to
let it go. So hold still and let me see how badly
you're hurt."

She still tried to scramble off the table, but he
was stronger than she was, holding her there, and
she gave up fighting.

"Shit," he muttered.

"Shit," she echoed, looking down at the blood-
matted leg of her jeans. No wonder it was throb-
bing.

"Stay put," he said, and by now she wasn't fighting. He went to a drawer, grabbed a bunch of things

and turned back, cutting her pants leg to her knee with a pair of scissors before she could protest.

There were three gashes on her leg. At least the bleeding had stopped, though her entire foot was soaked in blood.

"Lie back on the table."

"I've heard that before," she said in a caustic voice.

"Behave yourself, Jamie." He pushed her, surprisingly gentle, and she lay back, closing her eyes. It wasn't the same push that had sent her hurtling forward into that room. Different hands, yet who else could it be? Who else was here?

"Did you push me?"

He was cleaning the scrapes with infinite care, and he didn't hesitate. "You know I did. And if you try to sit up again I'll sit on you."

"I don't mean now. I mean on the third floor. Did you push me into that room?"

Only the slightest hesitation, so slight that most people wouldn't have noticed it. "I didn't want you up there," he said finally. "Why would I have pushed you in? Especially with the floor rotting away like that. The roof over the place has leaked for years, and I just got it redone this spring. I haven't had enough money to take care of the damage on that floor, and I assumed no one would be wandering up there or I would have warned you. What in hell made you go up there in the first place?''

''I heard someone moving around up there. I thought you'd gone upstairs for something.''

''I was in the garage.''

''I didn't hear you down there.''

''You think I'm lying?'' The question was very casual, but she didn't miss the edge.

''No,'' she said. Hoping she meant it.

''You know this place has rats. They've taken a particular affection for you. You must have heard one moving around up there. The place is probably teeming with them. No one ever goes up there.''

She shuddered. ''Why don't you get rid of them?''

''I told you, there's plenty of poison lying around. That's why they suddenly show up dead at your feet. What can I say—you and rats have a certain affinity.''

''Are you talking about Nate or about you?''

''Take your pick. Why don't you find some nice banker and marry him and make your mother happy?''

''Nothing would make my mother happy,'' she said flatly.

"Well, you've learned that much over the years. Sit up."

She actually didn't want to. She wanted him to climb up on the table and kiss her, to wrap his arms around her and soothe her irrational fears. Because there was nothing to be afraid of, was there?

But she sat up, looking down at her bandaged leg, looking up into his shadowed face. He had her blood on his hands.

"Are you all right?" he asked finally, almost unwillingly. "You look as pale as a ghost."

"There's no such thing as ghosts, right? Nate's dead and gone—he can't come back."

"He's dead and gone. I identified his body, Jamie. There wasn't any doubt, despite the condition he was in."

"Condition?" she echoed in a faint voice.

"Come on, Jamie, you know what shape he was in. He was beaten to a bloody pulp. The Duchess herself wouldn't have recognized him, except for the jewelry and the clothes."

"So there couldn't have been a mistake?"

Dillon shook his head. "I was here at the time, Jamie. Nate didn't leave."

The first trickle of doubt began to form in the pit of her stomach. "What do you mean, you were here? You knew what was happening?"

He didn't look at her. "I wasn't Nate's baby-sitter. He stayed on the third floor, remember? I work in the garage with the music cranked up."

It wasn't an answer, not a real one. He'd gone to the sink, washing her blood from his hands, and she could see the tension in his tall, lean body.

"You're lying to me," she said.

He glanced at her over his shoulder. "What are you accusing me of, baby girl? Killing Nate? Luring you upstairs to try to kill you? Couldn't I have just strangled you in bed?"

It shouldn't have made her blush. Doubt filled her body, and she made herself slide down off the table. Her ankle hurt, but it bore her weight.

"I don't know what to believe. All I know is you're lying."

He turned around, leaning back against the sink. "Yeah?" he said. "And do you want me to show you how much you care?"

"What do you mean?"

He started toward her, a slow, stalking gait, and she froze. He was threat personified, and all her instincts said "run." And all her instincts said "stay."

He came right up to her, towering over her, his body brushing hers. He leaned his head down and whispered in her ear. "You don't care whether I killed Nate or not. You don't even care if for some crazy reason I want to kill you. All I have to do is touch you and you don't care about anything but me.'' He slid his hand between her legs, and even through the denim of her torn jeans she quivered, swaying toward him.

He brushed his lips against the side of her neck, and she arched. ''It's called power, baby girl,'' he whispered. ''Sexual thrall. I own you, and it doesn't matter what I did, what I will do. All that matters is you'll do what I say. Won't you?''

He was stroking her, and she could feel herself getting damp. He moved his lips to the corner of her mouth, and he moved one leg between hers, pressing. ''Won't you?'' he said again.

She wanted to touch him. She wanted to put her arms around his waist and pull him tighter against her body, she wanted to sink down on the floor and finish what she'd started earlier. She wanted to do anything he asked of her, and more.

But she couldn't. She looked up into his dark eyes, and she wanted to disappear into the darkness, into the heat and power. But she couldn't.

''Did you have anything to do with Nate's death?'' She could barely get the words out.

She expected him to pull away. He didn't. He pushed his leg between hers, pulling her forward so that she rode against his hard thigh, and she moaned. "Do you trust me?"

God, she wanted to. She wanted to empty her mind and her heart of everything but Dillon. He was going to make her come this way, and she didn't want to. She wanted him to stop, to talk to her, to tell her there was nothing to be afraid of, nothing to worry about, that she could trust him with her life.

"Do you trust me?" he asked again, his leg sliding against her, harder, and she felt the quivering of an incipient orgasm begin to wash over her. She was having trouble breathing, and if she weren't supported by the table behind her and his leg between hers she would have collapsed.

She was almost there, and he knew it. He knew everything about her body in this short time. "Do you?" he asked, one more time, brushing his mouth against hers, and she wanted more, she wanted his tongue, she wanted everything. Everything but losing herself.

"No," she whimpered.

"No? No, don't do this, or no, you don't trust me?"

"I...I..." She could barely speak, she was shaking so hard. He could finish it if he wanted to, but he was holding her just on the edge, taunting her.

"No, I don't trust you," she said. "And no, don't stop."

He pulled away from her, so abruptly she fell back against the table. She looked up at him, dazed, but he'd already stepped back.

"Sorry, baby girl. You can't have one without the other."

And he walked out into the night, into the snow, without another word, slamming the door behind him.

16

He hadn't taken a coat, and he didn't give a shit. He didn't get cold easily, an advantage in this climate, and the flannel shirt would be enough to get him away from Jamie. He should have known, of course. She'd been raised by the Duchess, side by side with Nate. There was no way she could have come through life untainted, no matter how innocent she seemed. Fucking him was all well and good—she'd do anything he wanted her to if he just touched her the right way. Anything except trust him.

Crazy that that would bother him. Why the hell would he need her to trust him, when all he really wanted was her ass? To burn off twelve years of frustration in the shortest possible time.

Maybe it was because she'd trusted Nate, believed in him as she'd never believe in Dillon. Nate was the most treacherous creature Dillon had ever known, including the thugs he'd met during the year and a half he'd spent in prison, and Jamie still thought he walked on water. And she looked at Dillon and saw a bad boy and a good time.

Hell, he shouldn't object. Isn't that how he saw himself? Isn't that all he wanted to be to her?

Mouser would smarten him up. He could always count on Mouser to make him see things clearly, whether he wanted to or not. And Mouser would always go to a meeting with him. He'd walk over to his place and talk him into driving him to St. Anne's. It was getting cold. He'd run over to his place before he froze his balls off.

But Mouser's place was dark. He lived on the first floor of a decrepit apartment building, and he slept with a light on. He was afraid of the dark—a weakness he admitted to few, but Dillon knew it. Yet his apartment was pitch black.

He knew where Mouser kept the spare key, and he heard the cats before he even opened the door. It had always been a source of amusement to him, Mouser's fondness for cats. He was a sucker for any stray that wandered by—it was no wonder he was so protective of Jamie. He currently had three cats who were now weaving their way around Dillon's ankles, making plaintive, hungry noises.

He'd always told Mouser he didn't like animals, and of course Mouser didn't believe him. He leaned down and picked up one scraggly bundle of fur, rubbing the head of another, and headed into Mouser's tiny kitchen.

The cat food dish was empty. Which was crazy—Mouser doted on his felines. He never would have left them without food.

He poured some food into the bowls, and was immediately rewarded with a couple of loud purrs, another body weaving around his ankle, while a third decided to sharpen his claws on his shin before settling in to eat.

He flicked on the light in the kitchen. Supposedly cats could see in the dark, but Mouser wouldn't want them left in an unlit apartment.

He should leave him a note before heading out to the meeting. But he had a cold, certain feeling that Mouser wasn't coming back.

Mouser's upstairs neighbor, a plump widow with a similar fondness for strays, promised to look after the cats until Mouser returned. At least they wouldn't starve to death in the apartment. Mouser would never have forgiven him if he let that happen.

He walked down the snowy street, heading toward St. Anne's. It was a long walk, he didn't have a coat, and he didn't give a shit. Too much had happened in the last twenty-four hours. He was usually the most cynical, pragmatic, grounded person he knew. Now he was having morbid fantasies and was on the verge of falling in...

Hell, no. He just needed a meeting to help clear his head. He'd swing by Mouser's apartment on the way home, where he'd find his old friend with a perfectly reasonable excuse for why he'd disappeared. And when he went back to the garage, if Jamie wasn't gone, he'd pick her up, drop her in her car and lock the doors behind her.

Or maybe he wouldn't pick her up. Touching her tended to get him into trouble. If she hadn't left he could drive her out with words easily enough.

But he was counting on her to leave.

He lit a last cigarette before heading into his meeting. Sunday night at St. Anne's was a crowded one, and the coffee was awful, but it would be hot. And maybe things would start to make a little sense.

Jamie sank down into one of the kitchen chairs, staring at the door in disbelief. He'd simply walked out on her. Brought her to that point, so that her nerve endings screamed, her skin prickled, and she could barely breathe, and then walked away.

He must have gotten over his obsession awfully fast. It hadn't taken much to get him past twelve years of wanting, she thought bitterly. Whereas in her case, she was just starting.

Fuck him. Fuck them all. She was tired of feeling vulnerable, needy, helpless. He'd let the air out of her tires? She'd seen the compressor, and she was equipped with a brain and determination. She could figure out how to fill the tires with air and then get the hell out of there before he returned. That's what he wanted, wasn't it? That was what they both wanted.

And if she couldn't, then she'd simply take any car she could start. Except for the yellow Cadillac. If that was her only choice she'd walk barefoot through foot-deep snow rather than get back in that damned car.

She'd never been alone in the huge old building before, at least, not that she'd been aware of. Without Dillon's music thundering through the place it felt empty, desolate. Almost haunted.

Her sneakers were bloody from her fall through the floor, but that was the least of her worries. She shoved her feet back in them, then headed into the garage, refusing to look behind her. She never could rid herself of the feeling that someone, something, was watching her, and now, in this empty place, that feeling was more powerful than ever.

She could hear the old building creak in the cold. The faint sound of movement overhead—more rats, presumably. The howl of the strong Wisconsin wind, rattling the windows and shaking the garage doors. And the sound of her footsteps as she walked across the cement floor to her poor old Volvo.

She kept her gaze averted from the Cadillac, deliberately. She could have kicked herself for her behavior earlier. She'd done just what he wanted, playing into his hands perfectly. He got to have her in the back seat of his goddamned convertible, where he should have had her years ago. Dillon, not Paul.

Oh, not that she'd had anything to do with it, she mocked herself, heading toward the stereo. Whose idea was it to go down on him, when the very thought used to disgust her? Who was still teetering on the brink of arousal, and which of them had walked away without a second thought?

Fooling herself was a waste of energy. She may as well face the facts—she'd always wanted Dillon Gaynor, and chances were she always would. He was a teenage fantasy come true. But it was time to grow up.

She couldn't stand the eerie silence of the garage. She wasn't about to put on Nirvana, but he had some REM as well as some U2 CDs, and she put one on at random, cranking the volume up loud before she approached her car.

The compressor was a little more complicated

than the kind they had at gas stations, and it didn't come with a pressure gauge. There was no way she could tell how much air she put in the tires, but she figured she'd just fill them by sight and then stop somewhere once she got out of this place and have a professional adjust them.

Three of the tires filled easily enough, but the fourth decided to give her shit. After the third try she realized the damned tire had been slashed.

Why would Dillon do that when he'd only wanted to slow her down? Why would he ruin one of her tires? He was more likely to take a sledgehammer to the front windshield—if there was one thing Dillon Gaynor wasn't, it was petty.

And if there was one thing Jamie Kincaid wasn't, it was defeated. She'd changed tires before—she could change them again.

She stood up, feeling suddenly light-headed. Not enough food, she thought absently, putting a steadying hand on the bumper of the car. Except that the very thought of food made her stomach lurch.

She'd take care of feeding herself as soon as she got the hell out of there. She walked around to the trunk of the Volvo. There was a dark stain spreading on the cement beneath it, and she cursed beneath her breath. So much for Dillon's assurance that her car was running better than ever. It had some kind of oil leak, or brake fluid. Something dark and viscous in the shadows beneath the car.

She was just about to open the trunk when the stereo switched to the next song. And she froze.

Bono's plaintive voice filled the garage, and Jamie didn't know which hurt more, her churning stomach or her heart. The music was love and sex, howling through her soul.

Her head wasn't feeling too hot, either, but she pushed away from the Volvo, determined to stop that damned song before it made her burst into tears. She would have run, but for some reason she seemed to be moving in slow motion. The smell of exhaust that always permeated the garage was stronger than ever, and by the time she managed to figure out how to turn off the thundering stereo that had been so easy to work a short while ago, she was ready to pass out.

There should have been silence in the empty garage. But there wasn't. A car engine rumbled ominously.

She started toward the cars parked along the left side of the garage, only to realize that the sound was coming from all around her. More than one car engine was busy pumping carbon monoxide into the room, and it was no wonder she was either going to throw up or faint.

Her best bet was to get the hell out of there before she passed out. She tried to run toward the kitchen door, but it was like running in Jell-O. She stumbled, and her feet got tangled up beneath her, and she went sprawling onto the cement floor.

She tried to push herself up, but her arms were like spaghetti beneath her. She sank back again, her cheek resting against the rough pavement, and she felt her eyes begin to close. If she didn't get up she was going to die. It was that simple. There was only one person who could have turned on those engines, one person in this big empty building. Dillon must have come back when she wasn't looking, to finish what he started earlier.

It didn't make sense. He had no reason to want to kill her. But maybe a man named Killer didn't need a reason. And maybe he was just tired of having to deal with her.

She tried to move, to drag herself toward the door, but she couldn't. She tried to open her eyes, and she thought she could see someone standing just inside the closed doorway.

"Help...me...." she said in a croak, but the narrow figure didn't move. Any why would she think he'd help her, if he was the one who'd done this to her?

Her eyes felt like lead, but she forced them open, staring at the man in the shadows.

And then she knew she was dying, and there was nothing she could do about it. Because Nate was there, standing over her, waiting for her to join him. And she stopped fighting.

He looked down at her with real affection. It didn't matter that she and Dillon had been going at it like rabbits. She'd always been his little sister, she'd always thought he was wonderful, and he'd liked that uncritical appreciation. Of course, she had no idea who and what he was. Adoration based on ignorance wasn't worth much in the long run.

Aunt Isobel, on the other hand, knew exactly who he was. And what he'd done. The things he'd keep on doing. And she loved and protected him, anyway. Smothering him with her unquestioning protection. And not just for her dead sister's sake. She saw him as her real child. She'd married her second cousin to keep the Kincaid line strong, and in the end she'd been unable to conceive. Only Nate was left, and he was the center of her life. Jamie had always been more of an afterthought, at least as far as Isobel was concerned.

Dying had been the best thing that had happened to him in a long time. For the first time he'd been

released from Aunt Isobel's obsessive devotion, and
it was enormously freeing. He'd recommend death
to almost anyone—his ghostly existence was by far
his favorite part of his life so far.

Jamie had passed out completely, and he walked
over to her, staring down at her sprawled body.
There was a special pleasure in killing someone
who loved you—a thrill that couldn't be found any
other way. Jamie had given him that gift, and he
felt almost tearful with gratitude. He squatted down,
touching the pulse at the side of her neck. Slow.
Almost nonexistent. He rolled her onto her back.
Dillon had been inside her—he'd watched them. If
he screwed her dying body it might almost be like
screwing Dillon. Something he'd wanted for a long,
long time.

But the room was filled with poison, and he
couldn't linger. Besides, Dillon might come home.

He pulled her loose T-shirt up, took a knife and
sliced through her bra. She had marks on her
breasts, from Dillon's mouth, from the roughness of
his beard.

The knife was very sharp. He'd cleaned it after
he'd finished with Mouser, sharpened it again. He
was a man who appreciated his tools and took loving care of them.

Her skin was pale, soft. It shouldn't just be Dillon's mark on her flesh. He took the razor sharp tip of the knife and pressed it against Jamie's skin.

When he finished he pulled the T-shirt back down, and the tracings of blood began to soak through the cotton. He leaned over and kissed her slack mouth, using his tongue. And then he rose.

Carbon monoxide shouldn't hurt a dead man. How many times could a man die?

But he wasn't ready to see Dillon. He'd go back to one of his vantage points and wait for him to return. Wait for him to find Jamie's body. And then the fun would begin.

When Dillon left the church basement the snow had started falling again. It was going to be a hell of a winter, if late November and early December were anything to go by. He didn't mind—he preferred the deep snow to the icy rain that had been prevalent back in Rhode Island. Hell, he preferred everything in Wisconsin to life in Rhode Island. Except for Jamie Kincaid.

And now here she was. And there she'd go. He'd fill her tires when he got back, unless of course she'd figured out how to do it herself. If she was determined enough she'd manage it, and he'd left her in a very determined state.

He should be feeling better. Usually after a meeting he felt grounded, centered, not the total fuck-up he really was. But not tonight. Tonight he'd checked his watch, and he hadn't listened to a word the speaker had said. And when everyone headed out for coffee afterward he begged off, for the first time in years. The after-meeting coffee times were almost better twelve-step programs than the actual meetings. But all he could think of was that he had to get back. Had to find Mouser. Had to make sure Jamie was safe. Make sure that his irrational, eerie suspicion didn't have an ounce of truth to it.

He headed back at an easy run. He had to keep himself warm, didn't he? And running was the best way to do it. He wasn't really worried that anyone was in any kind of danger. After all, who could possibly be a threat to Jamie?

But he knew. Deep inside, he knew, and he felt sick that he'd left her alone.

She would be getting her behind out of his garage, out of his fucking state, as fast as she could. Maybe once he found out what was really going on he might go after her. Though probably not. Once he managed to get rid of her, he'd be a fool to seek her out. She had too strong an effect on him, and distance was the best cure for that.

He could hear the music from almost a block away. Nirvana, cranked up almost to ten, shrieking in rage and pain. What was she doing in the garage? And what was she doing listening to Nirvana when her tastes ran more to mournful girl singers than screaming rockers?

Maybe she'd managed to fill her tires and drive away. But the garage door would be open—she wouldn't have bothered closing it behind her, she would have just gotten the hell out of there. In fact, the snow was piled high against the bottom of the door, sealing it.

Sealing it. The kitchen door was locked, when he never locked it, and even when he used his key it was jammed. He slammed his body against the door, once, twice, and if finally flew open, the chair that was blocking it splintering beneath the force of his body.

He could smell it—the carbon monoxide seeping under the doorjamb. He didn't hesitate—Jamie hadn't left, and she wasn't upstairs. She was in that garage filled with poisoned air.

He kicked the door open. The blue haze of car exhaust floated a few feet above the cement floor and it took him a moment to see her, sprawled on her back between the row of cars.

Later, he couldn't remember scooping her up and racing out of there with her. She was still breathing, and her pulse was steady, but he had no idea how long she'd been in there.

Even the kitchen stank of exhaust, so he simply carried her outside and put her down in the snow. She stirred, and he left her for a moment to grab a pile of coats to cover her with.

Four of his cars were running, filling even the cavernous spaces of the garage with carbon monoxide. He turned the damned music off first, then tried to turn off the cars.

None of them had keys in the ignition. Someone had managed to jump-start them, and he knew damned well that was beyond Jamie's capabilities. In took him only a moment to rip out the wiring that kept the motors running. He forced the garage door open, letting the poison out into the night air, and then ran to Jamie's body. She was shivering— no surprise since she was lying on a pile of snow, and he threw the coats aside and pulled her into his arms.

She moaned, and her eyes fluttered open. She couldn't seem to focus, and he knew he had to get her to a hospital, fast, when she suddenly yanked herself out of his arms, turned and vomited in the snow.

He held her, anyway, and she was too weak to fight him. She didn't have much in her stomach, and he realized belatedly that he hadn't been feeding her properly. When she'd gotten rid of everything and there was nothing left but dry heaves, he pulled her back in his arms, and she buried her face against his chest as he stroked her damp, flushed face.

"I need to get you to a hospital," he said after a while. He was kneeling in the snow, holding her, and he was cold, wet and uncomfortable. And he didn't want to move, didn't want to let go of her.

She shook her head, the movement unmistakable against his chest. "No," she said. "I'm fine."

"You passed out. God knows how much of that shit you've got in your system. We'll take your car, and if they agree you're okay then you can get right away from here."

"We can't take my car. You slashed the front tire, remember?"

His heart had stopped racing and his brain had finally started working. "I didn't slash your tire."

She didn't say anything, just turned her face closer to his chest, like a kitten seeking comfort. He had to ask her the question he didn't want to. He doubted her automotive skills extended to jump-starting antique automobiles, but who else could it have been? Who else was there?

"Were you trying to kill yourself? Tell me the truth, Jamie?"

She looked up at him then, her eyes bright with unshed tears. "Just because I'm stupid enough to be in love with you doesn't mean you're worth committing suicide over."

He blinked in surprise, but she didn't seem to realize what she'd said. "Someone was there. I had the stereo on loud and I didn't hear anything until it was too late."

"You were listening to Nirvana?"

"Hardly. U2."

At least he still knew that much about her. His mind was still reeling with what she'd said before. "Then someone was trying to kill you."

"Yes," she said, her face pressed against his plain white T-shirt and his pounding heart beneath it. "Was it you?"

So much for her astonishing declaration of love. "I wasn't here, remember? And if I were trying to kill you I wouldn't have saved you, would I? It wouldn't make much sense."

"Nothing makes sense," she said wearily. "I don't suppose we can go back inside? My butt is soaking wet."

"The hospital—"

"No. Just fix my goddamned tire and I'll get out

of here. Never darken your door again," she said in a defeated little voice.

He wanted her to tell him she loved him again. With some kind of shock he realized that no one had ever said that to him when he wasn't making them come. Anyone could think they were in love when they were climaxing. But Jamie Kincaid was sitting with her butt in the snow, her lungs just beginning to clear from poisoned air, her stomach hurting from throwing up, and she could say she loved him. Even if she thought he was trying to kill her.

It was too strange for him to even begin to take in. Instead he stood, scooping her up with him, and she made an expected sound of pain.

"Are you all right?" He sounded anxious, and he didn't like it. He couldn't help it.

"Fine. I could probably walk...."

"I'll carry you." To be honest, he wanted an excuse to hold her tight against him. That excuse would leave when she did, as soon as he fixed her tire, but for now he was going to indulge himself.

The kitchen was cold now. The open doors that had let out the gas had brought in the icy night air. He kicked the door shut, then closed the door to the garage as well. "It'll warm up in a minute...." he began, but she started struggling.

Instinctively he tightened his hold, until she managed to mutter "bathroom" and he had no choice but to release her. She disappeared into the lavatory beneath the stairs, and a moment later he heard her puking again.

She didn't really have much left to throw up. She'd locked the door, and while locked doors didn't usually stop him, he decided to leave her in privacy, at least for a while. He wasn't squeamish, but she was, and he could do that much for her.

The garage was icy cold, too, but most of the smell had vanished. He closed the sliding door again, leaving it open just a narrow crack to let the last of the poison escape, and then turned to look at her Volvo.

She hadn't lied—the front right tire had been slashed. Beyond repair, as a matter of fact, though he had any number of tires hanging around that he could substitute. But if he hadn't slashed her tire, then that left only Jamie herself. Maybe looking for an excuse to stay?

Wishful thinking. She'd managed to figure out his air compressor enough to fill the other three tires, which certainly suggested she wanted to leave. But who could have slashed the tire?

The logical culprit was Mouser. Loyal, interfering Mouser, who thought he knew what was best for Dillon no matter what Dillon said. And he had the stupid, romantic idea that Jamie was the perfect woman for him.

But Mouser had disappeared, without a word, when he seldom traveled out of their abandoned neighborhood. And Mouser wasn't the type to destroy, even in the name of true love.

He'd get Jamie settled, then come back and fix the tire. If he couldn't talk her into going to the hospital, couldn't club her over the head like a caveman and drag her there, then he'd get her tucked up in bed and then get to work. The question of the hour was, which bed?

It wasn't a question at all, really. She wouldn't want to sleep where a dead rat had rested—she'd rather sleep with a live one. And he wasn't going to be there—he'd keep himself busy in the garage, getting her car in working order, rewiring the cars that had been jump-started, trying to figure out what the hell happened.

She'd emerged from the bathroom and joined him in the garage, looking even paler. As if she'd seen a ghost. "Go on up to bed," he said. "I'll get your car running again and you can leave first thing in the morning."

"And I'm supposed to trust you because…?"

"Because you don't have any other choice." At

least it was an honest answer, though he wasn't sure he wanted to hear it.

"The rat bled all over my mattress."

He cocked his head, looking at her. "You know the answer to that one. You can even lock the door. I'll sleep down here on the sofa."

She couldn't help it—she glanced at the sofa in the corner, and a wash of color flooded her pale face. It fascinated him. How could she still blush after everything he'd talked her into doing?

"All right," she said. And before he could reply she whirled around and disappeared up the narrow stairs, with more energy than he would have thought possible.

He wanted to follow her, so damned badly. He didn't want to screw her—he just wanted to lie in bed with his arms around her, just for a short while before she left.

But he wasn't going to touch her again. He was going to keep his promise, the one he made to himself, not her. The one where he decided she was more trouble than she was worth, that she did him more harm than good. The one where he decided to let her go so he could finally get over her. The one where he decided to let her go because that was the best thing he could do for her.

The garage was cold from having the doors open

to the night air, and he was damned tired. It wouldn't take him long to fix Jamie's tire, and the other cars could wait until after she left. In the meantime he was going to do what he'd told her. He was going to stretch out on the battered old sofa and sleep for a few hours before he dropped with exhaustion. Nothing was making any sense, and nothing would until he got a little sleep.

The tattered green sofa was faded and lumpy. And the last time he'd stretched on there Jamie had been beneath him, clutching him, terrified and unwillingly aroused.

She wasn't there now, he reminded himself. And he couldn't very well avoid every place in the building where she'd been—he'd have to burn the place down and move out.

No, he could lie on the sofa and not think about her. As soon as he fell asleep.

And only if he were that lucky.

17

Jamie didn't even glance into her abandoned bed-room. She knew where she was sleeping that night, and it didn't matter whether or not she had any choice. It was just one more night, and it wasn't going to make any difference. It wouldn't change her, and it wouldn't change Dillon. He could do anything he wanted to her and it wouldn't make any difference. Make it any easier or harder to leave, when she knew that was her only choice.

It was cold up there, but she opened the window, anyway, to dispel any lingering carbon monoxide. She'd somehow managed to cheat death once al-ready that night—she'd be an idiot to risk her life all over again. Though maybe she was, simply by staying there.

She was too tired to do more than strip off her snow-damp jeans and crawl into his bed, pulling the covers up around her. Her chest ached, throat hurt, and she was so damned cold. She reached inside her T-shirt to unfasten her bra, only to find that it was already free. Dillon must have unhooked it to give her room to breathe, though it wasn't as if the bra was that tight to begin with. And for some reason the back clasp was still fastened—it was open at the front.

Her T-shirt was damp as well, and her chest felt as if it were covered in icy fire. She pulled the covers up over her shoulders and turned off the light, closing her eyes. Willing sleep to come.

There was a lot to be said for having an iron will, but forty-five minutes later Jamie accepted the fact that you couldn't force sleep, no matter how determined you are. She should have remembered that. She lay there in the dark, listening to the sounds of the building as it settled into the cold night. Waiting for the sound of Dillon's footsteps on the creaking wooden stairs.

But he didn't come. And she told herself that was relief she was feeling, and she should go to sleep now, and first thing in the morning she'd get out of there. And she stared into the darkened bedroom and waited for him. Until she realized he wasn't coming—he really was going to spend the night down there on that lumpy old sofa, in the remnants of the carbon monoxide.

She sat up in the darkness, clutching the covers around her. The entire evening had become hazy—

she remembered trying to fill the tires with air, listening to U2 in the background. She remembered feeling dizzy, and then that damned song came on. And then she didn't really remember anything more, just odd dreams, with a ghostly Nate watching her as she crawled toward him, reaching for help.

There must have been other dreams, visions as well, but she couldn't remember them. Someone had turned those car engines on, the noise covered by the blasting of the stereo. Someone had tried to kill her.

As a murder attempt it was kind of half-assed. Anyone could have come by and found her. As Dillon had done, the perfect hero. But Dillon was no hero.

There were two possibilities. He'd done it, either to rescue her and fool her into thinking he was a good guy, or maybe he'd wanted to get rid of her and then thought better of it.

The other choice, the unthinkable choice, was that someone else was there. Someone who really wanted to kill her. Someone who wouldn't stop. Someone who'd either come up here and finish the job, or who'd kill Dillon as he slept in the garage. Helpless, except that she could never imagine Dillon as helpless.

So that left her with two choices herself. She could crawl out of bed and lock the door, push the furniture against it and wait for morning. No one would be able to get in and finish what they started.

That was the smart thing to do. If it really had been Dillon it would keep him at bay, as well as anyone else who wanted to hurt her.

But she wasn't going to do that. Her jeans were almost dry when she pulled them back on, and they were toasty warm from the heating duct where she'd placed them. She picked up the comforter and wrapped it around her shoulders, dragging it behind her as she walked down the darkened hallway.

She could still imagine those eyes watching her, and she realized that she'd always had the sense that someone was there. She'd like to think that it was Nate's ghost, looking out for her, but she wasn't quite that naive. Whoever was watching her was no benevolent spirit.

The kitchen was cold. There was a single light over the sink, and the window was open a crack, letting a blast of icy air inside. The door to the garage was open, as well, and while she could hear the furnace working overtime, it was making little progress against the night air that flooded the building.

She stopped in the open doorway to the garage.

The smell of exhaust had disappeared, and there were no engines running, no poison gas filling the room. The garage was dark—only a small desk lamp provided some illumination. Dillon lay stretched out on the sagging green sofa, sound asleep, a thin blanket covering him.

Not enough warmth in a cold space like this, she thought, shivering. At least Dillon didn't seem to be troubled with sleeplessness, or a guilty conscience, or worried about someone trying to kill him. Maybe he'd been out getting drunk—she hadn't been in any condition to notice whether he'd been using or not.

But then, she hadn't seem him drunk since she got there. Hadn't even seem him take a drink—the one time she thought he had it had only been iced tea. If she didn't know better she'd think that Dillon didn't use alcohol anymore.

She shivered, standing there, her bare feet icy on the cement floor. She glanced at the shadowy frame of her car—he hadn't done anything about it yet, and she had no guarantee that he would.

There was nothing to stop her from leaving this place, right now. Walking to the nearest pay phone, calling a taxi and making it to the airport, where she could either spend a fortune on a flight or a smaller fortune on a rental car. Either way, the price would be cheap compared to her life. And her soul.

Her chest hurt, her feet hurt, her heart hurt. While he slept the sleep of the innocent on that huge old sofa, she was standing there freezing to death, awash in misery.

She walked across the garage, the covers trailing behind her, until she stood over him. He looked almost innocent in sleep, but Dillon Gaynor had never been innocent in his life.

She was about to turn and leave him, when his voice broke the silence.

"I'll share my covers if you'll share yours."

His eyes were open, and he was watching her, lying on his side, up against the back of the sofa. A million arguments cropped up in her mind, and then they all vanished. Just for tonight she didn't want to fight.

And he knew it. He lifted the threadbare blanket and she climbed onto the sofa beside him, pulling her covers around them both. It was a big sofa, but still only a sofa, and she had to move close to him so as not to fall off.

He didn't say a word. Simply tucked her against him, her head on his shoulder, his arms around her, holding her loosely, protectively. He reached up and brushed the hair away from her face with a gentle hand, and unconsciously she rubbed her face against his hand, almost purring like a kitten.

And then she sighed, letting out the tension and fear and distrust. Letting go of everything. And just before she fell asleep she felt his lips against her forehead, and she wanted to cry.

He could see them in the darkness. Ghosts had better vision, and shadows didn't stop him. They were asleep on the sofa, wrapped up close together, and the slow rage that fueled him was cold as ice. But then, he was always cold. That's what happened when you were dead—all the heat left your body. Haunting the icy upper floors of Dillon's garage was only fitting.

He'd watched them. He'd watched his sweet little cousin go down on Dillon on the floor of the garage. He'd watched them in the bedroom, heard the sounds she made when she came. But mostly he'd watched Dillon, his hips thrusting, his mouth kissing her, his hands holding her, touching her, loving her.

But this was worse. This was tenderness, and unbearable. Dillon didn't know about tenderness, any more than Nate did. He knew about sex—Nate had never had any doubts about that. But this was something else, something unacceptable.

He should have killed her twelve years ago, when he'd planned to. It had just been bad luck that the police had stopped them, but he could have followed through later. He thought the danger was over—she would never see Dillon again. And Dillon would get over his fucked-up obsession for an innocent teenager.

But it hadn't happened that way. And he was the one who died, thanks to Dillon.

He should have cut deeper with the knife, let her bleed to death on the cement floor of Dillon's garage. He'd thought the carbon monoxide would have done it, but Dillon had come back sooner than he'd expected.

But this time he wouldn't let go of it. This time he'd planned backup—he was older now, and he didn't make mistakes that couldn't be corrected. Jamie would be dead in the next few days.

And Dillon would have no one left to love. No one but him.

It was strange, Jamie thought. How could she feel so warm, so safe, so peaceful, when things were so wrong? She didn't want to wake up—it felt too good to lie where she was, pressed up against Dillon's warm body, his arms holding her.

But she couldn't stay there—they both knew it.

It was almost dawn—the garage was filled with a murky light, and she turned her head to look at him. His eyes were open, dark, lost eyes, and he was watching her.

He moved his head, and she knew he was going to kiss her, and then she'd kiss him back, and then she'd be lost, and at the last minute she put her hands against his chest, pushing away from him.

There was blood on her hands. Blood on his plain white T-shirt. Blood everywhere, and she let out a wordless cry of horror. She scrambled away from him, landing on the hard floor of the cement, shivering.

"Blood..." she said finally. "You're covered with blood."

He sat up, pushing the covers aside, and looked down at his shirt. And then he looked at her.

He got up and walked to one of the workbenches. When he turned around he was holding a knife.

She didn't make a sound as he approached her. She tried to move backward, away from him, but the sofa blocked her, and she could do nothing but huddle there in terror and wait for him to kill her.

He could read the panic in her face. He grabbed her arm, hard, and pulled her into a sitting position, then pushed her against the sofa. She held up her arms, instinctively to block the knife.

"Jesus Christ," Dillon muttered, grabbing her wrists in one strong hand and holding them out of his way. And then he took the knife and cut her T-shirt down the center, so that it fell apart.

"Jesus Christ," he said again in a softer voice, releasing her wrists, dropping the knife. "What the fuck happened to you?"

She reached down to pull her T-shirt back around herself, and then stopped. If his shirt had been streaked with blood, it was nothing compared to what she was wearing. Her once-white T-shirt looked like red tie-dye. It didn't even seem to matter that she was half naked in front of him. She just looked down at the shallow tracings on her chest with numb horror.

"Lie down," he said. She didn't move, so he pushed her back onto the sofa, too shocked to argue. She wanted to cover herself up, at least cover her breasts, but she couldn't bring herself to do it. She simply lay back and closed her eyes, and waited.

A minute later Dillon was sitting on the sofa beside her, laying a warm wet towel over her chest. He pushed her torn T-shirt and bra straps off her shoulders and down her arms, tossing the ruined clothing onto the floor.

"You're pretty damned trusting for someone who thought I was about to cut your throat." There was no bitterness in his voice, in his face, when she opened her eyes to look at him. No emotion whatsoever—he'd closed himself off from her. As always.

"Just lie there for a while. I brought a sweatshirt of mine you can put on—I'm afraid my wardrobe doesn't consist of bras, but you don't need one, anyway."

"Go to hell," she said wearily, turning her face away.

He stood up, and she wanted to reach out and grab his hand, to hold it. She wanted, needed to touch him, to feel some kind of connection.

But she didn't move. "Who did this to me?"

He shrugged. "Whoever locked you in the garage with the cars running."

"Was it you?"

He didn't blink, didn't answer. He just turned away from her.

"I'll change the tire on your car, and then you can leave whenever you want to," he said, moving away.

She sat up, holding the damp towel against her chest. "What are those boxes in the back seat?" she asked, trying to sound as cool as he did. As if being cut with a knife was an everyday occurrence.

"Those are Nate's things. I thought you wanted

to take them back to the Duchess...." His voice trailed off, and he was staring at her car, an abstracted expression on his face.

"What's wrong?"

"I thought I put those boxes in the trunk," he said, his voice remote. He seemed to have forgotten her. He was concentrating on her old Volvo, heading toward the trunk, and she could see the dread in his body.

"There's no spare tire in the trunk," she said, forestalling him. "I had a flat last week and I forgot to pick up a new one."

"I'm not looking for a spare," he said in a dull voice. And he opened the trunk, staring down into it in silence.

She dropped the towel, grabbed the sweatshirt he'd brought and pulled it over her head. She started toward the car, and he spun around, shielding it.

"Don't come any closer, Jamie!"

His voice was raw with grief and rage, and there was no way she was going to obey him. She tried to push past him, but he caught her arms in an iron grip and dragged her away, hurting her. But not before she could see what lay in the trunk of her car.

He dragged her across the garage to the yellow Cadillac, and she started to struggle. He ignored her flailing, wrapping his arms tight around her, ignoring her grunt of pain as he pressed against the wounds on her chest. He picked her up and dumped her in the front seat of the car. Behind the steering wheel. He leaned over and started the car, and she sat still, staring up at him.

"This puts the top up," he said in a monotone. "The rest of it is pretty standard. It has a full tank of gas and snow tires, though it gets lousy mileage. You need to get out of here, right away."

"Who was that…?"

"In your trunk? Mouser. Or what's left of him." He closed his eyes for a moment, and she could see the pain wash over him. And then he focused on her again, all business. "Where's your purse?"

"I don't remember."

He reached into his back pocket and tossed his wallet into her lap. "There are credit cards and plenty of cash. Enough to get you back to Rhode Island. Just dump the car somewhere—I don't need it anymore. It's served it's purpose."

"But what about my car?"

"It's going to disappear. Mouser has no one, and he wouldn't want ugly questions surfacing that no one can answer."

The Cadillac was purring like the perfectly maintained machine it was. As it had twelve years ago. "Did you murder him?"

She'd been frightened of him before, but in comparison to this it had been no more than a mild nervousness. The look he turned on her would have frozen anyone.

"I've never hit a woman," he said in a contemplative voice. "I'm more than willing to start with you. Get the fuck out of here and don't come back."

"I don't have any shoes."

"What?"

"I can't drive off into a snowstorm in bare feet."

His reply was short and obscene. "Put the fucking top up." A moment later he threw a pair of his own sneakers into the open window.

"These won't fit—"

"Shut the fuck up and get out of here before it's too late."

There was nothing left to say. Except the obvious. "Then who killed Mouser? Who tried to kill me?"

"You're smarter than that, Jamie. You should have figured it out by now."

"Well, I haven't. I don't have the faintest idea what's going on. Enlighten me."

"Looks like your dreams might come true, after

all, baby girl,'' he said bitterly. "Maybe I made a mistake. Maybe your darling cousin Nate isn't dead. But if you don't get out of here, you will be. I can't protect you, Jamie. Stay here and die, or run like hell.''

He spun around, went over to the huge garage door and opened it. She backed the car around, heading it toward the open door and the snowy morning. The heat had come on, pouring down on her bare feet, and she pushed her hair out of her face. Her face that was wet with tears she hadn't even realized she'd cried.

She wouldn't see him again, she knew it. She needed to put the car in Drive and get the hell out of there.

She didn't move. He came back to the car, still wearing the T-shirt stained with her blood. He leaned in the window of the car, put his hand behind her neck and kissed her, a hard, desperate kiss that lasted an eternity and only a moment. And then he drew back.

"Get out of here, Jamie. And don't ever come back.''

And putting the car into Drive, she tore out of the garage, onto the empty, snow-covered streets.

18

Dillon stood in the open garage door, watching until the taillights of the old Cadillac disappeared into the snowy morning. And then he closed the doors and locked them. Locked himself in with the dead body of his best friend. With the murderous ghost of his oldest friend.

Except that he didn't believe in ghosts. Not in ghosts that could use a knife, the way someone had used a knife on Mouser. He recognized Nate's signature—Mouser wasn't the first person Nate had killed. Though from what little Dillon had discovered, he preferred to hurt women.

He reached for his cigarettes, and he noticed his hands were shaking. He figured he had two choices. One was to call the police and try to convince them that he, a convicted felon, had nothing to do with the dead body in his garage. The second dead body in the last three months. For some reason he didn't think Lieutenant MacPherson was going to be listening, no matter how reasonable he'd seemed. And they certainly wouldn't take his word for it that Mouser had been killed by a dead man.

Even more important, they'd drag Jamie back to Wisconsin. It was her car, it would be covered in her fingerprints. Maybe they'd be satisfied with someone taking a long-distance deposition. After all, an upper-class innocent like Jamie wasn't the type to kill a stranger.

But he couldn't take the chance. He'd be fine if he could just be certain he never had to see her again. She made him crazy, mean and stupid and out of his mind, and he couldn't afford to let that happen. He'd accepted the fact long ago—she wasn't for him. The fact that he'd had her, in just about every possible way, for the last two days was a boon he'd never expected. And didn't dare try to repeat.

He patted his pockets, looking for his lighter, but it wasn't anywhere. Must have fallen out of his pocket in the sofa. When he'd slept with his arms around Jamie.

He hadn't slept much. Hadn't allowed himself to. There was something dangerous, evil in the old building, and he didn't dare relax his guard.

And if he was going to be honest with himself, he had to admit that he wanted to watch her. Feel her slow, steady heartbeat against his chest. Listen to the soft sound of her breathing.

He'd left the trunk open, too busy keeping Jamie away to worry about it. He reached up to close the lid, looking down at what was left of Mouser.

"Sorry, old friend," he said softly. "I should have known what was going on. I should have warned you."

But Mouser wasn't going to be answering. There was nothing Dillon could do for him at this point, and he was damned if he was going to cry. He hadn't cried since he was eight years old and his mother had left him with his drunken old man. He certainly wasn't going to start now.

He started to put the cigarettes back in his pocket, then stared down at the crumpled pack. Mouser was always lecturing him about his smoking, telling him it was going to kill him. But it was Mouser who was dead, wasn't it?

"Here, buddy," he said, tossing the pack of cigarettes into the trunk. "It's the least I can do for you."

It was only a little past dawn when he drove Jamie's car out of the garage, into the empty streets. He stopped and closed the doors behind him—there was still a pool of dried blood where the car had sat, and he didn't want anyone wandering in and seeing it until he had a chance to do something about it. He drove silently, grimly, through the growing light, needing a cigarette. At least it was a distraction—he could think about how much he was craving nicotine. It was a small pain compared to everything else, but it was a piece of suffering he could offer up to the angry gods who seemed determined to screw him over. Him, and everyone he'd ever cared about.

Wisconsin was a damned flat state, but there was Tucker's Ravine, right on the edge of the county line. The scar in the land ran deep and narrow, and the trees and shrubs were a jungle in the summer. If he aimed the car just right it would disappear into that crevasse and not be found for decades. They wouldn't be able to identify Mouser—he had no family, no record. Dillon didn't even know his real name. Fingerprints would be long gone, and hell, maybe the wreck would never be found. He was counting on it.

He drove to the very edge of the bluff, climbed out and stepped back. It wouldn't take much to send it over the edge, and he'd been thoughtful enough to fill the gas tank when he thought Jamie was going to drive away in it.

He walked around to the back of the sedan and began to push. There was a slight rise up to the very edge of the ravine, and the Volvo was a heavy mother. It finally began to move, and he felt the front wheels drop over the side.

He knocked on the trunk, a useless gesture of affection and farewell, as the car disappeared over the edge.

He watched it go, turning end over end, disappearing into the deep scar in the land, the noise muffled by the snow and the trees. The final explosion came from far away, and the flames were barely visible from the top of the bluff. He stood and watched until the fire died down, and there was nothing more than a faint plume of smoke.

It was snowing harder now. His hair was wet, as were his shoulders and his feet. He hadn't bothered to change into boots, and his sneakers weren't the best choice for deep, drifting snow. He didn't give a shit. He wanted a cigarette, he wanted Mouser to be alive, he wanted Jamie. And he wasn't going to get any of those things.

The six-mile hike back to the garage was physically miserable. The snow was a mixed blessing. It would cover up all trace of the Volvo's descent into the ravine, and it kept people off the road who might see him. He only had to dive off the side of the road twice as cars passed. He didn't expect anyone to find Mouser, but it was never a mistake to be careful.

The snow wasn't going to be a treat for Jamie, though. The tires on the Caddie were good, and she was used to driving a rear-wheel-drive car, but there was a big difference between a full-size American car and a compact Volvo. And she wouldn't be in the most stable state of mind. She'd just seen her first dead man, and she probably thought he'd killed him.

He didn't give a shit what she thought. As long as she was gone, she was safe. And when it came right down to it, that was all that mattered.

It was late morning when he finally made it back to the garage. He was shivering—the snow had soaked through his sneakers, his shirt, plastered his hair against his head. He'd shoved his hands in his jeans pocket to keep them warm, but it hadn't done much good. He closed the door behind him, leaning against it as he stared at his deserted kitchen.

He'd stretched Jamie across that table and almost had her. He'd played cards with Mouser, laughed and joked with him over the years. He'd sat at the table, smoking cigarette after cigarette as he listened to the muffled sounds of Nate being beaten to death.

He crossed the room and heaved the heavy oak table over, sending coffee cups and plates smashing to the ground. He splintered one chair against the hard surface of the overturned table—the next one took more effort before it shattered into pieces. He went through the room, methodically smashing everything he could lay his hands on—the microwave, the dishes, the food. He even managed to tip the refrigerator over so that it crashed open onto the floor, the door snapping off as food and milk spread over the littered floor.

He stood in the middle of the chaos, trying to catch his breath. It should have made him feel better—destruction should have wiped his emotions clean. Instead the fury bubbled inside.

He could go into the garage, take a tire iron to the stable of old beauties. But he wouldn't do that. He'd already managed to hurt and destroy the people he cared about. He didn't need to smash the only material things he cared about, as well. He'd done enough for one day.

He stepped over the debris, heading into the garage for the small comfort the logical workings of a car could provide. But all he saw was the sofa where he'd slept with Jamie, their covers still intertwined. The pool of dried blood where her car had sat, holding its terrible secret.

Then he saw the word, written in blood on the cement floor. It had been hidden by the car, and he wondered when Nate had done it. Probably some time when he'd been upstairs screwing his brains out.

Dungeon. It was Nate's name for his childhood home, the one that had been destroyed in the fire that had killed his parents. The real name was Dungeness Towers, named by Nate's great-grandfather, a Scottish immigrant who'd amassed a fortune in shipping and built a monument to his own importance. The last time Dillon had seen it, there hadn't been much left but two of the towers and the carriage house that had once served as a small-scale chophouse for stolen cars and a drug center. Dillon had taken care of the cars—Nate had found people to steal them, Dillon had stripped them down and turned them out again in record time. He was young and in love with danger—he wanted to be the one to boost the cars, as well, but Nate's cool head had prevailed.

He hadn't been particularly interested in Nate's sideline of dealing drugs. He'd dealt weed and a few other things through high school, but Nate was getting into more dangerous stuff, and Dillon had lost his taste for it. Rebuilding stolen cars was enough excitement for him at the time.

They'd both called it the Dungeon. Nate had always said when he died he'd go back and haunt the old place.

Dillon closed his eyes and remembered the sight of Jamie's scraped torso. He'd rather think about her breasts, but the marks were more important. Fortunately she hadn't seen what was scratched into her skin. "Whore." "Traitor." "Dungeon."

Another message, meant for no one but Dillon. Who else would be looking at Jamie's bare chest?

He was going to have to go after him, sooner or later. It was a summons, an invitation, a dare. From a dead man, who knew that Dillon had betrayed him to his enemies and done nothing to save him.

And if he didn't go, then the ghost of Nate Kincaid would keep going after Jamie.

It was a confrontation long overdue. They'd both been selfish, self-destructive monsters when they were teenagers. But Dillon had grown up, learned a little about what was important.

Nate had stayed a dangerous little boy, out for revenge and anything else that took his fancy, no matter what the cost.

He had no choice. Maybe he could live alone here with Nate's ghost haunting him, leaving dead rats as a token of affection.

But he'd lost Mouser, and if he didn't do something, Jamie would be the next to go.

He didn't believe in ghosts, not really. Which left only one possibility. That Nate was alive, someone else had died, beaten and blood-splattered in that upstairs room. And if Dillon didn't do something about it, more death would follow.

He'd go after him, in his own sweet time. For now, Jamie was gone, safe, and there was really nothing Nate could do to hurt him. At least for the moment. The smartest thing to do was not to fall into his trap. To stay put at the garage and wait for his ghost to continue haunting him.

Because he would. He'd keep on, inexorable. Until Nate got what he wanted.

Dillon.

Jamie drove blindly, concentrating on the snowy roads and the poor visibility. The interstate system was better once she reached it, and the heavy morning traffic managed to snag the one part of her brain that was holding on to Dillon. Killer. Who had killed Mouser?

It couldn't be Dillon. Please God, it couldn't be Dillon.

She stopped for breakfast at McDonald's, almost taking off part of the drive-through as she tried to navigate the huge car. The Egg McMuffin didn't sit well in the pit of her stomach, but the coffee was warm and full of caffeine, giving her enough energy for another two hours. She was almost at the Indiana border, she had to pee and the car was running on empty. She pulled into a gas station and reached for the wallet Dillon had dumped in her lap.

Credit cards. Who would have thought a bad boy like Dillon Gaynor would end up with credit cards? She pulled out the gas one and paid at the pump, watching with horror as the Caddy sucked up thirty dollars' worth of fuel.

Fortunately the bathroom was inside the minimart and reasonably clean. As she washed her hands she stared at her reflection in the mirror.

She looked like holy hell. Like a ghost. Or someone who'd seen one.

Slowly, carefully, she peeled Dillon's sweatshirt over her head to get her first good look at her chest.

It was little wonder it had felt like fire. The tracings across her pale skin were red and angry, though the bleeding had stopped. It could have been worse, she thought. Whoever had done this to her hadn't gone near her breasts. He'd cut and scratched every part of her chest but her small breasts, and she couldn't help but feel that was deliberate. That whoever had done this to her didn't want to touch her breasts. Didn't want to touch anything about her that made her a woman.

She had no idea where that thought came from, but it was clear and solid. And then she peered closer at the marks.

There were letters, words there. She couldn't read them in the mirror—they were both scrawled and backward. She squinted, trying to mentally reverse them. The first one was easy enough. *Whore* was a simple word, though it had to be the first time in her sheltered life she'd been called that. It almost felt like a badge of honor, when she thought she was going to die frigid and untouched. At least she got one thing out of her sojourn in Wisconsin. She most definitely wasn't frigid. Nor was there any part of her that was untouched.

She couldn't read the word across the top of her stomach. The *D* stood out, as well as a bunch of vowels, but it was nothing she could understand. She squinted her eyes, trying to reverse the image. It looked like *Dungeon,* but why in the world would someone write that into her skin? But then, why would someone scratch anything into her flesh? She pulled the shirt back down over her, shutting out the questions.

She bought a six-pack of Diet Coke and a box of doughnuts and headed back to the car. Dillon's wallet held more than credit cards—there was a thick wad of money. His driver's license.

She stared down at the small plastic card. The picture didn't do him justice, but it was still the first photograph she'd ever seen of him. He'd been scowling at the camera, he hadn't shaved, and his hair was too long. And she stared at it, long and hard, and knew she wasn't going to give it back.

She flipped through the rest of the cards that were tucked in the plastic windows, then stopped. Why the hell would Dillon have the Serenity Prayer in his wallet? She looked further and found the answer to that question. A meeting list for south-central Wisconsin. The bad boy had reformed.

At first she thought there was nothing else in the wallet, until she noticed an extra flap in the leather. She pulled it up, and then wished to God she hadn't.

It was a picture of her, one she'd never seen before, hadn't even known had been taken.

But she knew when. It had been a summer afternoon when she was twenty. Dillon had disappeared from her life, forever, she thought. Her father had died, and her mother was holding the post-funeral reception in the garden of their house in Marshfield. It was a beautiful spring day, and Jamie was wearing pale yellow—her father's favorite dress. Her mother had had a fit, telling her it was disrespectful, but for once Jamie had held firm. Her father had loved it, and she had loved her father, and no amount of pressure from her mother would make her dress in sober black.

She was talking with one of her mother's friends, holding a cup of tea in one hand, smiling with her mouth, not her eyes. She could remember how she felt at the time, the desperate longing to smash the teacup on the ground and run away, but she'd held firm and done her social duty to her mother's eventual grudging approval.

Nate must have taken that picture when she hadn't realized it. And somehow Dillon had ended up with it, hiding it away in his wallet.

She didn't want to think how he got it. She couldn't begin to understand him, and the smartest thing she could do was not even try. At least, not until she was safe at home.

She plugged in the pay-as-you-go cell phone she'd bought with Dillon's money, gave it a few moments to build up a minimal charge, and then dialed home. It was almost a shock to hear her mother's voice on the other end.

"Where are you, Jamie?"

"On my way home. I'm afraid I don't have Nate's things. There...there wasn't anything there." She never lied, and she was lying to her mother.

"Don't be ridiculous. Dillon said he had two full

boxes of Nate's possessions. I want those things, Jamie. They're all I have left of him.''

"They're gone," she said flatly. "And so is Nate." And then she froze, as Dillon's words came back to her. That Nate might not be dead after all. Someone had been haunting Dillon's garage, leaving dead rats, trying to hurt her, carving words into her skin. Murdering Mouser. And Dillon was many things, but despite his nickname, he was no killer.

But Nate couldn't be. Couldn't be alive, couldn't be trying to hurt her. He was a brother to her, family. She'd learned the hard way not to trust him—he'd never told her the truth about the night of the prom, or about a million other things. And he was dead. Dillon had identified him.

Identified a body that was beaten into an unrecognizable mess. What if Nate had turned the tables on whoever tried to kill him?

"Jamie, are you listening to me?" Her mother's voice was strident in her ear, and it came to her that Isobel hadn't asked her how she was. Hadn't asked anything about her, only about Nate. And she didn't know whether it was Dillon's power of suggestion or the truth finally hitting home, but she realized that she had always been an afterthought, at least for her mother. Her father had loved her, she knew that much, but Isobel had always been fixated on Nate. And Nate had taken advantage of it.

"I'm here," she said faintly. The skin at the top of her stomach was hurting again—the scratchings were deeper there, still seeping some blood. "Does the word *dungeon* mean anything to you?"

"Of course it does. Don't you remember? It's what Nate used to call the family home. The place that burned, the Kincaid family estate. It was called Dungeness Towers, but I suppose Nate was too little to say the real name, so he called it the Dungeon."

"What happened to it?"

"Jamie, I'm not interested in ancient history, I'm interested in what happened to Nate's possessions...."

"Where is the Dungeon?" She overrode her mother's arguments ruthlessly.

"In Connecticut. After Nate died I inherited the place, but I haven't had the heart to do anything about it. It's just a bunch of ruins, probably quite dangerous. Once I'm feeling a little stronger I'll have the place bulldozed and sell the land. After all, my sister and brother-in-law died there—I hardly have fond memories of the place."

"What about Nate?"

"Nate loved it. He didn't think I knew, but he used to go camping there. And take his awful friend

Dillon. I should have made him raze the place years ago.''

''Where in Connecticut?''

''A little country town called Danvers. Why should it matter?''

''It matters,'' she said grimly.

''Jamie, I want you to go back to Wisconsin and insist on—''

Jamie pushed the off button on the cell phone and set it down on the seat beside her. It was growing dark, and, even though the snow had stopped, the roads were still slick. She was going to do the smart thing. She was going to find a discount store and buy herself a change of clothes, toiletries and shoes with Dillon's credit card. Then she was going to find a motel, eat a huge meal and get a good night's sleep.

And that's where her wisdom would end. Because tomorrow she was getting back in Dillon's car and driving to Danvers, Connecticut. To the Dungeon, where she'd been summoned.

To face the ghost of Nate Kincaid. Who'd never died in the first place.

19

Nate Kincaid was beginning to come to the unpleasant conclusion that he might not be dead, after all. He'd spent so long in the upper reaches of Dillon's garage, watching, waiting, a spectre biding its time, waiting for vengeance. And when he'd needed strength, corporeal power, he'd somehow managed to leach it from some unknown source.

But he shouldn't have had such a hard time dragging Mouser's bloody body into the trunk of Jamie's car. He shouldn't have felt the delicious pressure of the knife as he carved his message into Jamie's skin. And it wouldn't have been so hard to stop when he did.

But if he'd cut deeper, slashed harder, there would have been too much blood, and Dillon wouldn't have understood his message. He would have been weeping over Jamie's dead body, totally immune to the challenge Nate had given him.

Killer was a fool. A weak, sentimental fool, when Nate had always considered him the only man who even approached his equal. He mooned after Nate's little cousin like a adolescent, always would. Until she was finally gone, and the cloud would lift from Killer's usually hardheaded brain.

He could have killed her any number of times. The night Paul Jameson had raped her had been perfect, except for the interference of the police. He'd thought of her high school graduation and the lavish party Aunt Isobel and Uncle Victor had thrown for her, but he'd never had an opportunity—too many people milling around.

He'd come close the day of Uncle Victor's funeral. He'd spent the time taking pictures—he'd wanted to bring one final one to Dillon as a parting gift. But once more fate had interfered, this time in the shape of his indulgent Aunt Isobel. If he didn't know better he'd suspect she knew what was going on in his mind. But Aunt Isobel was a simple woman—she had the sense to appreciate his uniqueness, but she'd never guessed the extremes he was capable of. Nothing stopped him, not idiot laws or interfering people or maudlin emotions.

He was ready to bring things to a head—he'd waited too long as it was. Too long for what was rightfully his due, too long to get revenge on those who'd tried to thwart him. He knew which category Jamie belonged in. She'd been the only one who'd managed to distract Dillon from Nate's agenda, the only one that Dillon hadn't gotten over. Uncle Victor's favorite. And she'd loved him, her cousin, with uncritical devotion. For that alone she had to die. He wasn't quite sure why—he only knew it was necessary.

But Dillon was another matter. Was he the object, or the barrier? The goal, or the hindrance? Maybe he'd never know. But he knew one thing—if he couldn't have Dillon, he could at least kill him.

Old oil soaked into concrete like water into a sponge. The bloodstains and scrawled message now lay hidden beneath a thin, viscous coating of recycled oil, and no one would be able to see it.

The first thing he'd done was search the garage from top to bottom. No sign of Nate, either ghostly or human. No sign that anyone had been in the upper reaches of the building, watching.

He took Jamie's suitcases and dumped them in a trash bin halfway across town. If anyone got to them before they reached the compactor there wouldn't be anything to identify her. He didn't know if she'd be pissed at the wholesale destruction of her clothes, but he didn't care.

Of course, he wasn't going to be appreciating that body anytime in the near future. And if he had to be honest, he didn't really want anyone else doing so, either. Hell, maybe she should keep to the baggy clothes.

That wasn't his business, either. Still, it grieved him to let go of the racy underwear. Hell, if miracles happened and he ever got near her again he could always buy her some new stuff. Though he liked her best in nothing at all.

He didn't believe in miracles any more than he believed in ghosts. Jamie was gone, out of his life for good. Now he just had to wait for Nate to make his move. The word scrawled on the garage floor was only a first step. He just had to wait for the other shoe to drop.

Nate Kincaid had never been the forgiving sort, and he would have known that Dillon had given him up to the enforcer who'd come looking for him. The game of cat and mouse was just hint of things to come—he was circling around, making his way closer and closer toward his object.

Dillon had no fear that Nate would stab him in the back, cut his throat while he slept. Nate would want him to know what was happening, would revel in it. No, Dillon would get plenty of warning. All he had to do was wait.

It was late afternoon, and he had his head under the hood of the '63 Mustang, when he heard the banging at his front door. The doorbell had stopped working years before, and half the time Dillon played the stereo so loud he couldn't even hear when someone showed up.

But for some reason he didn't want music. Not Nirvana blasting away—he'd never hear Kurt Cobain without picturing Jamie lying unconscious on the floor of the garage.

U2 was even worse—too fucking mournful when he was already missing Jamie. He'd get over it, he always did, all he needed was time. At least in time he'd have a sense of closure.

He laughed out loud at the ridiculousness of that thought. For a man who didn't believe in ghosts or miracles he seemed damned eager to believe in fairy tales. There wouldn't be closure with Jamie until they were both dead. And maybe not even then.

The pounding was continuing unabated. "Hang on, I'm coming!" he called, grabbing a rag for his filthy hands. "The door's unlocked—come on in."

By the time he reached the kitchen he realized that might have been a tactical mistake. Most people around here knew he seldom bothered to lock his door, and most people were too smart to mess with him. Which meant it was either a stranger or the police, and he wasn't in the mood for either.

It was the police, in the personage of Lieutenant MacPherson, one of the few cops with a brain that

Dillon had ever met. This unbelievably shitty day had somehow managed to get worse.

"Had a big party, Gaynor, or is this your idea of housekeeping?" MacPherson closed the door behind him. He was alone, which was a good sign. If he'd come to arrest him he would have brought backup.

Dillon glanced at the trashed kitchen. "I got pissed off," he said, leaning against the door to the garage.

"At anyone in particular? Should I be looking for a body?"

Dillon didn't even blink. "She took my '56 Cadillac and left. Untouched."

"Untouched?"

"Well, unhurt," Dillon amended. "What's it to you?"

"I heard you had someone staying here. I thought you might have decided to settle down, get married, raise a family." MacPherson reached into his pocket and pulled out his cigarettes. He didn't bother to ask—he already knew Dillon's kitchen was a smoker's haven from his previous visits. The scent of fresh cigarette smoke hit Dillon with a longing almost as powerful as his longing for Jamie.

"I'm not the marrying kind, Lieutenant. You should know that."

"I'm not sure what I know. Had a couple of

questions for you, though.'' He blew the smoke out, and Dillon was half tempted to move closer, just to get a taste of secondhand smoke. He thought of Mouser and stayed put.

''Ask away. Do I need to call my lawyer?''

MacPherson laughed. ''Do you have a lawyer?''

''No.''

''Then let's stop playing games. You know anything about a dead body in a car down in Tucker's Ravine?''

Shit. That was too damned fast. ''Nope. What kind of car?''

MacPherson laughed. ''Trust you to get to the essentials. Some kind of Volvo, they think. It's pretty welled burnt, and it must have been stolen in the first place. Someone's filed the VIN numbers off it, not to mention anything else that might identify it. Done by a professional, my men say.''

''I haven't stolen a car in almost ten years, Lieutenant.''

''And I'm supposed to believe you? As a matter of fact, though, I do. I just thought you might know who in town was in the habit of boosting cars.''

''One stolen car doesn't make it a habit.''

''It's not the only car that's gone. The Volvo was found last night, and then this morning we got word that an Audi was stolen. The damned car was loaded with every antitheft device known to man, and it was still taken.''

"What does the owner say?''

"The owner's in the hospital with a fractured skull, and we're not allowed to talk to him until he stabilizes. We figure he came across the thief at the wrong moment. Lucky he's still alive—he was pretty badly beaten.''

Dillon shrugged. "That's a shame.''

"He'll survive. I just kind of remembered that you used to specialize in Audis, back in the day.''

"Nothing was ever proved. You know that, MacPherson.''

"Yeah, I know that. I also know how to add two and two.''

"I didn't steal someone's Audi and beat the shit out of the owner.''

"I'm not saying you did. I'm just thinking you might have a good idea who did.''

"Can't help you.''

MacPherson crossed the littered floor to the sink and ran water over his cigarette butt, rendering it useless. Just as well—if he'd simply stubbed it out Dillon would have probably salvaged it and smoked what was left. He was that desperate. "No,'' MacPherson said, "I didn't imagine you could help. I just figured it was worth asking.'' He headed back to the door, the broken dishes crunching under his feet. "Oh, and one more thing."

"Yeah?" He knew cops, and specifically MacPherson, well enough to know that this one would be the zinger.

"We're thinking of doing a DNA test on some of the evidence from Kincaid's murder. We're thinking it might not have been as straightforward as we thought."

"I identified the body. Are you saying I lied to cover for him?"

"We both saw the condition of the body. His own mother wouldn't have been able to recognize him. No, I think if it's not Kincaid, that you probably made an honest mistake."

"You think I'm capable of honest mistakes, MacPherson?"

"I think you're a testament to the powers of redemption, Gaynor. You were a loser punk, throwing your life away, and now you're a productive member of society. I don't want to see you get into trouble again."

"I'm not about to."

MacPherson stared at him for a long moment, then nodded. "Take care of yourself, then."

Dillon locked the door behind him. He had no cigarettes, no wallet, but he kept a wad of cash in his safe for emergencies, along with a phony driver's license and registration for half the vehicles in the garage. He hadn't ever thought he'd need it, but a lifetime of habit couldn't be changed.

With luck he wouldn't need it. With luck he'd drive to Connecticut, to the ruins of the Dungeon, and have a final confrontation with his old buddy Nate. He'd been hoping Nate would be coming to him—he'd be easier to deal with on his own turf, but he should have realized it wasn't going to be that easy. The bloody word on the floor was a summons, as were the bloody scratches on Jamie's soft skin. The Audi was the final message.

Dillon had been adept at stripping down the Audis that Nate had brought him. Other people brought in Mercedes, Ferraris, even classic American cars. Nate only stole Audis.

His only consolation was that Jamie was safely out of the way. She didn't even know what the Dungeon was. By now she should be halfway home, and by tomorrow she'd be letting the Duchess fuss over her, and she'd be counting her blessings at her lucky escape.

Except he'd never seen the Duchess fuss over anyone but Nate. And there was no way he was going to count on Jamie being safe without checking.

He hadn't heard the Duchess's voice in twelve

years, and he could have happily spent the rest of his life without that particular pleasure.

"Is Jamie there?" He didn't bother trying to disguise his voice—she'd never paid him enough attention that she might remember. He knew she couldn't have made it home yet—not unless she ditched the car and flew. But a stranger wouldn't know that. At least he could find out if Isobel had heard from her.

"Who's calling, please?"

Trust the Duchess to add that "please" in her peremptory tone, making it even more of a command rather than softening it.

"I'm an old friend of hers from college," he said easily. "James MacPherson. Could I speak to her?"

"She's not here."

He'd been set to hang up the moment he heard her voice, but the chill that had been sitting in the pit of his stomach suddenly exploded.

"Where is she?"

"I don't remember her mentioning any James MacPherson," she said, her voice suspicious. "And I'm not about to tell a perfect stranger where my daughter is—"

"Where the fuck is she?"

"Dillon." It wasn't a question, it was a statement.

He didn't bother denying it—the panic was too

strong. "Is she on her way home? Do you know where she is?"

"As a matter of fact, I do. She's stopping on her way back, but I have no intention of telling you where—"

"Shit." He closed his eyes. "Did she go to Connecticut? To the Dungeon?"

The Duchess's silence was answer enough. He slammed down the phone, cursing himself and everyone he'd ever known. How stupid could he have been? Nate's message hadn't just been for him. It had been for Jamie, as well. Nate had always despised his little cousin, even before jealousy over Dillon had come into it. He would have known exactly what Dillon and Jamie had been doing the last few days, and his hatred would have grown to unmanageable levels. It wasn't just Dillon he wanted to kill.

If he didn't get to the Dungeon in time, Jamie was going to be dead. It would be no consolation that he'd tear Nate to pieces with his bare hands this time, to make sure no mistakes were made.

But it wasn't going to happen. He was going to get to the Dungeon before anything happened.

He had to.

20

The snow followed her east, like a hungry ghost, waiting to devour her. She kept expecting to drive out of the storm, but it kept pace with her, and when the finally turned on the AM radio in the old Cadillac, the weather reports weren't encouraging. The storm was moving east, and another one was coming up from the south to join it.

When she was young she'd loved snow. It covered everything with a beautiful whiteness, it closed schools and made everything a wonderland.

But now, for all its whiteness, it seemed a dark, oppressive thing, slicking the roads, shadowing the sky, drifts of doom and disaster falling around her.

It was early afternoon when Jamie finally reached the town of Danvers, Connecticut, but it was already growing dark. She got off the interstate and headed down the secondary roads, expecting something like her home in Rhode Island. Old colonial houses, stately trees, New England at its best.

The town looked deserted. The main street consisted of deserted storefronts, most of them boarded up. Some well-meaning person had put up Christmas decorations, but half the lights were out, so that the outline of the snowman looked like a question mark.

She stopped at a gas station, to gas up the ever-ravenous tank of the Cadillac, and was surprised to have someone appear to fill it, just as she was about to climb out of the car.

"I'll take care of that, ma'am," the wizened old man said. "We're a full-service gas station. Want me to check your oil?"

"It's fine. I checked it last time I stopped for gas."

"Sure is a beauty," the man said. He had to be in his late sixties at the very least, old enough to have known a car like this in his youth. "How's she run?"

"Just fine."

"Must have been restored by a master craftsman. You would have paid a pretty penny for this beauty."

"It's a loan."

The man let out a low whistle. "The guy must be in love with you, then. No man would let a car like this out of his sight for anything short of true love."

Jamie's laugh was without humor. "I'm afraid he doesn't believe in true love. He believes in cars."

"And there's a difference?" the man said. He had the name Wilfred embroidered across the pocket of his old-fashioned uniform. "This baby's worth fifty grand, easy. Be careful of her."

Jamie blinked. The old man must be nuts—an old American car couldn't be worth that much. And Dillon wouldn't have let her take it if it was. Not to mention telling her to dump it when she didn't need it anymore.

"This town looks pretty dead," she said casually, changing the subject.

"It is dead. Factory closed down twenty-five years ago, and each year more businesses close, more people move away. Used to be five gas stations in town—now I'm the only one left and I hardly have any business. Everyone's moved closer to the cities. Hell, even the rich folks who used to come here don't bother anymore. The land's useless for growing anything but tobacco, and no one wants to buy tobacco with all those do-gooders around trying to make rules for people that aren't any of their damned business."

"People are like that," Jamie said in a noncommittal voice, reaching into Dillon's wallet for a couple of twenties. It was a good thing he'd had plenty of cash as well as credit cards in his wallet—the car seemed to go through a tank of gas every hundred miles, and it liked premium gas.

"What's a young lady like yourself doing in a ghost town like this?" Wilfred asked, topping off the tank. "We don't get many people wandering off the beaten track nowadays."

She'd had long enough to come up with a variety of excuses, and she trotted out her favorite. "I'm looking for the ruins of an old place called Dungeness Towers."

"The Dungeon? Why would you want to go there? Nothing left but a couple of towers ready to collapse and maybe a few ghosts. It's dangerous out there—the police posted the place years ago. Doesn't mean that kids don't still go out there to make out, maybe look for ghosts. But it's not a place for a lady. Especially not after dark, in the middle of a snowstorm."

Jamie glanced out the huge windshield of the Cadillac. "I think the snow's stopped."

"It'll start again," Wilfred said gloomily. "What do you want with the Dungeon?"

"I'm a writer," she said blithely, she who could never lie. "I'm doing a feature on the robber barons of Connecticut, and I've worked my way around to Dungeness Towers."

"Robber barons? I guess you could call old James Kincaid a robber baron. He built the factory that kept everyone around here employed. He wasn't so bad, but that son of his was a cold-blooded bastard. He sold it off to some corporation who didn't give a damn about Danvers or the economy of a small town. He bought it for a tax break and closed it."

"But the son still lived here, right? At the Dungeon. Died here, didn't he?"

"Yup. He and his wife. The place caught on fire one year, and the two of them were trapped in one of the towers. It was a snowy night, and the fire department couldn't get there until it was too late. That poor kid was sitting out in the snow, huddled up, listening to the screams of his parents as they burned to death. I always wondered what happened to that boy. Thing like that must have scarred him."

The stinging sensation beneath her shirt was a sudden surprise, when she was close to forgetting about it. The scratches were closing up, healing, but every now and then she felt a flash of fire across her chest.

"It must have been hard on him," she said neutrally. The young boy she'd grown up with hadn't seemed the slightest bit traumatized by watching his parents burn to death. She'd always assumed he'd been away from home when it happened. Not that he'd actually been there, the only witness, the only survivor.

"If I were you I'd skip the Kincaids," Wilfred said. "They were a doomed family, and there's nothing left out there that anyone wants to know about. Ten years ago some drug dealers camped out there, and the police suspected someone was running a chop shop out of the old garage, but they never caught anyone."

"Chop shop?"

"The kind of place where they take stolen cars, strip them down and then send them out on the roads looking entirely different. It's quite a business, but you need to be fast and good to get away with it."

Jamie clutched the huge steering wheel of the Cadillac. It shouldn't have surprised her—drugs and stolen cars were an obvious way for Dillon to have earned a living. Not so obvious for Nate, which was probably why they got away with it.

"I still want to check out the place before it gets dark. Take a few photos. The light's always best just before dusk."

Wilfred shook his head. "Suit yourself, miss. The roads are in lousy shape—no one ever goes out there. Just don't say I didn't warn you."

"I've got a cell phone if I get into trouble."

"Won't do no good. There's no service around here. Too many hills, not enough people willing to let them put towers up."

"Well, I expect I'll be fine. The only people out there would be ghosts, and I don't believe in them."

"Don't you, miss? I wouldn't be too sure. People see lights out there sometimes, when no one should be anywhere around."

"No ghosts," she said firmly.

"Well, good luck, then. I'm afraid the motel down on Route 3 closed down a couple of years ago—the nearest place you'll find a room for the night is at least twenty-five miles away, near Cranston."

And that was exactly where she should go, and she knew it. She'd been driving all day, she was exhausted, and it was growing dark. A smart woman would find a place for the night and start out the next morning, in the clear light of day.

But she'd already proved beyond a shadow of a doubt that she was a complete idiot. Why mess up when she was on a roll?

"I don't suppose you'd feel like telling me how to get to the ruins?"

"Hell, it's your funeral. Take a left at the corner up there. Used to be a stoplight but it broke and no one's gotten around to fixing it yet, so be careful of the intersection. Not that you'll run into any traffic, anyway, not in this town. Head out that way for about three miles, and you'll see a narrow road off to the left. It'll be overgrown, and no one would have plowed. You probably won't even see it.''

''I'll take my chances. That's the driveway to the ruins?''

''If you could call it that. It's more than a mile long, and the farther in you go the worse shape the road is. I'd hate to see you hurt that pretty car of your boyfriend's.''

Boyfriend. Such a strange, teenage word. There was a time when she would have given anything to have the Bad Boy of Marshfield, Rhode Island, as her boyfriend. No matter what anyone else said.

But hell, better late than never. Better five minutes of fantasy than the brutal truth. ''My boyfriend will forgive me,'' she said. ''He loves me.''

Wilfred the Gas Station Man was right—she almost missed the turnoff. Getting through the intersection had been no problem, considering there were no other cars around to deal with the missing traffic lights, but the narrow path between the overgrown trees looked more like a path than a driveway. She was crazy to drive down that deserted road in the snowy dusk. But then, she knew she was crazy, from the moment she climbed into Dillon Gaynor's bed. From the moment she faced the fact that she was still in love with him after all these years, and part of her always would be, no matter what happened.

The Cadillac wasn't made for rough roads. She made it about a mile into the woods, the road getting narrower and narrower, when a downed tree stopped her. She managed to slam on the brakes in time, and sat in horror as the huge car continued to slide forward in the snow, stopping just inches before hitting the thick tree trunk that blocked the path.

She looked behind her into the darkness. There was no place to turn around—her only option was to back the huge car more than a mile down a twisty, overgrown road.

Which was what she was going to have to do, eventually. But in the meantime, she was this far. She might as well go the rest of the way, set her mind at ease. If Nate was still alive then he'd be there, waiting for her. He'd summoned her, and she'd always come when he called. He'd have answers, reasons for what happened. Reasons for carving words into her flesh?

But she couldn't be sure it was Nate. Maybe it was some sick act of Dillon's. Nate loved her—he'd never want to hurt her.

She turned off the headlights, and the forest was plunged into darkness. It wasn't yet four o'clock, but with the snow and the towering trees, no light penetrated into the overgrowth. She reached into the glove compartment, hoping for a flashlight, but came up with nothing, not even a registration. Lucky thing she hadn't been stopped, she thought grimly.

She flailed around under the front seat, and her hand wrapped around something narrow and cylindrical. She pulled it out, and then dropped it. It was a gun.

She turned the interior light on again to look at it. It had to belong to Dillon, and it certainly had to be illegal, since as far as she knew felons weren't allowed to own guns. She didn't like guns, but her father had, believing that everyone should at least know about them, enough to respect them.

Respect wasn't the emotion foremost in Jamie's mind, but at least she could recognize that it was well-oiled, cleaned and fully loaded. It was a nine millimeter with a clip, and she even knew how to fire the damned thing.

She reached back under the seat and came up with a box of bullets and the flashlight she'd been seeking. Did Dillon know he'd sent her off with a handgun? Things had been crazy when he'd gotten rid of her. He'd probably forgotten.

Except that wasn't the sort of thing Dillon forgot.

She flicked off the lights again, pulled her cheap winter coat around her, and climbed from the car. She shoved the gun back under the seat. Who was she going to have to use it on—Nate? Dillon? Not likely.

Her discount-store boots were a far cry from waterproof, and the snow seeped through the vinyl as she made her way down the path. There were no tire tracks, no sign that anyone had been down here in the past decade. She had no reason to trudge onward, cold, miserable, frightened. But she kept going, until she could see the towers against the snowy night sky.

There were two of them. Or one and a half—the second one was little more than a pile of rubble, and the first looked about to collapse, as well. At the foundation of the towers lay a litter of deep pits and charred wood, twisted metal, broken glass. No one had touched the place since the fire that had killed Nate's parents so many years ago. Odd, when her mother would have been the executor of her sister's will. She would have thought Isobel would have restored the place or had it torn down, but she'd left it as it was. Why?

Maybe the pain and horror of their deaths had made it too difficult to deal with. Or maybe Isobel had kept it at Nate's request. There was no way of knowing.

She skirted the vast expanse of the ruins, glancing up at the broken tower. It looked like some dark, Gothic sentinel, warning her away. But she'd been ignoring warnings for the past week, why change now?

At first she thought she was imagining the light in the darkness. She squinted her eyes, but the snow and wind had picked up again, making it almost impossible for her to see more than a few feet in front of her.

She kept going in the same direction. A tree branch slapped her in the face, and she cried out in pain, the sound jarring in the stillness of the snow-shrouded forest.

She was being an idiot. It was cold, dark and miserable out there, and she'd been through enough in the last week. She started to turn back, when the wind shifted, and she saw the light clearly. And she moved forward, her hands clutching the flashlight.

What had the old man said? That someone had run a chop shop out here? If so, she'd found the place. The two-story wooden structure must have served as a garage once, and the upstairs probably housed servants. The light came from the second floor, shining dully through the frosted window. And she knew she'd found what she'd been looking for. Answers.

She didn't make any effort to quiet her movements as she opened the door to the garage. The stairs were narrow and dark, not unlike the stairs in Dillon's place, but these were cold, unheated. If there were dead rats they'd be frozen solid.

The stairs creaked beneath her, but there was no sound from upstairs. She kept climbing, her heart hammering, until she came to the door at the top.

She could knock, of course, but that seemed stupid. Instead she just reached out and turned the doorknob, pushing the door open.

"Looking for ghosts, Jamie?" Nate asked from his seat by the window, a shotgun across his lap. "You found one."

21

———————

Dillon reached in his pocket for his cigarettes and came up empty. Which reminded him of Mouse, and why there were no cigarettes there, and he bit off a savage curse.

After ten years he hadn't lost his touch. He could still drive faster and better than almost anyone on the road, avoiding police and speed traps, weaving in and out of traffic so fast he could have been a ghost. It helped having the old Bel Air. For all its anonymous appearance, it was a monster underneath the hood, and he'd tuned it to a state of near perfection. He was gone before people even noticed him on the highway, chewing up the miles in a blur of speed.

He could even use his lack of cigarettes to focus on his goal. That nervous energy was focused straight ahead, on the Dungeon, and he drummed his fingers on the steering wheel, whistling beneath his breath.

Jamie had had a twenty-four-hour head start, but

she probably wouldn't have driven faster than sixty-five in the Cadillac. It could go one hundred and twenty, easy, but she'd be nervous of such a big car, and besides, the road conditions hadn't been ideal.

Whereas he could average ninety, going over a hundred when no one was around. He knew how to avoid construction, and he didn't stop for anything more than gas. Jamie would have spent the night on the road—she hadn't had a decent night's sleep since he'd first put his hands on her, and she'd be exhausted, both physically and emotionally. He could catch up.

He didn't need sleep, he didn't need food, he didn't need a damned thing. Nothing but Jamie.

Keeping her alive, he amended. The snow had slowed to lazy flurries, and he ignored it. He could drive on glare ice if he had to, he knew his way around spinouts, but at least there were regular tires on the car, with real treads, instead of almost tread-less racing tires. He sped through the miles, tapping on the steering wheel, humming tunelessly to the whine of the tires, the purr of the engine.

He couldn't even begin to think how this was going to end. MacPherson shouldn't be able to track the wreck of the Volvo—Dillon hadn't spent years in a chop shop for nothing. And if Mouser had any kind of history, it was from long ago, from a previous life. There'd be nothing to tie the dead body to Cooperstown, Wisconsin.

No, MacPherson might suspect, but he wouldn't be able to trace the Volvo back to him. Mouser had always said he wanted to be cremated, and that's what Dillon had done for him.

He was counting on Nate being true to form. Jamie was incidental—a means to an end. It wouldn't give Nate any satisfaction to kill Jamie before Dillon got there. He'd lose any advantage— if Jamie was dead there would be nothing to stop Dillon from killing him with his bare hands.

Then again, that might be exactly what Nate wanted. To make Dillon so crazed with anger that he'd be an easy mark. Because either Nate was going to kill him, or he was going to kill Nate. They both knew that. Maybe they'd always known it. Their relationship had always been so enmeshed, and Nate wasn't someone who let go easily.

He'd figured it out long ago—he'd never been particularly stupid, despite the asshole things he'd done as a kid. He knew that Nate had an obsessive relationship with him. For all his never-ending lineup of girlfriends, he'd always seemed focused on Dillon. Wanting to know who *he* was screwing, who *he* wanted.

He never should have told him about Jamie. But hell, he was seventeen and stoned out of his mind, and Nate was a master at getting useful information out of people.

He'd expected Nate to be furious, elder-brother protective when he found out Dillon had a wicked case of the hots for his then-fifteen-year-old cousin. Instead he'd been amused. And had taken to throwing them together, flaunting Jamie at Dillon's hungry eyes.

How many times had he kicked himself for that night? He'd known how Jamie felt about him—he knew the signs of a crush. He was a bad boy—a good-looking, fuck-it-all rebel—and girls loved him. It wasn't a surprise that Jamie would look at him surreptitiously, her gray eyes wide with virginal desire.

He'd been an idiot not to take her. Nate had thrown them together, and even if Dillon distrusted his motives, it still meant he could have had Jamie. And God knows, he'd wanted her so much it made him shake.

And he still did.

But he'd decided to be noble. She needed a jock, someone headed for Harvard. She needed her own kind, and he'd handed her over to a rapist.

And even worse, he'd seen the look of satisfaction in Nate's eyes when he'd taken his shattered cousin away.

He'd paid for that mistake. Not for beating Paul to a pulp, but for thinking Nate could be trusted. Nate had been the one to suggest Paul would be a good match for Jamie at her first wild party. That he'd look out for her. But Nate knew human nature better than any other human being on this earth, and knew exactly what kind of a bastard he had Dillon hand Jamie over to.

He hadn't been able to get out on bail, and the trial had gone quickly. In the end Nate had paid for a lawyer for him. He'd ended up with eighteen months, with time served taken into account, and he'd made it through. The only thing the lawyer couldn't fix was the felony conviction—the Jameson family was too powerful in Marshfield, Rhode Island, for that to happen.

Hell, it didn't matter. He didn't give a shit about voting, and he'd own a gun whether he was allowed to or not. He was off probation, self-employed, and he really didn't give a shit whether or not he could ever go into the army. What was past was past.

Except the past wasn't gone at all.

It was waiting for him.

He remembered the party at Dizzy's just after he got out of jail. Everyone was drunk out of their minds, high on any chemical they could find, and by the small hours of the morning most people had paired up. He'd been too drunk and too apathetic to take advantage of the various offers sent his way, and he'd passed out on the sofa. When he woke up, a couple of hours later, half the people in the room were asleep, the other half were fucking.

Which didn't bother him—nobody seemed to have trouble with inhibitions, and he figured if they didn't care, neither did he. Until his gaze focused, and he saw Nate in a far corner, banging some girl from the back. Which would have been fine, except that while he humped her he was staring directly at Dillon, a fixed expression on his face.

After that Dillon began to notice small things. How Nate always tried to entice him into a threesome with whatever girl he was with at the time. The possessive attitude when other people were around. Ending up with a night at the Dungeon, when everyone had fallen asleep, and Dillon had come out of a drunken stupor to find Nate in bed with him, curled up tight, with one hand on his crotch, jerking himself off with the other.

He hadn't freaked. He'd simply pulled away, rolled out of bed. He had an erection himself—no wonder when an anonymous hand had been stroking him in his sleep—but Nate could see it, and he redoubled his efforts, his eyes burning into Dillon's as he brought himself off.

Dillon shook his head slowly. "No, man. I love you like a brother, but...no."

He turned around and walked out. It was midsummer, and he was barefoot and still half out of it. He was afraid Nate would come after him, but he didn't. The upstairs of the garage was dark and silent.

And Nate had never mentioned it. Hell, maybe he didn't even realize it had happened, maybe it meant nothing and Nate hadn't even realized he'd crawled into bed with his best friend and not the girl he was currently screwing. That's the way he wanted to play it, and Dillon was willing to let it go. If anything he felt guilty—guilty that he might have misled Nate. Guilty that he couldn't give Nate what he wanted, when Nate had given him so much. Saving his butt when he'd faced a fifteen-year prison sentence.

Of course, he hadn't realized at the time that Nate had actually wanted his butt.

He'd left the Dungeon a few months later, heading out with an old friend. He hadn't told Nate he was leaving—he didn't want a scene. He managed to drop off the face of the earth, or so he thought, until Nate showed up at the garage five years later.

It was the first of many visits. He was dealing, big time, and Dillon was working on his day-by-day sobriety, a fact which amused Nate. Nate's favorite occupation was to use in front of him, and try to entice him into using as well. He liked to mock twelve-step slogans in a singsong voice, and bring women back to the garage and do them in Dillon's bed.

He'd tolerated it, to prove to himself he could, and for old times' sake. Just because he was in recovery didn't mean he couldn't have compassion for someone as messed up as Nate. Someone who loved him, even if it wasn't the way Dillon wanted to be loved.

Mouser had tried to warn him. Nate and Mouser had hated each other at first sight, a shock, because Mouser didn't hate anybody. He'd tried to warn Dillon, but he hadn't listened. Until he heard about the girl.

There was no proof, of course. If he'd had even a shred of proof he'd have taken it to the police, despite his distrust of them.

Mouser had been the one to tell him, just the facts, and Dillon hadn't wanted to believe him. Hadn't wanted to believe that Nate had anything to do with the nude body of a thirteen-year-old girl, found raped and murdered near Charles Street. Too damned close to the garage.

Any more than he'd wanted to believe that other girl's death had been an accident, back at the Dungeon. That was what had spurred him into leaving. He never knew her real name—she'd called herself Cheyenne but she looked more Scandinavian than Native American. She was strung out on any kind of drug she could find, any kind of man she could find, and she hung around the Dungeon like a camp follower. She'd been spending the last few weeks in Nate's bed when she disappeared. Her mutilated body had shown up in the woods by one of the standing towers. She'd obviously fallen, or been pushed, and her naked body was crushed by the stones she'd landed on. But it hadn't obliterated the knife marks.

Over the years he could remember other people, other disappearances that were never explained. Each one had seemed so random he hadn't connected them with anyone, but in hindsight he was sickened.

Nate had usually been too smart to mess with the wrong people. But he'd messed up on a drug deal in Chicago, he'd said when he arrived at the garage. Messed up badly. And men like Orval Johnson didn't tolerate mistakes. If he couldn't have money he wanted blood.

And Dillon could no longer ignore the truth of just what Nate was. When Johnson's enforcer showed up three days later Dillon had let him into the house, told him where Nate was, and sat alone in the kitchen, listening while he beat Nate to death.

He could have left. It would have been the smart thing to do, but he'd figured it was some kind of penance. For not realizing what Nate was capable of. For not putting a stop to it himself.

And in the end, Nate hadn't died. He must have known Johnson would be coming after him. Must have known time was getting short.

He was smart enough to know that getting a fresh start was the only way to go. So why had he showed up at the garage months after his death? Or had he ever left in the first place?

He didn't want to think about it. He couldn't think about anything but driving, chewing up the highway miles. To get there in time.

If Jamie had had any sense she would have turned and run. Except she'd known this was what she'd find. This was what she'd come after. Answers.

"Nate," she said, taking another step into the room, her voice broken.

He swiveled the gun around to point it directly at her chest. It was dark, it was a distance, but it looked like a gun that would manage to hit its target. And do impossible damage.

"Stay right there, precious," he said, his voice mocking. "It's not that I don't trust you. There's nothing you can do to me at this point, but I don't like to get close to people."

"If there's nothing I can do to you, why are you holding a gun on me?"

"Because there's a great deal I can do to you. When the time is right. Close the door, Jamie, and come on in. Haven't you got a word of welcome for your dead cousin?"

It was her last chance to run. She closed the door behind her. "Where have you been for the last three months?"

"Dead. Closer, sweetheart. I want to get a good look at you. I only managed to get peeps at you, when you were going down on my old buddy or when he was doing you from the back. Who would have thought my sweet, repressed little cousin could become such a whore?"

She'd already been cold, but his words drove the last bit of warmth from her body. "You watched?"

"I like to watch. You were getting quite inventive toward the end. But then, women never could resist Killer. I've been watching him fuck for years now, and women do anything he wants them to. I could never figure out why he kept his hands off you back then, when he wanted you so much, but I guess he made up for lost time this week.''

''Nate...''

''I want you to come here, Jamie, and sit in the corner like a good girl. We're waiting for a visitor. I knew you'd get here first—you always were a clever little thing. Killer would have had to deal with Mouser's body first. He'd know this was a trap, but it would take him a while before he figured out you'd be the bait. So I figure he'll show up sometime in the next twenty-four-hours, and we'll just wait here for him.''

''Why?''

Nate's smile was the same charming smile in his shadowed face. ''Because I'm going to kill him, of course. After I kill you.''

She skirted around him carefully, going to the spot underneath the window and sitting down, wrapping her arms around her knees. He smelled. Not like a dead person; like someone who hadn't bathed in months. He was almost skeletally thin, and his dark eyes bulged slightly in his bony face. Jamie looked away.

''It's cold in here, Nate,'' she said. She used the

reasonable voice she'd somehow slipped into, like a calm teacher dealing with a temperamental child.

"The dead don't feel the cold, precious. We don't need heat, we don't need food, we don't—"

"You clearly don't seem to need soap and water," she said in a caustic voice. "Which would be all well and good if you were really dead, Nate, but you're not. You're sitting there large as life with a gun across your lap, and I can see you and, God help me, I can smell you. You're not dead."

"You trying to piss me off, precious? I'm past all human emotions."

"Sure you are. If you're past all human emotions, why am I here? Why are you waiting to kill Dillon? If you're past all human emotions, why aren't you on some cloud playing a harp?"

Nate's laugh was eerily hollow in the chill air, and she would have almost thought he really was a ghost, if she couldn't see his breath on the frosty air.

"Silly girl. People like me don't go to heaven, if there even was such a thing. We go straight to hell."

"Then why aren't you there? Don't let me stop you—go ahead."

Nate chuckled. "You've gotten pretty feisty as you've grown up, haven't you? Though I remember you always did have a mouth on you. I just never imagined you'd use it on my old friend Dillon like that.''

''Are you trying to embarrass me, Nate? Because it's not working. I'm sitting here freezing to death, my supposedly dead cousin is holding a gun on me, and there's a good chance I'll be dead in the next few hours. Embarrassment pales in comparison.''

''Not a good chance you'll be dead, precious. A certainty.''

''Then why don't you kill me now?'' Stupid thing to ask, but she was trying to distract him, to keep him talking.

''Because I'm waiting for Dillon. It'll be that much more satisfying if he has to watch.''

''Or you could always kill Dillon and make me watch. There are all sorts of options.''

He shook his head. ''That wouldn't work. You see, I don't care about you. It doesn't matter if you suffer.''

It was ridiculous. She was sitting in a freezing room with a murderer and she felt as if she'd been slapped in the face. ''You don't care about me?'' she echoed.

''Don't be naive, Jamie. I tolerated you. If we hadn't been stopped for drunk driving that night I would have killed you then. You've been an annoyance my entire life, trying to steal Aunt Isobel's and Uncle Victor's love. It didn't work with Auntie—you always came second, you know. Uncle Victor was more suspicious, but then he died, and it didn't matter.''

Horror was beginning to work its way through the icy shock. ''You didn't kill him?''

Nate shook his head. ''He was on his way out, anyway. No need to hurry him along. Besides, been there, done that, got the T-shirt. I don't like repeating myself.''

''What are you talking about?''

Nate's skeletal smile was oddly innocent. ''My parents, precious. How do you think they managed to get locked in the house the night the fire broke out, and I got out safely? No one ever suspected a ten-year-old boy capable of such a thing. But I was. Oh, believe me, I was.''

She wanted to throw up. ''Why?''

Nate shrugged. ''Because they were there. They were talking about sending me away, so I just decided to take matters into my own hands. I knew Aunt Isobel would give me free rein. She always wanted a son, and there I was, blood of her blood.''

''Weren't you afraid she'd find out what you'd done?''

"Oh, I'm sure she guessed. And she still loved me better. Hush!''

In the distance the sound of a car broke the icy silence. "He was faster than I thought. He must really love you, precious.''

"He doesn't love me. He doesn't give a rat's ass about me.''

Nate shook his head, shifting the gun across his lap as the sound of the engine cut out and a car door opened. "You never were that stupid. Maybe he fucked your brains as well as your body. He's been mooning over you since you were fifteen. Of course, he was wrong about that. It wasn't really you he wanted.''

"It wasn't?''

He shook his head. Someone opened the door to the carriage house, and Jamie wondered if she'd have time to scream, to warn him. She'd die for it, like the girl in that old poem about the highwayman, but maybe it would be worth it.

"It was me he wanted,'' Nate said simply. "Me he loved. He just couldn't figure it out, so he went for the person closest to me. If he couldn't accept the fact that he loved me, he could fool himself into thinking he loved my cousin, the nearest thing to me.''

"I wasn't near to you. Not by blood, not by nature. I'm adopted, remember?"

A frown crossed his face. "Don't confuse me. He only wanted you because he couldn't deal with his feelings for me." His voice was getting shrill, and his grip on the gun tightened. As if he hadn't quite managed to convince himself.

"All right," she said in a soothing voice. "But why don't you put the gun down? You don't really want to shoot anyone, do you?"

Nate smiled, his good humor restored. "Of course I do, precious. I've never shot anyone before. I usually use a knife, though I'm not above taking advantage of whatever's available. I want to see what it's like to use a gun."

Someone was coming up the stairs, making no effort to cover the sound of his footsteps. It was a strange noise, a clicking, dragging noise, as if some huge monster was crawling up the stairs, moving closer and closer. But the monster wasn't the mysterious creature on the stairs, the true monster was sitting a few feet away from her, raising the shotgun as the door slowly opened.

"Come in, Aunt Isobel," Nate said sweetly. "I thought you might put in an appearance."

Jamie had opened her mouth to scream a warning, no matter what the consequences, but she sank back in sudden relief as her mother filled the doorway. She was supported by her two canes, hunched over in pain, and it must have taken a tremendous effort for her to get this far. She hadn't left the house without her nurse in five years.

"Nate," she said, her voice soft, not the usual strident demand that Jamie was used to. "Dear boy..."

"Aren't you going to say something to your daughter, Aunt Isobel?"

Her eyes slid over Jamie's figure, then back to Nate's. "You need to get away from here. I've brought money. You can just walk away—no one needs to know you're still alive. You should have told me. But it's not too late. You can start life over."

Nate's sweet smile was chilling, and he still held the gun loosely in his lap. "But Jamie would know. You don't think she'd keep quiet about it, do you?"

Her mother's glance was brief and dismissing. "Jamie will do what I tell her to."

Nate looked over at her, a smug look on his bony face. "You see, Jamie? You'll always come in second. Won't she, Aunt Isobel?"

"Dear boy..." her mother began, but the flash of light was shocking, followed by an explosion of sound. And Isobel Kincaid pitched forward, her canes rolling across the floor as blood spread out beneath her.

"You know," Nate said calmly, "I think I like shooting people." And he turned the gun toward Jamie.

22

Someone was screaming, a wild, keening sound. Jamie had surged to her feet as her mother pitched forward, and she realized belatedly that she was the one who was screaming.

"Shut up!" Nate shrieked at her, and he swung the gun at her, slamming her in the head with the butt of the weapon.

It felt as if her head exploded, but before she could do more than stagger back under the force of the blow he hit her again, and this time she fell, the floor hard and unforgiving as she went sprawling, her eyes unfocused, her head spinning. She blinked past the tears of shock and pain, and found herself staring at the body of her mother. The blood had spread from beneath her, so that it touched Jamie's fingertips, and she managed to scramble backward in panic, before Nate could slam her with the gun again. She couldn't stop him from shooting her, but she could keep him from bludgeoning her to death. Or at least make it damned hard.

He was looking down at the gun with a pleased expression. "I like using it that way, too," he said. "There's a nice crunch of skin and bones when it hits. Imagine a whole world that I'd never fully appreciated."

She was beyond talking. Her hands were covered with her mother's blood, and she rubbed them on her jeans. Her face felt numb, swollen, her mouth wasn't working right. She touched her lip with her tongue and tasted her own blood.

"What are you going to do?" she finally asked, her voice muffled.

Nate tilted his head to one side, like a curious robin, as he considered the possibilities. "Well, I may have been a bit hasty. We can't stay here now—the fun's gone, and she's made quite a mess, hasn't she? She'd hate that, wouldn't she? She was always so fastidious, so prim and proper. To lie facedown in a pool of blood would strike her as impolite."

"Is she dead?"

Nate shrugged. "I have no idea. If she's not dead yet she will be soon enough. Get up, Jamie. Stop cowering—it doesn't become a Kincaid, even a mongrel one. Aunt Isobel wouldn't appreciate it."

She managed to push herself up off the floor. Her head was still ringing from the force of his blows, and she couldn't see clearly. "Are you going to shoot me?"

"I'm waiting for Dillon before I decide. I'm kind of hoping I'll talk him into killing you himself, but that's probably an unreasonable fantasy on my part."

"Why would he want to kill me?" she asked, bewildered.

"He lost eighteen months of his life to you. He's spent years thinking about you, and Killer isn't the kind of man who likes to be vulnerable. He's finally managed to fuck you—he might just be ready to finish you off. Hate's the other side of the coin, you know, and Dillon hates you. You know that, don't you? Deep inside, Dillon despises you, wants you dead. That's why he sent you away, alone. He knew you'd end up here, knew what I could do to you. He wanted me to take care of loose ends, so we can be together."

She just looked at him. "You're insane," she said finally, and then realized it probably wasn't the smartest thing for her to say.

It didn't matter. He just laughed. "By some people's standards, I suppose. By your pathetically bourgeois standards. I like to think of myself as a visionary. Someone who does what needs to be done.'' He gestured with the shotgun. ''Come along, precious. We have a date with destiny.''

She wasn't sure she could stand, much less walk, but she didn't have any choice. She moved ahead of him, feeling the occasional prod of the gun barrel, and made her way around her mother's body to the narrow stairs. At any moment she expected him to shoot her, but he seemed content with using the gun as a cattle prod.

The moon had risen on the frosty landscape. Isobel's aging Mercedes was parked by the garage, the motor still running. She must have found another route in.

''She still has that old car,'' Nate mused. ''Which car did you come in? Not the Volvo, I assume. You'd be too squeamish to drive a hearse. I know—he would have sent you off in the Cadillac. What poetic justice! He did, didn't he?''

''Go to hell.''

''I wonder which one I'll take with me when I leave,'' he said in that dreamy voice. ''The Cadillac has fond memories, but I've always liked Mercedes almost as much as Audis. I suppose it'll depend on what Dillon shows up in.''

''He's not coming.''

He shoved the gun barrel harder into her back, and she groaned in pain. ''Of course he will. He'll come for you, and he'll come for me. It just depends who he's going to end with.''

He caught her arm and dragged her over to the Mercedes. He opened the door to turn off the engine, and the air was filled with the familiar scent of Isobel's perfume, Chanel No. 5.

"How could you have killed her?" Jamie demanded brokenly.

"I don't see why you care. She would have sacrificed you for me any day of the week. You were always second choice, your entire life. She didn't care about you.''

She turned to look at him, at the shotgun now pointed at her own chest. "But I still cared about her,'' she said simply.

"More fool you, then,'' he said. "Come on.'' He grabbed her arm and started dragging her across the ground, toward the rubble of the old mansion, the broken towers stark against the night sky.

Someone had boarded up the entrance, but he smashed through the flimsy wooden barricade, dragging her over the shattered wood, up the sharply angled staircase. She was still dizzy, and something had caught her jeans, tearing them. She could feel the warmth of blood on her shin, but she didn't have time to think about it, she could only follow Nate's scarecrow figure, his birdlike hand a manacle on her wrist.

Their sudden reemergence into the night air caught her by surprise. The last bit of tower was gone, leaving the area exposed to the wind and the weather, and snow had drifted against one of the partial walls.

"Now, isn't this nice? We'll be able to see Dillon's headlights from far away, and there's nice fresh air. We needed to get away from Aunt Isobel, you know. Dead bodies start to smell after a while."

She didn't bother arguing, or asking him how he knew that. She didn't need to.

"It's cold," she said instead.

"It is, isn't it?" he agreed, his voice rich with satisfaction. "Get on your knees, Jamie."

She'd been leaning against the broken wall, but at his words she straightened.

"Come on, Jamie. You did it for Killer, you can do it for me," he said, reaching for his zipper.

"You can shoot me right here," she said flatly. "Because I'm not touching you."

He laughed, unoffended. "You're awfully picky. I thought you might have developed a taste for it. Never mind, though. You're not my type. Hold out your arms."

She still didn't move. He put the shotgun down,

and she wondered if she was any match for him. He was taller than she was, but he was nothing but skin and bones in an oversize scarecrow's clothes. He should be weak, helpless.

But he wasn't. She'd felt the determined strength in him as he'd dragged her up the stairs. He had the benefit of insanity on his side, and that made up for a lot.

He began wrapping a thin, plastic cord around her wrists, pulling it tightly. "You might like this, precious," he cooed. "I'm going to tie you up so you can't move." He pulled the thin cord around her waist, up over her shoulder, a complicated configuration. He shoved her on the ground, but he seemed to have lost interest in his earlier, obscene suggestion. The rope was very thin and very tight, wrapped around her ankles and knees, elbows and wrists, until it ended up tight around her throat, so tight that she didn't think she'd be able to speak. Or maybe even breathe.

He stepped back to admire his handiwork, reaching for the shotgun. "You've probably noticed how tight that is, precious. If you struggle, or try to call out and warn Dillon, you'll strangle yourself. It'll crush your larynx and you'll choke to death on your own blood. Trust me, the gun will be much more merciful."

"Trust you?" she echoed in nothing more than a strained whisper. "You don't know anything about trust. Or mercy."

His smile was macabre as he approached her trussed-up figure, and he gave a short tug on the cord, one that cut off her air completely before he released it.

"Actually I know all about trust and mercy, Jamie," he said, sitting back on his heels. "I just don't have much use for them. Isn't that right, Killer?"

She hadn't heard him, hadn't seen him, but he loomed over Nate's figure in the night air, more like a ghost than Nate ever was.

"Trust and mercy?" he echoed, his voice cold and harsh on the night air. "Not really your style, is it?"

Nate ran his hand over Jamie's front, touching her breasts, and it was all she could do not to squirm. Any movement made the ropes tighten dangerously. He ran his hand down her stomach, between her legs, and then looked over his shoulder at Dillon.

"If you come any closer she'll die," he said casually. And in the moonlight she could see the glint of the knife. "I liked the gun, and making you strangle on your blood appeals to me, but when it comes right down to it, knives are always my weapon of choice. If you try anything, Killer, I'll cut her throat, and you'll just have to watch her bleed to death. We're too far from a hospital to give her even the smallest chance of surviving.''

"So I won't try anything," Dillon said, his voice just as emotionless. "What do you want, Nate?''

"Was she worth the wait, Killer? She's been your obsession for most of your life. The real thing must have been quite a letdown.''

"What do you want me to tell you? That she's lousy in bed? That I couldn't get rid of her fast enough? That you were right, she's nothing but a pain in the ass? Okay, I'm telling you that. It doesn't mean she deserves to die.''

Just what she wanted to hear, Jamie thought, staring up at him past Nate's hunched shoulders. She could feel tears sting her eyes and she wanted to laugh. She was about to die at her cousin's brutal hands and she was worried about what Dillon thought of her. She was as crazy as Nate.

"You could tell me that," Nate murmured, stroking the side of her neck with the blade of his knife. He turned back to look at him. "Is it true?''

Dillon didn't answer the question. "What do you want from me, Nate?'' he asked again. And he leaned forward and put the barrel of the handgun against Nate's temple.

Nate just smiled. "Who can move faster?" he said in a singsong voice. "Can you blow my brains out before I cut her throat? I don't think so. Which means we're at an impasse. Now, put that gun down before I slip and do something I'm not ready to do. Step back."

Dillon didn't move, and Nate ran the knife against her throat, deeper, so that she could feel the warmth of blood trickle down her shoulder.

"Step back," Nate said again, pleasantly.

Dillon moved back, against the far wall. "Very good," Nate said. "Now, put the gun down on the floor and kick it toward me."

She heard the clunk of metal on the rubble-strewn floor, the sound of it slid in their direction. Nate didn't bother to turn his head.

"I'll ask you one last time, Nate. What do you want from me?"

Nate lifted his head, and his mad, beautiful eyes were shiny with tears. "I want you to love me," he said, and plunged the knife toward her throat.

She rolled away from him, the knife glancing across her shoulder, and for the second time that night gunfire shattered the night. Whatever Dillon had dropped on the ground, it hadn't been the gun.

Nate rose, the knife still clutched tightly in his hand. "Just love me," he said in a whisper, as the bloody hole in his chest spread. The knife clattered to the ground and he pitched backward, toppling over the edge of broken wall, still clutching the end of rope that bound her.

She was dying. Choking to death, as he'd told her she would, as the ropes dragged her up against the wall, and she tried to make a sound, but nothing came out but a choked gasp.

And then the ropes loosened, and she could breathe again. Dillon was slicing through the cord with the knife that was still wet with her blood, his face totally blank.

She wanted him to hold her. She needed his arms around her, she needed to bury her face against his chest and sob. But his words came back to haunt her, and she lay very still as he sliced through the thin plastic cord.

"Is he dead?" The words came out on a strangled gust of air, and the pain was excruciating.

Dillon rose, glancing over the side of the tower. "Very," he said in a cool voice. He didn't reach down to touch her, didn't do anything but stand over her, waiting. But she didn't know what he was waiting for.

"My mother...' she said. "He shot my mother...."

"Where is she?"

"In the carriage house. Upstairs. I'm not sure if she's dead." The words were hardly distinguishable, but he seemed to understand.

"I'll check on her," he said. He was wearing a jeans jacket that had seen better days, and at the last minute he shrugged out of it, tossing it at her. "You look cold," he said.

Nothing compared to his icy demeanor. She could hear sirens in the background, getting louder and louder, and knew the police were coming, knew and felt nothing but panic.

She pushed herself up off the floor, trying to catch her labored breath. "You have to get out of here," she said. "The police..."

He seemed unfazed, and she realized he must have heard the sirens before she did. "I'll check on your mother," he said again.

"And then run. Nobody has to know you were here—I'll come up with something."

He shook his head in what could have been refusal, could have been disbelief. And then he walked out of her life without another word.

23

Jamie moved home for Christmas. They'd kept her in the hospital overnight, stitched up her various cuts and slashes, watched her for signs of a concussion, sent her back to Rhode Island with a police escort, including Detective Drummond, who spent the entire time questioning her and giving nothing in return but a thoughtful "hmm." She didn't tell him a damned thing, pleading shock and an unlikely amnesia, and after a while they stopped trying. She'd hoped she could protect Dillon, but she knew it was too late for that. She wasn't going to tell them anything to make it worse. The source of evil was gone—Dillon deserved to be left alone.

At least he'd gotten far enough away. He wouldn't have gone back to the garage—they'd find him there. No, he'd probably disappeared, created a new life for himself. When she saw him again, if she ever did, he'd be sixty years old and unrecognizable.

And who the hell was she kidding? The way he was going he'd be lucky to reach thirty-five.

Her mother stayed behind in the hospital for another two weeks, then returned home with the fanfare reserved for a duchess. She'd lost a lot of blood, but by sheer luck Nate's bullet had missed any vital organs, and when Isobel returned it was as if nothing had happened. Gracious, elegant and ruthlessly proper, she refused to even talk about Nate. And there was no way of ever knowing if she'd made the extreme effort of getting in her car and driving to Connecticut to save Jamie. Or Nate.

It didn't matter. Nothing mattered, just one day following the next. Nate was buried quietly in the family plot, and the only people in attendance were Jamie and Detective Drummond, who'd made the forty-five-minute trip from Danvers just for the occasion. And to ask more questions that Jamie refused to answer. Jamie's mother declared herself too frail to leave her bed to even attend the ceremony, but Jamie knew better. Isobel Kincaid just refused to accept the finality of Nate's death.

Days turned into weeks, and the police stopped asking questions. Everything had been tied up quite neatly, thanks to the wonders of DNA testing, and the short, violent life of Nate Kincaid was only a file in some storage vault. And there was no word from Dillon.

Christmas was shaping up to be a bleak holiday. Her mother insisted on a tree, even though neither of them felt like celebrating, and it was up to Jamie to buy it, decorate it, find a wreath and pretend that everything was normal.

There was something inexplicably lonely about the holidays when your heart was breaking, she thought, wandering through the parking lot and the rows of freshly cut Christmas trees. It was cold, and she pulled the jeans jacket around her. Isobel despised it without even knowing who it had belonged to, but Jamie had stopped listening to her mother somewhere along the way. She even took the jacket to bed with her at night. If Dillon could hold on to her old striped dress then she had every right to cling to the jacket he'd tossed her the last time she saw him.

The smell of the Christmas trees was heavenly, but for some reason it reminded her of Wisconsin. Her mother would never have anything less than a real tree at Christmas, and she decreed tiny white lights and the collection of German glass ornaments and French crystal that had been handed down through generations of Kincaids.

Jamie pulled a tree upright, but she wasn't looking at it. All she could see was Dillon, watching her.

She blinked, and it was nothing more than a dream. Part of her life that was past. So why was she crying?

She put the tree back against the fencing and walked back to her car. None of the well-proportioned trees would meet her mother's exacting standards—she'd have to drive to the next town over to check.

She was driving the Cadillac—always a mistake when she was feeling vulnerable, but Isobel's stately Mercedes wouldn't hold the size of tree she demanded. The thing ate premium gas like a starving man at a feast, and she pulled into the self-serve on the edge of town and pulled out her credit card.

She was a quarter full when the police car pulled up beside her, and she watched Lieutenant Drummond get out and head over toward her. Her stomach constricted, but she kept a calm expression on her face as the gas tank kept guzzling.

"Nice car," he said by way of greeting.

"It belongs to a friend of mine." Wrong thing to say. He gave her a swift, questioning look, and she could have bit her tongue. Lieutenant Drummond had handled the investigation into Nate's death and her mother's shooting, and he'd always been gentle and circumspect with her. But she didn't trust him.

"Lucky man," he murmured, and Jamie didn't dare ask him how he knew the car belonged to a man. "You staying around for the holidays?"

"Why? Am I supposed to?"

"No, ma'am. The case is closed, everything's all nice and tight. I was just being sociable."

"Sorry," Jamie said. "After the last few weeks I guess I'm a little bit edgy. I'm not planning on going anywhere. Just keep my mother company for Christmas."

Drummond shook his head. "Your mother's quite the character, isn't she? Scared the heck out of me, and I've faced some of the worst criminals you could imagine."

"My mother can be very intimidating."

Drummond grinned, running a hand through his thinning hair. "Well, I was over this way on business and I thought I'd stop and wish you a happy holiday, and find out how you're holding up."

"Thank you, Lieutenant Drummond. We're fine."

"No, I meant you, personally," he said. "And I figured I ought to tell you that Gaynor's been cleared of any charges in Wisconsin, as well. They decided your cousin must have pushed your car into the ravine before he left Wisconsin. I have my doubts, but I figure Gaynor's been through enough.''

She blinked. ''Gaynor?''

''Come on, Miss Kincaid. You didn't think we didn't know what was going on, did you? We had Dillon in custody before you were even in the ambulance. He was with your mother, waiting for us. Not that she was particularly appreciative. She was bitching him out, big time.''

''He was there? Where did he go?'' she asked faintly. She hadn't felt this disoriented since Nate had cracked her across the face with the butt of a shotgun.

''I'm afraid he spent three weeks as a guest of the state. Given his record, the D.A.'s office thought he might not be so innocent in the matter. But DNA testing cleared everything up—the wonders of modern science. He was released last Thursday, and he's back in Wisconsin.''

''He was in Connecticut all this time? In jail?'' She was going to throw up.

''Your mother knew. She said not to bother you with that information—it would only upset you.''

''She was right.''

''Anyway, good to see you. Happy holidays!''

''Merry Christmas,'' she replied absently.

There was a Wal-Mart just down the road, part of a new strip development that her mother had decried. Jamie found what she wanted in record time—a pink tinsel tree with flashing lights and a revolving base that played Christmas carols on a tinny computer chip.

Isobel was taking her afternoon nap when Jamie returned home. It took her fifteen minutes to set up the tree, another five minutes to write the note, and ten more minutes to pack. And then she was out of there before her mother even knew she'd lost her.

She threw everything in the back seat of the Cadillac, including the wallet he'd given her when he'd sent her away. She stopped and looked at the leather seats, remembering the first time she'd been there. And the last.

It started snowing when she reached the Wisconsin state line, and she almost laughed. The AM radio was playing Christmas carols, the heater was pumping out enough heat to warm half the state, and by the time Jamie pulled up to Gaynor's Auto Restoration it was almost midnight.

She turned off the car and sat there in the darkness for a moment. Mouser was gone, and she hadn't even had time to mourn him. Everything had changed. She'd been out of her mind to show up without warning, and she should get her ass out of there before he realized she'd arrived.

There were lights on in the garage, and she could hear Nirvana blaring. She could just walk in the open door, leave the keys and the wallet on the kitchen table and take off on foot. She wasn't about to give up the jacket. Of course, there was the problem of her suitcase. She could always stash that and come back and get it after she rented a car. It couldn't be that far to civilization, even if it seemed as if the garage was at the back end of beyond.

She climbed out of the car, and her sneakers sank into the snow. She grabbed his wallet and walked to the door.

She was right, it was unlocked, as it always was. But she was wrong, the kitchen wasn't empty. Dillon was sitting at the kitchen table. Looking up at her in shock.

She almost backed out again in panic, but it was too late. She stepped inside, into the warmth, and closed the door behind her.

"What the fuck are you doing here?" Where had she heard those words before? She swallowed. The room seemed different. Different refrigerator, and the table seemed even more battered than before. Only one chair, and it looked as if it were held together with duct tape. And no cigarette smoke in the air.

"Did you stop smoking?" she blurted out.

"A while ago." His voice was flat, uncompromising. "I repeat, what are you doing here."

She walked toward the table, carefully, as if approaching a hungry polar bear at the zoo. He looked about as welcoming. "I brought your wallet back. I don't know how much money you had in it, but if you let me know I'll write you a check—"

"Shut up, Jamie. I don't want your money. You could have sent the wallet. Hell, you could have had it dropped off at the correctional center."

"I didn't know you were there. I would have come—"

"And brought me a file baked in a cake?" he mocked her. "Just as well you didn't know. I wouldn't have wanted you there."

Another slap, but she'd become a glutton for punishment. "I also brought the Cadillac. I couldn't very well send that."

"I figured we were even. I destroyed your car— I owed you one. I should have realized the Cadillac would be the last car you'd want. Give me enough time and I can find a car just about identical to yours, though maybe with fewer miles on it."

"I don't care about my car."

"Fine. I don't care about the Cadillac. So where does that leave us?"

"Nowhere, I guess. I just thought we should have some closure. That we should say goodbye or something."

"Goodbye." It was immediate, flat and uncompromising, and she had no choice. She turned and headed for the door, almost tripping over a cat that wove its way around her ankles. She stopped to pick it up, and it purred happily, rubbing his face against hers.

"Where did the cat come from?"

"I have three of them. A bequest from Mouser. I figured I needed something to help with the rats since Nate's not around anymore."

His flat statement was so shocking she almost laughed. Instead she put the cat back on the floor, giving it one last stroke.

She didn't want to leave. Couldn't leave. But he was giving her nothing to hold on to.

"My mother's doing well," she said suddenly. "The bullet missed her heart."

"The Duchess doesn't have a heart. And I didn't hear me asking about your mother. I don't give a shit."

"No," she said. "Of course you don't. Sorry I bothered you."

"You always bothered me." She already had her hand on the doorknob, but something in his voice stopped her. Some last, crazy flash of hope.

"Ask me to stay," she said, her back to him, her voice so quiet he probably couldn't hear her.

But he did. "Stay."

She turned around to look at him. "Just like that?" she said.

He pushed away from the table. "Just like that." And he crossed the room and pulled her into his arms.

He didn't kiss her. He didn't need to. He just held her, against his warmth, his strength, and she felt whole for the first time in weeks.

He slid his hand up under her hair, rubbing the back of her neck. "This will never work," he murmured against her hair.

"Of course not," she said, rubbing her face against his chest. "But think how much it would piss off my mother and Nate."

She heard his laugh, deep in his chest. "Good enough for me," he said, kissing her, hard.

And it was good enough for her.